PRAISE FOR *DEATH RID*
BY JANET DAWSON

"VERDICT: With a nod to Agatha Christie, Dawson has created a stand-alone historical that's perfect for Western collections with its detailed descriptions of the midcentury train-routes.... Her stately pacing and elaborate attention to clues make this a must-purchase for any library with historic–train aficionados."
—*Library Journal*

"*Death Rides the Zephyr* is an entertaining tale of spies, counter-spies, and intrigue which also captures nuances of a transcontinental train trip in the early '50s."
—*Railfan & Railroad* Magazine

"*Death Rides the Zephyr* is an engrossing murder mystery with enough suspicious people to provide multiple suspects. A late-in-the-story catastrophe raises the stakes and the suspense. The book is also an unapologetic paean to railroading, recreating the train travel experience of the 1950s. The pace of the narrative matches the pace of a train trip."
—*Gumshoe* Magazine

"This historical mystery is really a love song to a bygone way of life. ...The real star is the train, which is lovingly described, from its layout to its ingenious bedrooms to its cuisine. That's worth the price of admission."
—Roberta Alexander, *Oakland Tribune*

"Dawson's extensive research into train life is translated into a moment-by-moment account of life on the California *Zephyr*, and we are privileged to see every aspect of being a Zephyrette....Train lovers will love this glimpse of a life spent riding the rails on this unique streamliner."
—*Historical Novels Review*

MYSTERY FICTION BY JANET DAWSON

THE JERI HOWARD MYSTERY SERIES
Kindred Crimes
Till the Old Men Die
Take a Number
Don't Turn Your Back on the Ocean
Nobody's Child
A Credible Threat
Witness to Evil
Where the Bodies Are Buried
A Killing at the Track
Bit Player
Cold Trail

SHORT STORIES
Scam and Eggs

SUSPENSE FICTION
What You Wish For
Death Rides the Zephyr

COLD TRAIL

A JERI HOWARD MYSTERY

by

Janet Dawson

PERSEVERANCE PRESS / JOHN DANIEL & COMPANY
PALO ALTO / MCKINLEYVILLE, CALIF.
2015

A Perseverance Press Book
Published by John Daniel & Company
A division of Daniel & Daniel, Publishers, Inc.
Post Office Box 2790
McKinleyville, California 95519
www.danielpublishing.com/perseverance

Distributed by SCB Distributors (800) 729-6423

Book design by Eric Larson, Studio E Books, Santa Barbara
www.studio-e-books.com

Cover photo by Mark Hillestad

10 9 8 7 6 5 4 3 2 1

LIBRARY OF CONGRESS CATALOGING-IN-PUBLICATION DATA
Dawson, Janet.
Cold trail / by Janet Dawson.
pages cm
ISBN 978-1-56474-555-2 (pbk. : alk. paper)
1. Howard, Jeri (Fictitious character)—Fiction.
2. Women private investigators—California, Northern—Fiction.
3. Missing persons—Investigation—Fiction.
4. Murder—Investigation—Fiction.
5. Mystery fiction.
I. Title.
PS3554.A949C65 2015
813'.54—dc23
2014041661

To my brother, Roger Dawson

ACKNOWLEDGMENTS

I appreciate the assistance of Sarah Andrews, who is a great friend, mystery writer extraordinaire, geologist, and gold mine of information on all things concerning the community of Graton as well as western Sonoma County. I also wish to thank Bette Lamb, potter and ceramicist, for her expertise; Norm Benson, retired forester with the California Division of Forestry; Hazel Jens and the ladies of the Graton Community Club; and Julia Turner, for trekking around Sonoma County with me as I did location research for this book.

COLD TRAIL

ONE

I FELT COLD, AND IT WASN'T ONLY BECAUSE OF THE morgue's temperature. The pathologist, a middle-aged woman in green scrubs, walked to the oversized stainless steel refrigerator and opened the door. She pulled out the drawer that held a covered body.

"You know there was a fire," the pathologist said, by way of warning.

I nodded, glancing at Griffin and Harris. They were detectives with the Sonoma County Sheriff's Office Coroner Unit. They'd met me here on this sunny Tuesday in August and they had prepared me for the condition of the corpse I was about to view.

"The body was burned," the pathologist said. "That's why we weren't able to get fingerprints. But the damage is mostly to the lower part, the legs, the hands and forearms. The head and chest are... Well, you'll see."

"I understand," I said. "I'm ready."

The pathologist reached for the sheet that covered the body. My hands tightened into fists. I shoved them into my pockets. I breathed in the scents of formaldehyde and decay as the pathologist uncovered the dead man's head and torso. I stared at the face, willing myself to move past emotion and examine what was there.

The dead man had thick brown hair that fell past his ears. The ends looked singed. So did his eyebrows and eyelashes. His eyes were open and staring, a pale blue. His mouth was open, too, his teeth exposed in a disturbing rictus. The teeth were stained by tobacco. His skin had been reddened by the fire, but I could make out a faint crescent-shaped scar on the man's lower left jaw. His earlobes were long and fleshy, and they'd been pierced.

He hadn't died in the fire, though. He'd been shot. The bullet had entered his chest near the heart.

I let out the breath I'd been holding. I shook my head.

"It's not him."

"You're sure?" Griffin asked.

I nodded, relief and disquiet washing over me, as I concentrated on cataloging what I'd seen and what I knew. "You told me this man is six feet tall and a hundred eighty pounds. That matches my brother's description. But the hair is too long, and too dark." I raised a hand to my own short auburn hair. "Brian's hair is like mine, a bit lighter. And it's thinning on top. His eyes are blue, but darker. He doesn't have a scar on his chin. Or pierced ears." I gestured at the dead man's open-mouthed grin. "Brian has a crown on the upper left side of his mouth, and his two upper middle teeth are slightly larger than the others. This guy's teeth are more even. And they're stained. That tells me this guy was a smoker."

I looked at the pathologist. She nodded. "Definitely a smoker," she said. "The victim doesn't have any crowns. Just fillings. He's missing a tooth on the upper right, way at the back."

"I don't know who this man is," I said. "But it's not my brother."

Griffin nodded and exchanged glances with Harris. "Thank you, Doctor. Thanks for coming in, Ms. Howard."

The pathologist covered the body and returned the corpse to its resting place in the refrigerator. The detectives and I headed for the door.

Outside in the corridor, I turned to them. Harris was the taller of the two men, with a broad coffee-colored face and big shoulders inside the jacket of his blue suit. He looked older, too, in his forties. Griffin was my height, about five feet eight inches, and appeared to be in his late thirties, with a wiry, athletic build under his gray suit. He had short blond hair over a tanned face, looking as though he spent a lot of time outdoors.

I reined in my emotions as best I could. "May I see the bracelet again?"

Griffin took the evidence bag from his pocket and handed it to me. I held it up in the bright fluorescent light, examining the bracelet inside the clear plastic bag.

The bracelet was made of brushed stainless steel, with a rectangular plate and a stretch band, like a watch. It had come through the fire with a layer of soot, and I saw a bit of burned fabric caught in one of the links. There were also scratches on the links where the bracelet band had broken, as though the bracelet had caught on something stronger than it was, metal probably. The link must have separated as the bracelet was pulled away. It looked as though some of the links were missing.

The front of the plate was engraved with the medic-alert symbol, a serpent-entwined rod as wielded by the Greek god Asclepius, a deity associated with healing and medicine. Next to this was the name BRIAN. The back of the plate was also engraved, with a name—BRIAN HOWARD—and information noting my brother's penicillin allergy. Below this was the identification number that led the detectives to the MedicAlert Foundation and ultimately to Brian's family.

I willed the inanimate object to tell me where my brother was. But it didn't. I handed the bag to Griffin.

"It's Brian's bracelet, all right. Where did you find it?"

"On the floor inside the boat's cabin, near the corpse." Griffin put the evidence bag back into his pocket. "We think maybe it was in the victim's pocket."

"When did this happen? And where?"

"Early Sunday morning," Harris said. "Newman's Marina near Lakeville. The boat was tied up at a dock there. There was an explosion and a fire, probably due to a propane leak somewhere in the boat's cabin, according to the Lakeville Volunteer Fire Department. After they got the fire out, they found the body and called us. We figured it for an accident until the pathologist did the autopsy. Now it's murder."

"To the best of my knowledge," I said, "my brother didn't know anything about boats. He's not a sailor. I can't imagine why he'd be at a marina on Saturday night."

"You can't think of any reason why your brother's MedicAlert bracelet would turn up at a homicide?" Griffin's expression was bland.

I shook my head. "No. Not a clue."

The detectives exchanged looks. "In the meantime," Harris said, "our body's still unidentified. We're back to square one."

I sighed. "So am I."

THE DETECTIVES AND I WALKED THROUGH THE DOOR at the end of the corridor. It led to another hallway. Several members of my family waited there, stress and anxiety etching lines on their faces and circles under their eyes. They looked up as I approached them, their faces full of questions and fear.

"It's not Brian," I said.

"Oh, thank God." My mother, seated on a nearby bench, slumped over, her hands clasped tightly together on her lap. My father sat beside her. Now he covered his face with his hands. Then he straightened and put his arm around my mother's shoulder.

My brother's wife, Sheila, stood next to the bench, her face stricken. She didn't speak. Then she turned away and leaned against the wall, her palms and forehead against the painted surface. Aunt Caro, my father's younger sister, had been standing on the other side of the bench. Now she walked to where my sister-in-law stood and put her hand on Sheila's arm.

"Let's get out of here," I said.

Then I could figure out what to do next.

Mother got to her feet and reached for Dad's hand as he, too, rose. Together, hand-in-hand, they walked slowly toward the front door of the Sonoma County Coroner's Office. Caro and Sheila followed. I told Griffin and Harris I'd be in touch. Then I walked out into the midday sunshine.

In the parking lot, my parents were climbing into Dad's car. Caro had her arm around Sheila, who was standing at the open door of her Honda Civic hatchback.

"I have to go back to Petaluma. I left the kids with a neighbor." Sheila glanced at me and Caro, as though expecting us to argue with her. Then she tossed her shoulder bag onto the passenger seat, slid into the driver's seat, and fastened the lap belt and shoulder harness.

"I'll talk with you later," I said.

Sheila didn't acknowledge my words. She started the car, backed the Honda out of the space, and drove out of the parking lot.

"Something's going on there," Caro said. It wasn't a question.

I nodded. "Yes. Not sure what it is. But I'll figure it out."

"I'm sure you will. I'll see you back at the house." Caro embraced me. Then she walked to Dad's car and got in. As soon as they drove away, I reached for my cell phone and called my friend, Dan Westbrook.

"It's not my brother," I told him. "Yes, I'm relieved. But I still don't know where Brian is. Thanks. I don't know when I'll be back. I'll talk with you later, when I know more."

I disconnected the call, got into my Toyota, and drove toward the parking lot exit. The coroner's office is on Chanate Road, in the northwest part of Santa Rosa. As I headed into town, I recalled that quick exchange of looks between the two detectives.

I knew what they were thinking. If Brian wasn't their corpse and his MedicAlert bracelet was at the crime scene, these two detectives had reached what was for them the next logical step.

My kid brother was a person of interest, maybe even a suspect, in a homicide.

―――――――

MY BROTHER, Brian, had disappeared a few days earlier. I wasn't even certain when he'd gone missing, and until yesterday, I hadn't known he was gone. I didn't have any idea where he was or why he'd left. Or why his MedicAlert bracelet had been found with an unidentified body on a burned boat at a marina in rural Sonoma County.

I reviewed what I did know.

Brian called my cell phone on Friday morning. But he didn't leave a message. I returned the call later in the day. His phone went straight to voice mail, so I left a message for him. He didn't call back.

I'm a private investigator, working out of Oakland. A couple of weeks earlier, I had finished up a big case that resulted in a big check deposited in my business account. I'd cleared up several small cases as well. I decided to take advantage of my light work-load and take some time off. So I rescheduled several appointments, cleared a week in my calendar—this week—and arranged for my tenant to feed my cats, water the plants, indoor and out, and take in the mail. I was going to take a vacation, time away from the day-to-day routine, and quality time with Dan, since our friendship had evolved over this summer into something more than just a friendship.

On Saturday, Dan and I drove up to Lassen Volcanic National Park. The park is located in the northeast part of the state. The annual snowfall at Lassen is usually the heaviest in California. There are permanent snow patches on Lassen Peak. We planned to spend the week hiking, relaxing, exploring the park and the surrounding area.

Things didn't work out that way.

Yesterday—Monday—we hiked the trail up Lassen Peak. It's the southernmost active volcano in the Cascade Range. The mountain had rumbled frequently between 1914 and 1917. A powerful eruption on May 22, 1915 spewed boulders that were too hot to touch for days afterward. The cloud of ash produced by the volcano drifted as far as 200 miles.

Lassen Peak is likely to erupt again, one of these years. I was reminded of this frequently during the hike, since the area has constant geothermal activity, with boiling springs, mudpots and fumaroles.

The trail Dan and I hiked was a five-mile round trip with an elevation gain of two thousand feet, and we were on the mountain most of the day. Though it was early August, we encountered snow on the ground at the higher elevations.

It was nearly five when we got back to the cabin where we were staying, at the Mill Creek Resort, not far from the park's southwest entrance. We stripped off our hiking clothes and headed for the bathroom. The hot shower felt good on my aching muscles, and so did Dan's shoulder massage. We dressed and made plans for dinner.

Only then did I look at my cell phone. I had four missed calls and two voice mails from my sister-in-law. I listened to the voice mails, with growing alarm. In the first message, Sheila sounded concerned. In the second, worried. She wanted to know if I knew where Brian was.

I called Sheila. "No, I don't know where he is. What's going on?"

Sheila told me, her voice trembling, that she and the children had left Brian at home in Petaluma twelve days earlier. She had driven to Firebaugh, in the southern part of the Central Valley, to visit her parents. When she returned from her trip on Sunday afternoon, Brian was gone. He'd left a note saying he was going away for a couple of days. He didn't say where he was going, just that he would be back on Sunday.

He never showed up.

Sunday night gave way to Monday morning. Still no Brian. He wasn't answering his cell phone. Calls went straight to voice mail. Text messages went into the ether.

I asked for more details, firing questions at my sister-in-law. She told me she had talked with Brian several times while she was in Firebaugh, most recently on Monday of last week. She hadn't spoken with him since then, although he'd called two days later. He'd disconnected when the call went to Sheila's voice mail. But the missed call showed on her phone's list of recent calls.

Usually when Sheila and Brian were apart, they talked with each other more frequently. If that routine had been broken, something was amiss. I pressed Sheila for answers, sensing that she was leaving something out. She seemed reluctant to answer my questions. Finally, she told me she and Brian had had a fight, a big one, during that phone conversation a week ago. But she didn't want to discuss that over the phone.

Fine, I thought. But we will discuss it, in person.

I told Sheila to file a missing persons report with the Petaluma police. Then Dan and I packed our gear into his Subaru wagon and checked out of our cabin, heading west out of the mountains to the town of Red Bluff, where we had a quick dinner before driving south on Interstate 5. From there it was another three hours, or more, driving time to Oakland. Dan was at the wheel, pushing the upper limits of speed. I called Sheila several times during the drive, hoping for news. But Brian hadn't called, nor had he come home.

Sheila hadn't contacted my parents. I had to make those calls, letting them know that their only son was missing.

The first call was to Castro Valley, where my father lives. Tim Howard is a retired professor who'd taught history at California State University in Hayward, now known as Cal State East Bay. Dad was at home. He told me he'd drive up to Sonoma County first thing in the morning. He said he'd call his sister in Santa Rosa, so we could use Aunt Caro's place as a rendezvous.

My mother was where she usually was in the evenings, at her restaurant, Café Marie, in her hometown of Monterey. She, too, made plans to leave things in the hands of her capable staff and drive north.

It was after ten o'clock that night when Dan dropped me off at my home in the Rockridge section of Oakland, on Chabot Road, just off College Avenue. My cats, Abigail and Black Bart, meowed at me indignantly, acting as though I'd been gone for weeks instead of days. They had received food, water, litter box care and lots of attention from Darcy, my tenant, who lived in the studio above the garage. Regardless of how long I'd been away, they still needed reassurance that I loved them. They also wanted feeding again, just because. I fell into bed, stroking furry cats who snuggled close to me in bed. I worried about my brother until I drifted into an uneasy sleep.

I got up at six-thirty on Tuesday morning, fed the cats again, and sent a text message to Darcy to let her know I was home. I was on my second cup of coffee when the phone rang.

It was Sheila, nearly hysterical. She was calling to tell me that Brian's MedicAlert bracelet had been found with a corpse.

After finding the bracelet, Detectives Griffin and Harris had notified the MedicAlert Foundation to find out if the registry had contact information for Brian Howard. Then they saw the missing persons report Sheila had filed on Monday with the Petaluma police. That report had mentioned the bracelet, which Brian always wore since the family had discovered his penicillin allergy, back when he was a kid. The detectives had then contacted the Petaluma Police Department. The detective in charge of that case had called Sheila, asking if she or a member of the family could come to the morgue to look at the body. Neither my sister-in-law, my mother, or my father could face the prospect of identifying my brother's body. It was left to me.

But the man in the morgue wasn't Brian. Now I had lots of questions and no answers. And I was following a trail that was already several days cold.

THREE

HE FELT AS THOUGH HE'D STEPPED THROUGH THE looking glass.

All he'd wanted to do was get away for a few days. Away— from trouble, arguments, pressures.

How had everything gone so wrong?

Now all he wanted to do was get away from here.

"This is a mistake," he said. "I'll just leave now."

Why did they look so hostile? One of them had a gun.

He backed away. Then he ran. But they were quicker.

They manhandled him through the door. His bracelet caught on something sharp. A nail. It scraped his wrist. The band of the bracelet broke. He heard it fall, saw the glint of the metal links on the wood plank floor.

He struggled against his captors, but they overwhelmed him. Then his forehead slammed against something, so loud he heard the crack. He saw stars. Pain lanced through him like daggers.

Everything turned black.

FOUR

MY AUNT AND UNCLE LIVE IN THE ST. ROSE NEIGHBOR-hood, just north of downtown Santa Rosa. Caro is Dad's younger sister. Her real name is Caroline, but when she was born Dad had trouble with the longer name and called her Caro. The name stuck.

Caro writes historical novels. Her husband, Neil, is retired from the Santa Rosa City Planning Department. Their three children are grown and out of the house. As it happened, my uncle was away from home this week. An avid tennis player, he was competing in mixed and men's doubles at the National Senior Games.

My parents are divorced, a few years now. Despite their break-up, they've remained friends. I've always had a close bond with my father. My relationship with Mother has been prickly in the past, but we're getting along better these days.

When Sheila called this morning, I grabbed my keys and ran out to my car. I got on the freeway and headed north. I called the Sonoma County Coroner's Office from the road, arranging for the family to meet the detectives there at eleven.

Now it was past noon. In Caro's comfortable living room, Mother and Dad sat side by side on the sofa, holding hands as though they were each other's lifelines. They're both in their late sixties, both vigorous, active, in good shape. Today they looked haggard, as though they'd aged overnight.

Caro came in from the kitchen, carrying a tray with a pitcher of iced tea and glasses. She set the tray on the coffee table in front of the sofa, filled glasses, and handed them round. I took a sip and set the glass on the end table. I pulled out my phone and a small notebook.

"When was the last time either of you saw or talked with Brian?" I asked my parents.

"The last weekend in July, on Saturday," Dad said. "That was a couple of days after Sheila and the kids went down to Firebaugh. Brian and I went birding at Abbotts Lagoon."

I wrote the date and the information in my notebook. The hike out to the lagoon off the Pacific Ocean at the Point Reyes National Seashore was a popular one for Bay Area birders. Dad has become a birder since he retired and it's keeping him active.

"We met at the Bovine Bakery in Point Reyes Station," Dad continued. "I guess it was around seven-thirty. We had coffee and pastries, talked a while. Then we left my car there in town and drove his old Jeep, the one he uses for camping."

"What did you talk about?"

Dad thought for a moment. "We just talked, you know. He told me all about the family camping trip to Yosemite in June. And he said he was looking forward to starting his new teaching job in Petaluma."

"Did he say anything about plans to go away for a while?"

"Yes, he did. He said that Sheila was due back from Fire-baugh on Tuesday, and they were going camping again, at Plumas–Eureka State Park up by Graeagle."

"But Sheila didn't come back from Firebaugh until Sunday," I said.

"I'm sure he said Tuesday," Dad said. "They must have had a change in plans. Brian said he had a reservation at a campground up there. He was looking forward to the trip. One last family outing before school starts."

A change in plans, I thought. Did that have something to do with the argument Brian and Sheila had on the phone a week ago?

"Did he hint that there might be anything going on between him and Sheila?"

Dad shook his head. "No. Believe me, I would have remembered that."

"He didn't say anything to me," Mother said. "But I thought there might be."

I turned to Mother. "How so?"

She leaned against the back of the sofa, her brow furrowed. "Brian and I talk on the phone about once a week, sometimes more often. The last time I spoke with him was a week ago Sunday, the day after your father saw him. He told me Sheila and the children had gone to Firebaugh—again. I remember him saying that, 'again.' And the way he said it." Mother sighed. "It sounded as though he was upset that she was going away. She's been back and forth to Firebaugh a lot during the spring and summer, because her father's ill. But he didn't elaborate. We talked about other things, including this new job he's starting in Petaluma. He's excited about it."

"I don't talk with him as often as you do," I said. "He did call my cell phone last Friday, but he didn't leave a message. I called him back but he didn't answer, so I left a message. Sheila says she hasn't talked with him since last Monday. That was eight days ago. So as far as we know, no one in the family has talked with Brian since Monday a week ago. Unless..." I looked at Caro.

My aunt shook her head. "I haven't seen him since the Fourth of July. We had a big barbecue, invited the relatives who live up in this area. Brian, Sheila, and the kids came over." Caro stood and took a step in the direction of the kitchen. "I'll fix lunch. If anyone's hungry."

I put my cell phone and the notebook in my purse. "I'll pass. I'm going down to Petaluma to talk with Sheila. I'll check in later."

FIVE

UNTIL RECENTLY, MY BROTHER AND HIS FAMILY LIVED
in Sonoma, in the eastern part of the county, where Brian taught
middle school, in the Sonoma Unified School District. Then, at
the end of this most recent school year, he had accepted a job in
Petaluma, teaching at a junior high school in the Petaluma Joint
Union School District. He was supposed to start the new job in
mid-August. Classes started around the third week of the month,
and teachers usually began the school year a few days earlier. This
was the first week in August, so I figured Brian was due at his new
school the following week.

Brian and Sheila made the move from Sonoma to Petaluma
the last weekend in June, about six weeks ago. For the time being,
they were renting a house in East Petaluma. It was located in a
development of tract houses off McDowell Road, near Lucchesi
Park and the Petaluma Valley Hospital. I had an address, though
I had not been to this house before. It looked small, but the situation was temporary. Once Brian and Sheila sold their house in
Sonoma, they'd buy a bigger place here in Petaluma.

But first I had to find my brother and figure out what was behind his disappearance.

I parked my Toyota in the driveway behind Sheila's Honda,
walked to the small front porch, and rang the bell. A moment
later, Sheila opened the front door. She had changed out of the
slacks and shirt she'd worn to the coroner's office, and now she was
dressed in a faded T-shirt, blue cotton shorts, and slip-on sandals.

My sister-in-law looked exhausted and on edge. The events of
the past forty-eight hours were taking their toll. Without a word,
she motioned me inside.

The front door opened onto a small entry hall. To my left a
short passage led to the double car garage. Sheila led the way
into the house, crowded with furniture from the Sonoma house
and boxes that had yet to be unpacked. One corner of the dining

room had been turned into an office, containing a desk with draw-
ers on the right side. Above the desk's kneehole was a computer
with a large flat-screen monitor and an ergonomic keyboard and
mouse.

A sliding glass door off the dining room was open. Just the
other side of the screen was a square wooden deck and the big
backyard. There was an oak tree in one corner of the yard, a rope
hammock hanging from a sturdy low branch. Another corner of
the yard held a mature fig tree, branches heavy with fruit. Between the two trees was a garden patch surrounded by a red brick
border. At some point someone—Brian?—had been weeding, I
noticed, seeing a low plastic bucket full of dried vegetation.

My eight-year-old nephew, Todd, was in the middle of the garden patch, digging in the dirt with a trowel. My niece, Amy, who
was six, played on a swing set just this side of the oak tree.

"I've got lemonade in the refrigerator," Sheila said. "Do you
want some?"

"Yes, that sounds good."

We took our glasses out onto the deck. Amy left the swing set
and came running. I set my glass on the table and leaned down to
hug my niece. Amy circled my waist with her arms. She looked up
at me. "Hi, Aunt Jeri. Is Daddy with you?"

"No, sweetie. He's not."

Amy looked perplexed. "Daddy went away when we were at
Grandma's house. I want him to come home."

"I know you do." I looked past Amy at Todd, who had left off
digging in the garden. He hung back, dirt on his hands, T-shirt,
and shorts, a troubled expression on his face. "Are you planting
something, Todd?"

"Just digging." He shrugged, opened his mouth and then shut
it, as though he was going to say something else and thought better of it.

"What is it, Todd?"

He took a deep breath. "Aunt Jeri, did Daddy go away because of me? Because of something bad I did?"

I knelt in front of him and put my arms on his shoulders. "Oh, no, Todd. I don't believe that at all. I can't imagine that you would do anything bad. What makes you think that?"

"Well..." He looked at his mother.

Sheila was shaking her head. "Todd, honey, we've been over that. You didn't mean for Cameron to get hurt. It was an accident."

"Then why did Daddy go away?" he asked, tears brimming in his eyes. Next to him Amy look as though she, too, was about to cry.

"Your mom and I are going to talk about that," I said. "But we need to do that grown-up to grown-up. So it would help if you kids would leave us alone for just a little while."

"Okay." Todd took Amy's hand and led her away from the deck, to the swing set. He settled her into one of the swings and began pushing her.

I reached for the glass of lemonade. The weather on this August afternoon was hot, and the cold, icy lemonade tasted good, its sweet-and-sour tang lingering in my mouth. I sat down in one of the chairs. "What's this about an accident with Cameron?"

Sheila ran a hand through her short brown hair. "A kid who lives down the street. Todd met him last month, just after we moved in. A couple of weeks ago, they were playing in our front yard, just roughhousing, the way boys do. Todd pushed Cameron. The kid fell and cut his forehead. Then we had his parents over here yelling at us. A great start to living in this neighborhood." She sighed. "It's just one damn thing after another."

"We need to talk about Brian." She looked past me and didn't say anything. "Sheila, I need some answers."

"So do I," she snapped, her voice sounding ragged. "And I don't have any."

"Sheila, what's going on?"

"When you figure it out let me know."

I set the glass on the table and leaned forward. "Sheila, I am here to help. I want to find Brian as much as you do."

She glared at me. "I'm not sure I want to find him."

I was taken aback by the anger simmering in her brown eyes. "You don't mean that."

"I do. At least I think I do. Damn it, how could he do this to us?"

SIX

WE SAT SILENT FOR A MOMENT. WHAT WAS BEHIND Sheila's anger? It had to be fueled by something beyond the immediate shock of Brian's disappearance.

I thought back to the fight they'd had during their last phone conversation. It had been a bad one, she said. Was their marriage in trouble?

"Sheila..." I began.

"I didn't want to move here," she said. "I didn't want to leave Sonoma. We had a great house there, lots of friends, a wonderful life. We lived there ten years, ever since we got our first teaching jobs, after we graduated from Davis."

A wonderful life, I thought. The phrase made me think of the classic Frank Capra film *It's A Wonderful Life*, starring Jimmy Stewart as George Bailey, who decided, after various trials and tribulations, that he really had many blessings after all. However, the film had a dark edge to it. Maybe Sheila's recollection of good times in Sonoma didn't jibe with those of my brother. Maybe that was the undercurrent running beneath all this.

I'll be thirty-six this year, and Brian just turned thirty-two, so my kid brother is four years younger than me. Sheila is the same age as Brian. They met when they were undergraduates at the University of California in Davis, in the Central Valley near Sacramento, and they married the summer after they graduated. After receiving their teaching credentials, they both got jobs in Sonoma, Sheila teaching elementary school, Brian in middle school. Then, with the arrival of their children, Sheila became a stay-at-home mom, planning to go back to work at some point, when the kids were older.

So they'd lived in Sonoma long enough to put down roots in the community. Sheila was a small-town girl who liked small-town life. She was born and raised in Firebaugh, an agricultural town in Fresno County, with a population of about seven thousand people. Sonoma, with its historic old plaza and wineries, was about eleven thousand people. Petaluma was much larger, with a population of about fifty-eight thousand. The distance between Sonoma and Petaluma was only about fifteen miles, but the difference between the two communities was even more dramatic to Sheila. To her, Petaluma was a big city, and she didn't like cities.

"I don't understand why Brian would give up a perfectly good job in Sonoma to move to another district here in Petaluma," she said. "It's not a promotion."

"More of a lateral move?"

She nodded. "The salary is about the same. Plus, he's got to start over at the bottom of the pecking order, since he's new to this district. I just don't get it. Why did he do this?"

"Surely you discussed it before—"

"No, we didn't," Sheila interrupted. "I wasn't consulted. This whole job change and move, it came at me out of the blue."

I sipped my lemonade. She was angry about the move, but there was something else going on here, I was sure of it. But I didn't have any idea what it was, not yet anyway. Brian could have commuted to Petaluma from Sonoma, but it sounded as though he wanted to leave the town as well as the job. I wondered why.

Okay, I thought. Let's focus on the job situation first. It wasn't like Brian to do something as important as changing jobs and moving his family without talking it over with his wife. My impression was that my brother viewed marriage as a partnership. He was conscientious, a fine, four-square, upstanding, all-round nice guy.

Or was he? I was his sister. Despite viewing him as a bratty annoyance when we were kids, I had a different view now that he was older. I thought Brian was a good guy. Certainly I would admit that my opinion was colored by our family relationship. But I'd never seen my brother behave in a fashion that would explain this situation, or my sister-in-law's anger.

I set my glass on the table between us. "You say Brian had a perfectly good job in Sonoma. Think back. Are you sure he didn't say something that indicated he was thinking about making a change? Was he dissatisfied with the job in Sonoma? Did something happen?"

Sheila frowned. "Well…yes. Just over a year ago, in April. The principal of the school where Brian was teaching suddenly died of a heart attack. Brian was very upset. He really liked the man who died. They were friends, and they had an excellent working relationship."

"April of last year." In my head, I counted back on the calendar. "So that would be about sixteen months ago. After his friend the principal died, did Brian bring up the possibility of changing schools?"

She nodded. "That's when the subject came up. But he just mentioned it, in passing. Not anything definite. He didn't like the man who was assigned as the temporary principal, and hoped the guy wouldn't get the permanent assignment. But last summer, the temporary assignment became permanent."

"Did Brian want the principal's job?"

"I don't think so," Sheila said. She thought about it and shook her head. "No, I can't picture it. Brian likes teaching kids. He hates all the administrative stuff that gets in the way of teaching. He doesn't want to be a principal. He'd have to deal with all the politics and the district hierarchy. Teachers get enough of that anyway. Being principal would drive Brian crazy."

"Why didn't he like the new principal?" I asked.

Sheila shrugged. "Clash of personalities, maybe. I remember Brian saying this guy is a bully, a martinet, a petty tyrant. You know the type, one of those by-the-book disciplinarians who's difficult to work with. Brian doesn't like that kind of work environment."

"So Brian talked about changing jobs," I said, "but you didn't think he was serious."

She threw up her hands in a frustrated gesture. "He made a couple of offhand remarks about it, at the start of the school year, and again later in the fall. I didn't think much about it, just that maybe he was considering a transfer to another school in Sonoma. I don't remember him saying anything about it after that."

Late fall, I thought, followed by the distractions of Thanksgiving and Christmas. I asked the question that had been running through my mind. "Is it possible Brian didn't mention his plans because of the situation with your father?"

Sheila looked startled and I figured she hadn't considered this. In January, after the Christmas decorations had been put away for another year, her father had been diagnosed with cancer. In the months since his diagnosis, Sheila's father had had surgery, radiation, and chemotherapy. I gathered from what Brian had told me that the prognosis wasn't good. During that time, Sheila had been going to Firebaugh constantly, sometimes for long weekends, other times staying a week or more, usually taking the children with her, but not always. That sort of thing could put a strain on a marriage, too.

"I guess so," Sheila said. "This business with my father hit me hard. I'm the youngest, and the only girl out of a family of four boys. I'm Daddy's little girl. And he's always been so big and healthy and vital. When he got diagnosed with cancer, it was such a blow."

Sheila sighed. She rattled the ice cubes in her glass. "I know I've spent a lot of time going back and forth to Firebaugh. For all I know Dad may not last till the end of the year. Brian knows how important it is for me to be there for him, and help Mom."

"I just wondered," I said. "Maybe he didn't want to put anything else on your plate by talking about his problems at work."

"Even so, taking a new job and moving, that's a big deal. Yes, I've been gone a lot. But I thought he understood about that. I certainly didn't think he'd come home from work one day and announce that he had taken a job in Petaluma. It was a fait accompli. We're moving. I'm supposed to uproot myself and the kids, pack up everything we own, put our house in Sonoma on the market. He'd already rented this house, before he told me he'd taken the job. I hadn't even seen the damn place before we moved in."

That was out of character, I thought, frowning. "Just like that?"

"Yeah, Jeri, just like that. I didn't have any say in the whole damn fiasco. I'm pissed. Then he disappears. I feel..." She paused. "I feel like I don't know him anymore."

"What did you fight about, on the phone?"

Sheila's mouth tightened and she took a sip of her lemonade. "I left on Thursday, twelve days ago. I was supposed to come back last Tuesday. We were going camping before school started, up in Plumas County. We had a reservation at a state park campground up there, starting last Thursday."

"But you got home two days ago, on Sunday. You decided to stay in Firebaugh?"

She nodded. "When I got there, I found out my aunt, my dad's oldest sister, was coming to visit. She was due to arrive on Wednesday, the day after I was going to leave. She was bringing her daughter, who's my age, and her grandkids. I hadn't seen any of these folks in a long time, Jeri, because they live back in Ohio. So yes, I decided to stay longer. I called Brian last Monday and told him I'd be coming home Sunday instead of Tuesday."

"How did he react?"

"He was upset, angry. He didn't want to cancel the camping trip. He said he'd come and get the kids and take them camping. I said, no, I wanted the kids there to see my family. I asked him to come down to Firebaugh, but he didn't want to come. We argued and I hung up. Later that evening I called again and he didn't answer. In fact, I called several times over the next few days, and he didn't pick up the calls."

So Brian resented Sheila and the kids being gone, and Sheila's change of plans brought things to a head. Something else was lurking under the surface, though. I steered the conversation away from their argument and back to the move.

"How did Brian come to rent this particular house, without you even taking a look at it?"

"It belongs to Lance...and Becca." Sheila's mouth twisted, as though she'd bit into a particularly sour dill pickle. The tartness seemed to be reserved for Becca.

"Lance, Brian's buddy from college," I said. "He was best man at the wedding." I'd met Lance at Brian and Sheila's wedding ten years earlier. I dredged up a memory of a tall young man with sharp features and dark hair. "And Becca's his wife?"

"They dated the last year of college and got married a year after we did," Sheila said. "Lance was born and raised here in Petaluma. After school he went into business with his father, a real estate agent. Lance is now a big-deal Petaluma real estate tycoon and mover-and-shaker. Which is somewhat ironic, since he and Becca are such big environmentalists." She shrugged, reaching for her lemonade. "Lance is all right."

"But you don't like Becca," I said.

Sheila took her time answering, as though choosing her words. "Becca can be...overwhelming. She takes charge of things and bosses people around. Her way is always the right way. She's a true believer—always involved in some cause. Lately it's environmental stuff, everything from climate change to Sonoma County land use issues. Ever since we moved here, Becca's been recruiting Brian to join this or that organization. Right now Becca's energized about the Friends of the Petaluma River. She's a member and she convinced Brian to go to a meeting with her."

"Brian's always been interested in the environment and the natural world," I said. "He loves to camp and hike."

"I know that," Sheila said. "He takes the kids on nature walks. He enjoys birding with your father. Although I think that's not so much the birding as a chance to be with your dad, now that he's retired. But..."

The Friends of the Petaluma River sounded like a rather benign organization. Going to a meeting and joining the group would be normal activities for someone with my brother's interests, especially since he'd just moved to Petaluma. He had been active in community life in Sonoma when the family lived there.

But that didn't explain the frown on Sheila's face.

"Is there something else? Something you're not telling me?"

Sheila didn't answer right away. She set down her glass. Her mouth tightened again, and I saw tears in her eyes.

"I think Brian's having an affair."

I sat back in my chair. My kid brother, cheating on his wife? I didn't believe it. But that was Jeri, Brian's big sis. The private-eye Jeri took a different view.

"What makes you think that?"

"Something I found," Sheila said. "Wait here. I'll get it."

She got up and disappeared into the house, returning a moment later with a note card. She handed it to me. It was about four by five inches, and the front showed a delicate color sketch of a bird, a yellow-rumped warbler, a bird common to the woodlands in Northern California.

I opened the card. The inside was blank except for a hand-written message that looked as though it had been written in a woman's hand. In a few lines, she said she'd enjoyed talking with him, and that she hoped they could meet again soon. The signature read "All the best, Willow."

"How did you get this card?" I asked.

"I found it in Amy's room, right before I left for Firebaugh. She must have liked the picture. She said she took it from the recycling bin. When I read the message, it set off alarm bells."

"You might be reading too much into it. It sounds innocent enough." I set the card on the table between us.

"Am I? I asked Brian who Willow is. At first he didn't answer. He just seemed evasive. Then he said she was a casual friend, that he'd had coffee with her. Finally he admitted he'd had coffee with her several times. If that's all there was to it, why didn't he say anything about meeting her? He kept saying I was getting upset about nothing. But I *was* upset. I still am."

She seemed to be blowing up something trivial. But Sheila was definitely on edge. With everything tossed into the mix—Brian's dissatisfaction at work, Sheila's preoccupation with her father's illness, and the missive from the mystery woman—it sounded as though the conflict had been ripening into battle stage.

Had my brother's meetings with Willow moved into a different kind of relationship? Had Brian gone off somewhere to meet another woman? Sheila was certainly entertaining that thought.

But it was so out of character for my kid brother. So was the vanishing act. Besides...

"That still doesn't explain how Brian's MedicAlert bracelet wound up on a boat with a body," I said, thinking out loud.

Sheila's face crumpled and tears began to flow. "Oh, Jeri, do you think he's dead?"

I hastened to reassure her, although I'd reluctantly considered the possibility, then pushed it back into the darker reaches of my mind. "No, I don't think he's dead. I think we just have to keep looking, to figure out where he might have gone."

"I do love him," she said. "In spite of being angry with him, I love him. Oh, hell, I want him home."

"We'll find him," I said, as much to myself as to Sheila.

SEVEN

"WHERE DO WE START?" SHEILA WIPED TEARS FROM her face.

"Maybe Brian went camping on his own," I said. "Maybe something happened to his Jeep."

Maybe he was injured—or dead, somewhere out in the wilderness. I kept that thought to myself.

Conventional wisdom says that one shouldn't go hiking alone, especially in rugged or unfamiliar terrain. But people do it all the time. I'd done it myself, in Yosemite Valley. Yes, there's always someone around in Yosemite Valley. But I'd been there in March on that particular trip, in the middle of the week. There was snow on the ground, and fallen trees and rocks on the trail I'd chosen. I had felt isolated—until I encountered those hikers from Australia.

Brian was an experienced camper and hiker. No doubt he figured he was up for any sort of terrain, or conditions. But things happen out in the woods, or on the coast. It was possible he'd gone hiking and had a fall, breaking an arm or a leg and making it difficult for him to return to where he'd left the Jeep. Presumably he had his cell phone with him. But sometimes cell phone signals were few and far between, especially on the Northern California coast. He had been gone several days now. The cell phone could be out of juice. But he must have his charger. It wasn't in its usual place on the dresser, Sheila informed me, and he had a car charger in his Jeep. Maybe something else had happened.

Maybe, maybe, maybe.

None of this offered a plausible explanation for how his MedicAlert bracelet ended up on a burning boat with a corpse.

"I thought of that, about his going camping alone," Sheila said. "The note he left just said he was going away for a few days. It didn't say specifically that he was going camping. But he must have. I looked through the camping gear. Several things are missing."

"Let me take a look."

"It's in the garage." Sheila led the way back through the house and out to the double garage, with unpacked boxes stacked in the middle. Utility shelves held several clear plastic tubs. She pointed at an empty tub. "His sleeping bag is gone. The camp stove and the big cooler are gone. So is the tub with cooking stuff, the pots and plates and utensils. Both the lanterns are gone, but the tent is still here."

That told me he was going to be sleeping indoors, or that he'd gone camping with someone else who had a tent.

"His closet?" I asked.

"I checked," Sheila said, "and checked again. His hiking boots are gone. And his trek poles and backpack."

"Has his credit card or debit card been used since Friday?"

"That detective from the Petaluma Police Department asked me the same thing. Colman, her name is. I've got her card here. When I was talking to her yesterday, filing the missing persons report, I got the impression she figured Brian took off on his own. To get away from me." Sheila compressed her lips tightly and brushed away a tear. "Maybe he did."

"I don't think Brian would do that," I said. "You checked your bank account and credit card. What did you find?"

"There are no charges on the credit card," Sheila said. "Not since he used it at the hardware store two weeks ago. The last time he used the debit card was near here, on Wednesday of last week, to buy gas."

"Let me look at the desk and the computer. Is the desktop the only computer you have?"

"Yes," Sheila said. We went back to the house, to the desk in the corner of the dining room. "It's a Windows PC. We both have different log-ins to get onto the computer. As for email, we both have our own Gmail accounts. I don't know what his passwords are."

"I might be able to figure it out."

I sat down at the desk and turned on the computer and the printer as well. As the computer went through its start-up phase, I examined the desk and the surrounding area. On the right side of the keyboard and mouse, I saw an oversized pottery coffee mug, glazed in an iridescent purplish red. I picked it up. It was heavy and there was a faint brown residue inside. "Brian's mug?"

"Yes. He got that at some craft fair in Sonoma. He likes it because it's big and he drinks lots of coffee."

"Family trait." I, too, drink lots of coffee.

Sheila took the mug from me and looked inside. "Well, that needs washing." She turned and went to the kitchen.

I picked up a weekly calendar, and leafed through the pages. For the previous week, my brother had written in "Plumas," then he'd crossed out the notation. For this week, he'd written in two appointments, a lunch date with Lance tomorrow, Wednesday. On the calendar section for Thursday, I saw a name and phone number I didn't recognize, for a meeting at ten o'clock in the morning. For this coming Saturday, he'd written "Apple Fair." So Brian and Sheila had planned to take the children to the Gravenstein Apple Fair at Ragle Ranch Park up in Sebastopol. It was usually held the second weekend in August.

I looked at the books stacked on the desk to the left of the computer monitor. One was about mushrooming, finding and identifying wild mushrooms. I knew this was one of Brian's recent interests, along with birding. The other three books were hiking guides. The first was written by my friend Dan, about hiking at the Point Reyes National Seashore; *The Hiker's Hip Pocket Guide to the Mendocino Coast*; and *Day Hikes Around Sonoma County.*

Underneath the books I saw some papers. I pulled them out and examined them. They were printouts from the Internet, one containing information about the campground in Plumas County where Brian had intended to take the family camping. He'd written "CANX" and a date in black ink over the first page, showing that he'd cancelled the campsite reservation, the day after his phone argument with Sheila.

As for the other printouts, it looked as though Brian had been researching places to go for a short camping trip on his own. He had printed out information on campgrounds on the coast, in Sonoma County and Mendocino County.

Two brochures were stuck into the pages of the Sonoma County hiking book. Both were for Armstrong Redwoods State Natural Reserve and the Austin Creek State Recreation area. The two parks were adjacent, in an area a few miles north of the small town of Guerneville, on the Russian River. The larger brochure contained a map and descriptions of the parks' flora, fauna and trails. The smaller brochure was specific to the Bullfrog Pond Campground at Austin Creek.

I set the brochures aside and opened the lower desk drawer, which was deep enough for file folders. Here were bank records, information on the retirement savings Brian and Sheila were building, and details about their health plan. There was a tax folder as well. They had a will and durable powers of attorney, and they'd made arrangements for who would take care of the children should they die. Here too was a file about the house in Sonoma that Brian and Sheila were selling, and another containing Brian's résumé and information about his new job in Petaluma. I found folders for their vehicles, Brian's Wrangler and Sheila's Honda. I jotted down the license plate number and vehicle identification number for the Jeep.

I moved on to the shallow drawer and found a checkbook and an assortment of check registers. I also found a small notebook, two by three inches, with a red cover and lined pages. People frequently keep lists of user names and passwords, because these days there are so many of them, and it's difficult to remember all of them. My brother was no exception. Here was the key that would give me access to Brian's computer, his email, his financial records.

I looked at the little book in my hand. The sort of probing I would normally do in a missing persons case felt like an intrusion when the people involved were my brother and his wife.

But if I was going to find Brian, and a reason for his disappearance, I had to intrude.

I turned my attention to the computer monitor, which offered me the opportunity to log in either as Brian or Sheila. I consulted the little book. Brian had used a password that was easy for him to remember, a combination of his children's initials and birthdates.

The wallpaper was a picture of the two children, an outdoor shot, with Yosemite Falls in the background. It must have been taken during their camping trip earlier in the summer.

I began looking through the list of documents on the computer, in a folder labeled "Brian." Here I found correspondence and learned that as far back as last September, my brother had been updating his résumé and applying for jobs in the Petaluma school district.

At the bottom of the computer I saw a toolbar with the logo of the Mozilla Firefox browser. I clicked on this and the browser opened to Brian's home page, which was the Sierra Club website.

I clicked on the Bookmark tab. The drop-down menu gave me a list of folders, organized into subjects and topics of interest. One tab held financial links. Brian and Sheila had a bank account with Wells Fargo, and investments through Fidelity and Vanguard.

"How are your finances?" I asked Sheila as she returned from the kitchen.

"Okay for now. Lance is giving us a break on the rent. We need all the help we can get, financially. In addition to paying rent on this place, we're still paying the mortgage on the house in Sonoma. That's causing some real financial pain, I can tell you that." Sheila pointed at the calendar. "This meeting on Thursday is with the principal at the school where Brian will be teaching. He's supposed to start the new job next week. If he doesn't start that job, and we don't have his salary…oh, hell, I don't know what we're going to do."

"We can call and reschedule the meeting, that's all. The principal doesn't need to know why."

I turned back to the computer and found the link for Brian and Sheila's Facebook page. It contained pictures of the family. Here Brian and Sheila had posted more pictures of the Yosemite camping trip, and photos of other places the family had gone. Here was a visit to Monterey, where my mother lives, and pictures of the children at the aquarium.

I looked at the photos of Brian and Sheila's friends on the Facebook page. There were a lot of people I didn't know, but I found a picture of Lance Coverdell. Brian's college roommate and best man was tall and lanky, with a lean face and dark hair. In another photo, Lance was with Becca, his wife. She was nearly as tall as Lance, with long blond hair and a willowy figure.

Willowy, I thought. Willow? I peered at Becca's face. A tenuous connection at best. Surely not. Brian wouldn't have an affair. And certainly not with a friend's wife. But… What if Becca had a thing for Brian? What if she was using the name Willow? I mulled this over. I didn't know Becca at all. Come to that, how well did I know my brother? We didn't see each other that often. He had his life and I had mine. And Sheila didn't like Becca at all. She must have a reason for her antipathy.

I put these thoughts aside and turned my attention to the bookmarks in the browser. One caught my eye, called "Wish List." It turned out to be a list of locations, mostly various state and national parks in California and other states. I guessed that it was a list of places Brian would like to see. I copied the bookmark list into a document and sent it to the printer. If Brian had decided to go camping on his own, maybe he'd gone to one of these places. Somewhere close to home, though. He'd left on Friday and planned to return on Sunday. That meant he'd gone somewhere within a day's drive, probably closer. I opened another browser window and did a search on state parks in Sonoma County. I sent this to the printer as well.

Other folders in the bookmarks were labeled according to Brian's interests. He had a bookmark called "Organizations," which included links to a number of environmental and conservation organizations, including the Sierra Club. One of these was the Mono Lake Committee, which I also belonged to, and the Point Reyes Bird Observatory, headquartered here in Petaluma. One of the links was to the Friends of the Petaluma River. Becca belonged to the group and she'd encouraged Brian to join. According to the description on the website, the Friends was "a non-profit organization that is dedicated to celebrating and conserving the Petaluma River, its wetlands, and wildlife."

I found a link for Gmail and logged into Brian's email account. There was nothing here that was out of the ordinary. Nothing from anyone named Willow, or Becca for that matter. Just a message from Lance confirming the lunch date on Wednesday, tomorrow.

Brian and Sheila both had cell phones and accounts from a well-known provider. Using the password list, I logged into Brian's account and found a list of calls for his cell phone number. But it only went up to the end of their billing period. I printed out the list of calls and asked Sheila to take a look at it, to see if she recognized—or didn't recognize—any numbers. The area code for Sonoma County was 707. I lived in Oakland and Dad in Castro Valley, which was the 510 area code. Mother's area code in Monterey was 831, and Sheila's family in Fresno County was in area code 559.

I looked through the browser history on the computer, focusing on the past week. During Sheila's absence, Brian had accessed a number of websites that told me he was planning a trip. It looked like he'd done a search on state parks in Sonoma and Mendocino counties, and used other websites that showed campsite photos, trails, and hikes. He'd also looked at the State of California's website on state parks.

Sheila's voice interrupted me. "Do you want something to eat, Jeri?"

I looked up and then at my watch. "No, too much to do. I'm going to talk with the police. And have a talk with Lance Coverdell."

EIGHT

BEFORE LEAVING THE HOUSE, I JOTTED DOWN THE name of the Petaluma detective who had talked with Sheila when my sister-in-law had reported Brian missing. Then I drove to the police department on North Petaluma Boulevard. The department's Investigations Unit handled missing persons cases. Inside, I asked for Detective Marcy Colman. A few minutes later, she walked into the lobby and introduced herself.

She was a short, wiry woman about my age, mid-thirties, with a head of unruly dark curls. She had a slight frown on her face as she examined my business card, and I got the distinct impression she'd rather not have a nosy private investigator interfering in her case, even though the PI was the missing man's sister.

"It's been less than twenty-four hours since I spoke with Ms. Howard," Colman said, fingering the business card. "I've set the wheels in motion, but I have nothing to report so far."

"I've handled a few missing persons cases, so I know it takes time. Any luck with finding his Jeep? Or getting something from his cell phone records?"

She looked annoyed, as though she thought I was butting in and getting ahead of myself. "I don't have anything on the vehicle, not yet anyway. Someone is bound to spot it. I've contacted his phone provider as well. They may be able to locate the phone, if he still has it. Too early for any results, but I hope to have something later today, or tomorrow." She paused and gave me a measuring look. "It's possible your brother took off on his own, for reasons of his own. Your sister-in-law told me they'd had an argument on the phone last week."

I shook my head, disagreeing with her. "The body on the boat and the MedicAlert bracelet put a different spin on that theory. As well as some urgency."

"I talked with the Sonoma County detectives this morning. They filled me in about the body on the boat." Colman reached up and pushed some of her curls off her forehead. "You know your brother's a person of interest in that homicide."

Yes. And I was determined to find him before the police did, so I could get the full story.

"All the more reason to find him as soon as possible and clear this up," I said. "I'll check in with you later. And of course I'll let you know if I find out anything in my investigation."

"I'd appreciate that," she said.

When she'd left the lobby, I headed back out to my car. Working with Colman, and with Griffin and Harris, the Sonoma County detectives, was something of a balancing act. I had to tread carefully and not step on any toes in my eagerness to find Brian. However, they wouldn't share everything with me, so I wasn't inclined to share everything either.

I thought about Brian's phone. It could be at the bottom of the Petaluma River. And if the phone wasn't in the water, and the battery was dead, calls to Brian's number would go straight to voice mail, as was happening now. I'd already accessed Brian's cell phone records on his computer. But the records I'd found didn't tell the whole story. They ended with his last bill cycle. I needed to know if he'd used that phone since Friday, the day he left home.

———

BEFORE SHUTTING down the computer at Brian and Sheila's house, I'd done an Internet search for Lance Coverdell's real estate company. It was located in downtown Petaluma on Second Street between B and C Streets. I found a parking spot on Second and crossed to the opposite sidewalk. The real estate office was in the middle of the block. On either side of the center door, large glass windows were decorated with photos of houses for sale. I opened the door and stepped inside. At the front counter a twenty-something receptionist was talking on the phone, a headset over her short black hair. Behind her, the room had been partitioned into spacious cubicles, some empty, others with agents working at computers or talking on phones.

The receptionist disconnected the phone and smiled up at me. "May I help you?"

"I'm here to see Mr. Coverdell," I said.

"Is he expecting you?"

"No." I shook my head.

"He's not in the office right now. I expect him back at three, or a little after. Can someone else help you?"

"I do need to speak with Mr. Coverdell." I looked at my watch. Twenty after two. My stomach rumbled, telling me I should have taken Sheila up on her offer of lunch. It had been a long time since breakfast and I was hungry. "I'll be back at three."

I left the office and walked down Second Street, to the Great Petaluma Mill, an old feed mill that had been converted into a shopping center. I found a place called the Wild Goat Bistro, with a vacant table near a window. I scanned the menu, ordered a chicken club sandwich and iced tea, and made short work of both.

After I finished my lunch and located a rest room, I went outside. The Petaluma River ran through town. It was navigable from this location, known as the Turning Basin, all the way to the river's mouth, emptying into San Pablo Bay, near the Marin County town of Novato. Here at the Basin, people launched kayaks, canoes and paddleboards. Farther downstream there were marinas. Where I stood, I saw public docks, and plenty of restaurants with outdoor tables on both shores. It was a pleasant location to have a glass of wine and a good meal. But I had other priorities on this warm August afternoon.

I retraced my steps to the real estate office. A silver Toyota Prius, this year's plug-in hybrid, backed into a parking space a few yards in front of me. A man in gray slacks and an open-collared blue shirt got out of the car and locked it with a beep from his key ring remote. I recognized him from the photo on the Facebook page, though that picture hadn't caught the threads of gray in his dark hair.

"Lance Coverdell," I said.

"Yes?" He looked at me without recognition.

"Jeri Howard, Brian Howard's sister."

"Oh, yeah." He smiled. "The private eye. Brian's mentioned you. Plus, we met at the wedding. Of course, you weren't a private eye then. That was a long time ago."

"Ten years. When was the last time you saw or talked with Brian?" I asked.

His smile dimmed, as though he was taken aback by my question. He responded with one of his own. "Why do you ask?"

"Brian is missing."

Lance stared at me, the expression on his face one of consternation. Then he shook himself and gestured at the front door of his office. "I think you'd better come in and give me the details."

He held the door open for me, then followed me inside, where he greeted the receptionist and collected a handful of pink message slips. He glanced at them and told the receptionist he didn't want to be disturbed. Then he led the way past several cubicles to a small kitchen, offering me water. I accepted. He poured two glasses from a pitcher in the refrigerator and handed one to me. Then I followed him to his own office. He shut the door and motioned me toward a chair in front of his sleek wooden desk. As he settled into his own office chair, I saw two photographs in silver frames, angled on one corner of the desk. One showed Lance with Becca. The other picture showed Lance, Becca, and a little girl who looked like both of them.

He saw me examining the photos. "That's Becca. We got married a year after Brian and Sheila. And that's our daughter, Lucy. She's eight." He took a sip from his glass, then set it on the desk and laced his fingers together. "So what's the story about Brian?"

I gave him an edited version, leaving out the body on the boat. "It looks like Brian left on Friday. Sheila got home on Sunday and found a note from him, saying he was going away for a few days and would be back Sunday. He never showed up. Sheila filed a missing persons report on Monday and I came up here today to see what I could find out. When did you last see him, or talk with him?"

"Last week. Brian called me on... I think it was Tuesday. He asked if we could get together for lunch. He suggested Thursday, but I was busy all day. We finally agreed on tomorrow, Wednesday." Lance reached for his desk calendar and pointed at the notation.

"And before that?"

Lance flipped the pages of the calendar. "We talked on the phone the last week in July. Brian said he was planning to go birding with his dad, over at Point Reyes. And that Sheila and the kids were going to Firebaugh."

"Did he say that there was any specific reason for having lunch?"

Lance hesitated. Then he sighed. "Brian and Sheila are having some problems. I guess he wanted to talk about that. He and I had talked about it before."

"What has he told you?" I asked.

He took his time answering, choosing his words. "This business with Sheila's father being sick. I know on one level Brian understands Sheila being focused on her dad, because of the cancer. But on the other hand, he feels neglected, shut out."

"In what way?"

Lance took a sip from his glass. "Sheila has been back and forth to Firebaugh at least a couple of weekends a month, ever since the first of the year. She takes the kids with her, and Brian's left alone. That puts a strain on a marriage. He feels like he can't talk to her, so he talks to me."

"What else does he talk about, besides his marriage?"

"The job." Lance shook his head. "The past eighteen months, he's really hated that job in Sonoma. There was some major bad stuff going on in that school district where he was teaching. He felt like he had to get out, so he started applying over here. I know someone in the Petaluma school administration, so I put in a good word for him. I'm glad it worked out. He'll be much happier here, clean slate and all."

I took a sip of water and set down the glass. "Why would Brian need a clean slate? Sheila told me he didn't get along with his principal. What else was going on in Sonoma?"

Lance picked up a letter opener, playing with the blunted blade. "Last spring there was an incident involving a student. It hit Brian hard."

I frowned. "Incident" could mean a lot of things. I considered, then rejected, the possibility of any inappropriate contact between student and teacher. Brian wouldn't do that, I told myself. Not my kid brother. Maybe he'd had a physical confrontation with a junior high kid. I could see that happening.

"What kind of incident?" I asked.

"One of his students attempted suicide," Lance said. "I don't know the details. But Brian was really upset about it. Can't blame him. He kept saying he should have seen the signs, should have been able to prevent it. But sometimes you miss things. You can't be the hero all the time."

Yes, I could understand Brian's reaction to a suicide attempt by one of his students. He taught junior high. The thought of a kid that age trying to commit suicide...

But Sheila hadn't mentioned it. Did she know?

Or was Lance's story about the student's suicide attempt true? It was hearsay, his version of a conversation with Brian. I would have to double-check and verify that Lance was telling me the truth. If he was, it wasn't like Brian to make up such a tale. Such an incident involving one of his students would have bothered him a great deal. And normally he would have discussed something that serious with his wife. If he hadn't, that indicated a major rift in their marriage.

Suddenly the door opened. Lance looked up, annoyed at having been interrupted when he'd told the receptionist he didn't want to be disturbed. Then his face changed. He smiled at the woman who'd entered the office.

She was tall and slender, and her blond hair was piled into an untidy knot atop her head, skewered there with a pair of chopsticks. She wore a mauve T-shirt decorated with flowers over gauzy capri pants a shade darker, and a pair of sandals. Amethysts set in gold dangled from her earlobes, swaying as she walked into the office. Slung over one shoulder was an oversized handbag made of white straw, with a pair of sunglasses tucked into a side flap.

Becca ignored me and focused on Lance. "Did you hear about the fire out at Newman's Marina? One of the boats blew up and burned. I'm not surprised."

"Why do you say that?" I asked.

Becca turned and surveyed me with hazel eyes, as though it had just registered that there was someone else in the room with Lance. "Who's this?"

Lance rose from his chair, leaned forward, and kissed her on the cheek. "Becca, this is Jeri Howard, Brian's sister. Jeri's a private investigator. She's here because Brian's disappeared."

Becca looked shocked. "Disappeared? What happened?"

"He left home Friday." I summarized the story. "So, why aren't you surprised about the fire at Newman's Marina?"

Becca looked at me as though she was wondering what the marina had to do with Brian's disappearance. "Have you ever seen Newman's Marina?"

"No, can't say that I have."

"It's a marina and a roadhouse," Lance said.

"It's an eyesore and a mess," Becca said. "The guy who owns it doesn't keep up the place. I'm not surprised they had a fire. He's got oil, paints, solvents, propane, and God knows what else piled around the place. All that crap is contaminating the river. The roadhouse is a biker hangout. Word is, you can buy all sorts of drugs out there. The sheriff's department is out there constantly, dealing with fights."

"Walt Newman is a crusty old guy, that's for sure." Lance smiled and looked at me. "I'm a Petaluma native. My grandfather used to tell me stories about Newman's. The place had quite a reputation during Prohibition, lots of bootlegging and some pros-titution."

"It still has a bad reputation," Becca said. "I wish the county would shut him down. Maybe we will, with the protests about the land deal."

"What land deal?" I asked.

"There's a parcel for sale on the river south of the marina," Lance added. "It was owned by a farmer who died. His heirs want to sell it to the highest bidder. Old Man Newman's trying to buy it, to expand his operations. But the local environmental organizations are putting up roadblocks."

"We're putting together a bid," Becca said. "We want to preserve that land as wetlands and wildlife habitat."

"So the environmental groups are in the way of Mr. Newman's plans," I said.

"Mostly in court and through public opinion," Becca said. "Which reminds me, Lance. I want you to look at this op-ed piece I wrote for the newspaper."

She set her straw bag on Lance's desk and began rummaging. She pulled out a file folder. Something else tumbled out of the purse as well, a packet of note cards and envelopes tied with a blue ribbon that was caught on the corner of the folder. The cards spilled onto the desk and the floor. I leaned over to pick up a few of the cards, then sat up in the chair and examined them. They were ivory card stock, decorated with sketches of birds. One was an Anna's hummingbird, another a great blue heron, a third a spotted towhee, and the fourth scene showed a yellow-rumped warbler. This was the same card Brian had received, with a note from "Willow."

"Pretty cards," I said, handing them to Becca. "Where did you get them?"

"At a gallery up in Occidental." Becca stuffed the cards and envelopes back into her purse and handed the file folder to Lance. "If you could read this and give me your feedback."

"Sure." He set the folder on his desk. "Is there anything else we can help you with, Jeri?"

"One other question. Do either of you know someone named Willow?"

Something flickered in Becca's hazel eyes, I was sure of it.

"Not that I recall," Lance said. "Who's Willow?"

"I'm not sure." I turned to Becca. "Do you know who Willow is?"

Becca shook her head, her amethyst earrings swaying. "No, I don't."

I didn't believe her.

NINE

AS LAKEVILLE STREET HEADS EAST OUT OF PETALUMA, it becomes California Highway 116, or the Lakeville Highway. A few miles out of town, Highway 116 continues toward Sonoma, and the Lakeville Highway turns south along the river.

The Petaluma River is about eighteen miles long. Its headwaters rise near Cotati, a town northwest of Petaluma. The river becomes a tidal slough, emptying into San Pablo Bay, in the northernmost reaches of the larger San Francisco Bay. Lakeville is an unincorporated community located about four miles southeast of Petaluma, on a stretch of road that runs close to the river. The terrain here is open, with few trees. Farmhouses dot the terrain to the east, while to the west, between the road and the river, are sprawling hayfields and high marsh full of pickleweed.

I passed the fire station for the Lakeville Volunteer Fire Department. In a mile or so, I reached Lakeville. There wasn't much to it, a collection of buildings, some commercial, others homes, cabins really. A quarter mile further south I saw a wooden sign reading NEWMAN'S. I slowed my car and turned right into a gravel parking lot.

Newman's Roadhouse and Marina was situated on a low bluff overlooking the Petaluma River. The place looked as disreputable as Becca had said. The weathered wood exterior of the one-story building had once been painted blue, but now the paint was cracked and peeling. The front of the building faced the road, with a covered porch made of wood planks. On the left was the roadhouse part, with neon signs advertising beer and burgers. It was late afternoon and there were half a dozen Harleys clustered in front. Several rough-looking bikers lounged in the metal lawn chairs on the front porch. As I got out of my car, they gave me the eye.

The right side of the building looked like the marina office. I took the two steps up to the porch and tried the front door. It was locked. I peered through the grimy window and didn't see any movement inside.

That left me with the roadhouse. I walked along the porch, past a couple of bikers smoking and talking in low tones, and went into the bar. After the bright August sunshine, it took a few seconds for my eyes to adjust to the darkness inside. I saw three men and two women clustered around a table, and two more men playing pool at a table near the back. A dark-haired woman dressed in jeans and a tank top was at the bar, sipping on a beer and eating onion rings. She was chatting with the bartender, who was tall and bulky, with an array of tattoos snaking down each arm. He looked as though he could break up any fights and take on all comers.

"Help you?" he asked as I stepped up to the bar.

"I'm looking for Walt Newman."

"Not here," the bartender said. "Don't know where he is or when he'll be back."

I handed him a business card. "It's about that boat that burned here at the marina early Sunday morning."

He examined the card. "Private eye, huh. Insurance claim?"

"I do a lot of insurance work," I said. Which was true, though I wasn't handling the claim on this particular boat.

The bartender set the card on the counter next to the cash register. "Well, you're gonna have to pay the claim on that boat. It's a goner."

"Just talking to people, to get a handle on what happened."

The bartender shrugged. "I didn't see anything but I sure as hell heard it. We're open till two in the morning. Must have been about one when it happened. Propane explosion. That's what they say." He turned to the woman, who'd been listening. "What about you, Francie? Did you see anything?"

"Yeah, I was outside, on the dock by Barney's boat." Francie tossed back her long brown hair. "Heard a bang and that sucker went up. It made all the docks and boats rock and roll. People came running with hoses and buckets. Tried to put out the fire but it was burning like crazy. Didn't do any good till the fire department showed up. It's a wonder those other boats didn't catch fire. The dock's burned, too. They found a body." She shuddered. "Burned to death like that. What a way to go."

"Yes, I know about the body. Did you see or hear anything before the explosion?" I asked.

Francie shook her head. "It was a party, music playing, people talking, you know how it is. I didn't hear anything until the boat exploded. Like I said, I was at Barney's boat and it's tied up at the south end of the marina. The boat that burned was at the north end."

"I heard something." One of the pool players had left the table. Now he joined us at the bar, listening to the conversation. He was a short guy with a blond ponytail, wearing leathers and a vest that proclaimed his motorcycle club membership. "I was out in the parking lot, smoking. Right before the explosion, I heard something sounded like a backfire, either a car or a bike. Sounded to me like it was up at the north end. Maybe there was a spark and that's what set off the propane."

Backfire, or gunshot? My guess was that people assumed the man had died from the explosion or fire. His death by gunshot wasn't yet commonly known.

The bartender was shaking his head. "No, propane would need something direct to ignite like that. Had to be a leak in the cabin. The guy that got killed, I'll bet he stepped inside and fired up a cigarette. That would set off the propane."

"I'll know more when I see the report," I said. Or maybe Walt Newman could tell me more, when I caught up with him.

"You should talk with the guy who lives in the cabin at the north end," Francie said. "Chet something-or-other. What's his name?"

"Olsen," the guy with the ponytail said. "Chet Olsen. Yeah, his cabin is closest to that dock. That's number twelve. If anybody saw anything before the boat went up, it would be him."

"Thanks. Mind if I have a look around?"

"Suit yourself," the bartender said. "I'll give your card to Walt when he shows up."

I left the bar and walked down past the marina office, then
around to the rear of the building. A narrow gravel road led down
a slope to a cluster of cottages and cabins, people who lived here
at the marina. Narrow elevated walkways fanned out across the
marsh and the shallows, leading to a series of wider docks that
paralleled the river's bank.

I counted fourteen boats tied up at slips, a mixture of sail-
boats, cabin cruisers, and catamarans. In a wide area edged by
marsh, I saw several boats that were on racks, or dry-docked, evidently for repairs. Cans of paint and solvents were piled haphaz-
ardly near a shed, along with ropes, broken parts and sections of
boat. An overflowing plastic trash can held rags that smelled of
gasoline.

I walked north, past a boat launch ramp. There were several cabins of varying sizes, some better maintained than others. I
came to the end of the marina, where cabin twelve sat, about forty
feet from the walkway that led to the dock, which was some distance from the other docks, secluded from the rest of the marina
by some trees. Here were two more boats, tied up at this dock
where the wooden planks were charred and scorched. The boat
that had burned was gone, hauled off by the authorities, or the
owner. The two remaining boats were both cabin cruisers, both
looking fairly new. One was called the *Rosarita* and the other, the
Silverado. Both had a dusting of ash from the fire. I got out my
cell phone, which had a camera, and snapped several pictures of
the boats, making sure to get the names and hull identification
numbers. I took photos of the damaged dock as well.

The Petaluma River shimmered in the afternoon sun. The
river was wide here, with nothing on the other side except marsh.
I spotted a great blue heron, standing like a sentinel in the reeds
upstream. A snowy egret flew overhead and landed near the heron, then they moved slowly through the shallows, heads craned
downward as they searched the water for food. One of them struck
downward and came up with a fish wriggling in its beak. Then it
swallowed the fish, stretching its neck upward as the meal went
down its gullet.

I turned from the river and walked to the front door of cabin twelve. I knocked but there was no answer. I'd have to come back to see if I could talk with Chet Olsen about what he might have seen the night of the fire.

I retraced my steps to my car, feeling tired. No wonder, it had been a hell of a day. But I had a couple of stops, and phone calls, to make before returning home.

I looked through my phone's contacts for my cousin, Donna Doyle. She's a biologist—and a warden for the California Department of Fish and Wildlife. A few years ago, she'd been in the department's Central Region, which included Monterey and its environs. After that, she transferred to the North Central Region, working from the Sacramento area. Last year, she'd transferred again, to the Bay–Delta Region, which included counties from Santa Cruz in the south to Sonoma and Napa counties in the north, all the densely populated counties of the greater Bay Area, and the extensive Delta at the confluence of the San Joaquin and Sacramento Rivers. The regional office was located in Napa, with a second office in Stockton, on the Delta.

She didn't spend a lot of time in her office. She was usually out in the field. She answered after the third ring. "Agent Doyle."

"Hi, Donna. This is Jeri. What are you up to?"

"Looking for a poacher, up by Cazadero. But I'm heading back to the office now."

"You're in Sonoma County? So am I."

"Where?"

"Lakeville," I said. "South of Petaluma."

"I just passed Cotati heading toward Petaluma, cuz. Let's get some coffee and talk."

"Yes, I do need to talk."

Donna picked up on something in my voice. "What's going on? I heard your mom went out of town yesterday. Something about a family emergency."

The family grapevine knew about my mother's sudden departure from Monterey, but so far didn't know the reason.

"Brian's missing." After Donna's shocked exclamation, I filled her in on the story.

"Hell's bells," Donna said. "Listen, I'm almost to Petaluma. Meet me at the Petaluma Pie Company. I'm in the mood for something sweet."

TEN

DONNA WAS WAITING FOR ME OUTSIDE THE PIE STORE near downtown's Putnam Plaza Park, a small green oasis fronted by shops. It was just a few blocks from the real estate office where I'd met Lance Coverdell earlier in the afternoon.

Donna's father is my mother's older brother. Our extensive family tree is a mixture of Irish and Italian immigrants, the Doyles and Ravellas, and their offshoots are spread all over Monterey County. They had been in the area for over a hundred years. The Ravellas, from Sicily, were fishermen. The Doyles had migrated from Ireland at the time of the Great Famine, as had so many Irish Americans. They worked the canneries in Monterey and helmed small businesses.

My cousin is three inches shorter and three years older than I am, which means she's thirty-nine. Donna takes after the Doyle side of the equation. She is fair, with blue eyes, a round face and a snub nose, liberally dusted with freckles.

Since she spends a good deal of time outdoors, she is tanned and fit in her uniform, which has dark green trousers and a khaki shirt with a blue-and-gold patch showing the state of California divided into counties, with the state symbol, a golden bear. The belt around her waist contains, among other things, a gun.

As a warden with the California Department of Fish and Wildlife, Donna is tasked with protecting the state's wildlife and natural resources. She enforces laws relating to hunting, fishing, pollution, endangered species, and wildlife habitation destruction, and as such, she's an armed law enforcement officer with state-wide arrest authority. Typically she drives a state pickup truck, but she might also be found on anything from a horse to a boat to a helicopter or plane. She investigates crimes, like the poaching case she was working on now, collecting evidence and building a case. She also serves search warrants and arrests criminals. In addition to the entire state of California, Donna and her colleagues also have responsibility for the ocean 200 miles off the coast.

When I was in Monterey on vacation a few years back, Donna had gotten me involved in a case that involved pelican mutilations. It soon widened to include toxic waste dumping in Monterey Bay and a local murder.

"Hey, Jeri." She greeted me with a hug. We went inside the pie shop and ordered. Since it was the start of apple season, the choice was clear—apple pie for both of us. "Put some ice cream on mine," Donna told the server.

"Sounds good. Me, too," I said.

We paid the tab and carried our pie and coffee to a nearby table. "You should come over to Napa," Donna said. "You haven't seen our new house. Kay's really had a great time decorating it."

Kay is Donna's partner. They've been together for a number of years and recently got married. When Donna transferred, they had sold their house in the Sacramento area and bought another on the outskirts of Napa. Kay makes jewelry. She sells her creations to stores and online, and sometimes at arts and crafts fairs.

"I'd love to see both of you. But it will have to wait." I cut off a bit of my apple pie. It was delicious, particularly drenched with melting vanilla ice cream.

"Yeah, I'm really busy these days. This damn poacher." Donna grimaced. "The guy keeps slipping through my fingers, but I'll catch up with him soon. He's working up north of Guerneville, near Cazadero, killing deer, wild pig, whatever he can find. I just wrapped another case, some guys growing marijuana on state park land."

"Again? You told me you caught a pot grower last year, doing the same thing."

"Yeah, second time in two years. Same situation, different location. This most recent case was at Robert Louis Stevenson State Park in Napa County, north of Calistoga. These guys were clear-cutting the forest, grading the land to put in more plants, and damming a creek to divert water. You wouldn't believe the damage. Killing wildlife, toxic chemicals, trash everywhere. It just makes me crazy." Donna sounded equal parts disgusted and righteously indignant.

"That case last year was at Annadel State Park east of Santa Rosa, smaller plantation, but certainly the same kind of environmental damage. And who foots the bill to restore the land? The taxpayers. The bastard who had the pot plantation at Annadel got a slap on the wrist, because he had a slick lawyer. That's not gonna happen this time. I've got a good, solid case." She swallowed coffee and leaned toward me. "So what's the deal with Brian? He was due home Sunday and he didn't show?"

I nodded, cutting off another section of pie. "It looks like he was planning to go camping. Some of his gear is missing."

"If he went camping by himself, something must have happened to him," Donna said. "Car trouble, an injury, no cell phone service."

"Right, but there's a development that puts a different spin on that. This is for your ears only, Donna. I don't want this broadcast all over the family grapevine."

She frowned. "Absolutely. You have my word."

"Sheila filed a missing persons report yesterday. Early this morning she got a phone call." I told Donna that Brian's Medic-Alert bracelet had been found near the body on the burned boat. "So this morning we all met at the Sonoma County Coroner's Office. I had to look at the body for a possible identification. But it wasn't Brian."

"Hell's bells." Donna had been demolishing the rest of her pie while I spoke. Now she put down her fork and reached for her coffee. "Brian's bracelet was broken? I suppose it could have fallen off, somewhere, and this other man picked it up after the fact and stuffed it in his pocket."

"I thought of that, but it looked to me like the bracelet had been caught on something and torn off."

"A fight?"

"Could be," I said. "Listen, Donna, do me a favor. Can you

check around to see if Brian got a hiking permit or a campsite at any of the state parks in Sonoma County? I can give you the license plate number of his Jeep."

"Sure, I'll see what I can do."

I pulled out my notebook, where I'd written Brian's plate and vehicle identification numbers. She jotted them down in her own notebook.

"I'll check around and call you." A cell phone rang. "That's mine." She pulled her phone from a pocket and answered the call. "I'm in Petaluma, stopped for coffee. Sure, I can be there in…" She looked at her watch. "Half an hour, forty minutes tops." She disconnected the call. "I've got to go. I'll check in with you tomorrow."

After Donna left I finished the last bite of my apple pie, washing it down with coffee. Then I pulled out my own cell phone and made a call. It went straight to voice mail. "Hey, Rita, it's Jeri Howard. I'm in Petaluma, heading back to Oakland. I'd like to see you, so I'll stop in San Rafael."

I walked back to where I'd parked my car and drove through Petaluma to U.S. 101, heading south through Novato. When I reached San Rafael, the Marin county seat, I took the Fourth Street exit for downtown. A few blocks west, I located a parking spot on the street and fed coins into the meter.

Rita Lydecker's office was on the second floor of a building on D Street near downtown San Rafael. She hadn't called me back so I wasn't sure she'd be there, but as I approached I heard her loud, booming laugh echoing off the walls.

When I opened the door, Rita was on her cell phone, one hand running through her platinum blond hair as she leaned back in her office chair with her feet propped up on a cardboard box. Other boxes were piled here and there in the office. She motioned me to a chair that contained an empty box. I moved it to the floor and sat down. Rita had stopped smoking, but she still wore that jasmine cologne. Usually she dressed in silk with lots of gold jewelry, but today her barrel-shaped body was attired in a pair of khakis with a smudge at one knee and a T-shirt in an eye-popping shade of purple. Her hands were bare, no rings.

When she finished the call, she set the cell phone on the desk and grinned. "Jeri. Got your message. How are you?"

"Up and down." I gestured at the boxes. "Are you moving?"

"Gonna give up the office."

"You're not retiring?" Rita was older than me, early sixties, I guessed. She'd worked as a prison guard and a bail bondsman before moving into another career as a private investigator.

"Cutting back," she said. "I'm not getting any younger, girlfriend. I'll be sixty-five later this year. Old enough for Medicare."

"Really? I had no idea."

"Yeah, well, sixty-five doesn't seem that old the closer I get to it, but let's face it, my joints ain't as young as they used to be. Got arthritis in my knees and shoulder. Let me tell you, girlfriend, I know when it's gonna rain. The minute the weather gets cold and damp, I start aching. Anyway, I got things I want to do. Like that trip to Europe I've been promising myself for years. So I'm giving up the office. I'll operate out of my house. I've always been a solo operation. That's the beauty of being self-employed. I can roll my own schedule. So what brings you to my neck of the woods? A case?"

I nodded. "A missing persons case. Only this one is personal." I laid out the details for her, and she took notes, promising to do whatever she could to help me search for Brian. Between us we had a lot of contacts in the investigative community.

As I left Rita's office I called a number in Oakland. "Hi, it's Jeri. I'm in San Rafael, heading home. Okay if I drop by? Good, see you soon."

ELEVEN

FORTY MINUTES LATER, AFTER THREADING MY WAY through evening rush-hour traffic, I parked in front of a small Craftsman bungalow on Manila Avenue in Oakland's Temescal neighborhood, not far from busy Broadway. Sid Vernon, my ex, lived here, just a few blocks from Oakland Technical High School, his alma mater.

Sid bought the house after our divorce. Before and during our marriage, we'd shared an apartment in another neighborhood. The marriage itself had lasted only a few years. It wasn't working for me, so I left him. He resented that. But time heals wounds, or some of them, anyway. In subsequent years we'd gone from prickly post-divorce hostility to a friendly relationship.

I was Sid's second wife. His first lived in San Diego with her second husband. Sid's daughter Vicki, whom I still considered my stepdaughter, had graduated from the University of California at Berkeley, and was now a grad student.

I climbed the steps to the front porch and rang the bell.

The woman who opened the front door was in the running to become wife number three. At least it was looking that way. They had been together for a couple of years now. Graciela Portillo was, like Sid, an Oakland police officer. Whether that would make a good marriage or a difficult one, I didn't know. Grace and her son from a previous marriage had moved in with Sid last year.

"Hi, Jeri," Grace said through the steel mesh of the security screen door. At her feet, a small black-and-brown mutt woofed at me. "Hush, Maggie."

"Hi, Grace. How's the patient?"

Grace rolled her eyes.

"Yeah, that's what I figured."

"See for yourself." Grace unlocked and opened the door. "He's back in the family room."

I entered the house and offered my hand, palm up, to Maggie the mutt. She sniffed my hand and my clothing, no doubt catching the scent of cat, and wagged her tail. I made my way through the living room and kitchen to the family room, which had been added on the back of the house. A big flat-screen TV sat on a low stand, a sound bar on the wall behind it and a shelf full of DVDs next to it. In front of the TV were a recliner, a love seat and a worn armchair.

Sid was a big man with a pair of blue eyes set in a craggy face and tawny blond hair that was now going gray. I will be thirty-six on my upcoming October birthday, and Sid was nearing fifty. He'd been a cop for more than twenty-five years and in the Marines before that.

He was stretched out in the recliner, wearing a flowered Hawaiian shirt and khaki shorts on this late August afternoon. He didn't get up, and the reason was illustrated by the scar on his left knee and the lightweight aluminum walker next to the chair.

I sat down on the love seat. "So how's the knee replacement?"

He growled and grumbled. "Pain in the ass. Or the knee. Take your pick."

"It had to be done," Grace said, joining us in the family room, the dog at her heels.

"I know it did," Sid said. "Got tired of the knee hurting all the time. The docs said the cartilage was worn down to the bone. I blew out this damn knee one time too many. First time was chasing some perp in West Oakland, ages ago. Injured it several times over the years, and then the arthritis kicked in. This time, hell, I was just out for a walk with Gracie, around Lake Merritt. Took a step and wound up in the ER at Kaiser."

"Jeri, I've got a pitcher of iced tea in the fridge," Grace said. "Want some?"

"That would be great, thanks."

She turned to Sid. "How about you?"

"Sure, thanks, babe," Sid said. As Grace headed back to the kitchen he sighed. "Can't even have a damn beer because of the painkillers I'm taking."

On the table between the love seat and Sid's recliner was an iPad and a framed photo of his daughter. "How's Vicki?"

Sid's smile transformed his face. "You know she got that fellowship to study at Oxford. She's so excited about that. She stayed around for my surgery, then flew to London. I'm getting emails every day. She's been to the Cotswolds and now she's headed up to the Lake District."

"Let's see, the surgery was three weeks ago."

He nodded. "Yeah. I was in the hospital a few days, then rehab for a week. Sure was glad to get home. So here I am, recuperating. I go to physical therapy several times a week."

"How are you getting to the appointments?" I asked. I knew Grace's schedule was busy. She returned from the kitchen with a tray bearing three glasses. I took one. "Thanks."

"I'm taking him when I'm off," Grace said, setting a glass on the table next to Sid. Then she sat down on the armchair and sipped from her own glass. "My son's not old enough to drive, so some of the guys in the department are helping out."

"Wayne took me yesterday," Sid said. Wayne Hobart had been Sid's partner at various times when both of them worked Homicide.

"Let me know if you need a ride to physical therapy," I said. "I can make time."

"Thanks. I'll do that. Gotta do what I can to get back up to speed. I'm tired of sitting on my ass. I want to get back to work."

"I've got a job for you," I said. "My brother's missing."

"Brian? What the hell?" Sid frowned, the creases in his face deepening as I told him the story. Grace leaned forward, listening. I wanted her input as well. When I'd first met her, she was working the missing persons detail at OPD. Since they were both police officers they had access to resources I couldn't use. I was pulling out all the stops in my search for Brian.

I gave them what information I had. "The two Sonoma County detectives are Griffin and Harris. They're not very forthcoming with information. Neither is the Petaluma detective who is working on the missing persons case. And I know why. They figure because Brian's bracelet was found near the body, he's a person of interest. Or even worse, a suspect."

"I can't see your kid brother shooting some guy," Sid said. "He's the classic family man, a schoolteacher, for crying out loud. I bet he's never even had a traffic violation."

"Oh, he has. He got picked up for speeding once, but that was back in college. Not much of a misspent youth that I recall. And to the best of my knowledge he hasn't been in trouble since." I didn't share with Sid my sister-in-law's suspicions that Brian might be having an affair.

"If he's such a straight arrow," Grace said, "how does his bracelet wind up on the boat?"

"That's the big question mark," I said. "The link looked broken, like it had been caught on something. All I can think of is, Brian was in an altercation with the man. The bracelet fell off, or was torn off. The man put the bracelet in his pocket."

"That makes sense to me," Sid said. "But where's Brian?"

"I don't know. But I've got to find him."

"How can we help?" Grace asked.

"I need information, more than I've been able to pry out of Griffin or Harris. I can sense that they don't want me involved, but I thought maybe you two could help."

"Go around the back, you mean." Sid nodded. "I don't know anyone in the Sonoma County Sheriff's Office. How about you, Grace?"

She looked thoughtful. "I met someone from the DA's office a few months ago. I could call her."

"There's always Joe Kelso," Sid added.

"Is he still the police chief up in Cloverdale?" I asked.

"Yeah," Sid said. "I talked with Joe about a week ago."

Joe had been Sid's partner in Homicide, and best man at our wedding, which had taken place in the backyard of my parents' house in Alameda. Mother and Dad had divorced after I married Sid, going their separate ways. Around the same time, Joe had retired from the Oakland Police Department, but not from law enforcement. He and his wife, Brenda, had moved to Cloverdale, the northernmost town in Sonoma County, where Joe headed up a small police department. With a population of less than nine thousand people, Cloverdale was a different beat than Oakland.

"I'll call Joe," Sid said. "See if he can nose around and get more information. You going back up to Sonoma County tomorrow?"

I nodded. "I have some work to do first, and an appointment, but yes, after that. You can reach me on my cell phone."

MY HOUSE is on Chabot Road, near College Avenue in Oakland's Rockridge District. As I pulled my car into the driveway, Darcy Stefano was coming down the steps from her apartment above the garage. She'd been living in the studio ever since I bought the house, and the extra income helped pay the mortgage. She was an engineering student at Cal, due to graduate in a year or two.

"Thanks for the text letting me know you were back," Darcy said. "You came home early. I thought you were staying at Lassen all week."

"Something came up," I told her. "An emergency."

"A case, huh?" Darcy put her hands on her hips, clad in a pair of blue capri pants, and tossed her long dark hair off the shoulders of her white blouse. "You look tired."

"I am tired. It's been a long day."

"Take it easy and get some sleep." Darcy headed for her Volkswagen, parked at the curb.

I checked the mailbox and unlocked the front door. My cats met me on the other side, crying for food and attention. Abigail was an old brown-and-gray tabby. I'd had her since she was a kitten, choosing her from a litter right after she was born. Black Bart had chosen me. As a kitten, he'd shown up on the patio of the apartment where I lived before I bought my house. I fed him and then I caught him, bringing him inside.

I dished up cat food. Then I opened the refrigerator, surveying the contents—or lack of contents. Dinner at home didn't look promising. There was, however, an open bottle of Chardonnay. I poured myself a glass and went to the living room, putting my feet up. I sipped wine and looked at the photographs arrayed on the top of a nearby bookshelf. As I studied the picture of my brother and his family, I felt tears prickle, threatening to flow. I'd been holding my emotions in since yesterday, keeping it together for the sake of my parents and Sheila so I could talk with law enforcement and figure out what had happened to my brother. But now, in this unguarded moment at home, the family hero felt like having a good cry.

The cats were good at picking up my moods. Abigail jumped up and arranged herself on my lap, rumbling with a reassuring purr, while Black Bart tucked himself next to me. I rubbed the tears from my eyes, stroked both cats, and finished my wine.

My cell phone rang. It was Dan. "Have you had dinner yet?"

"No. I got home a little while ago."

"I'm on my way. We'll head over to College Avenue and get something to eat."

Dan Westbrook and I met in June while I was in Lee Vining, in the Eastern Sierra near Mono Lake. I had been working on another case, one that involved something that happened to my grandmother, Jerusha Layne, when she was working as a bit player in movies back in the 1940s. Grandma left Hollywood in 1942, to marry my grandfather before he went off to the Navy and the Pacific Theater in World War II. She died several years ago, so I went looking for one of her housemates, Pearl Bishop, who had also worked as a bit player.

Pearl, whose first marriage ended when her husband was killed at Guadalcanal, stayed in Hollywood, making a good living in movies and television until she retired and went to live with her son, Carl, and his wife, Loretta, in Lee Vining. Loretta was Native American, a Northern Paiute, part of the Mono Lake Indian Community, or Kutzadika'a, who had lived around the huge alkaline lake for hundreds of years. When Carl was growing up, he'd spent many summers with Pearl's family in Lone Pine, another Eastern Sierra town. As a result, Carl loved the outdoors. He'd gone to work for the U.S. Forest Service, working all over the state. Now he was nearing retirement.

When I found Pearl, I met Carl and Loretta, whom I liked a great deal. I also met her grandson Dan, eldest of Carl and Loretta's three children. He was there in Lee Vining that weekend, leading bird walks at the annual Mono Basin Bird Chautauqua. Like his father, Dan loves the outdoors and California's natural beauty. He even makes a living at it, writing hiking and camping guidebooks.

Dan lives in North Berkeley, so it took him only twenty minutes or so to get to my house. He is tall, with a rangy, lean body and a head of curly dark hair, threaded with silver. He has laugh lines around his blue eyes and a smile that won me over the first time I saw him. Since that first meeting, we'd been spending a lot of time together. I liked him a lot and could sense that the feeling was mutual. In fact, this friendship had turned into romance.

When I opened the door, he put his arms around me and held me for a moment. I sighed and relaxed in his embrace.

"How are you doing?" he asked.

"Hanging in there. But I'm really worried." I shut and locked the front door.

We walked down the steps. His green Subaru wagon was parked in the driveway behind my Toyota, but I live just a few blocks from College Avenue, so we walked down to that thoroughfare, holding hands and talking about where to have dinner.

We settled on a small café near the intersection of College and Claremont avenues. Once we were seated, we looked at the menu. I ordered one of the beers on tap and Dan did the same. The server returned with our beers and took our orders—salads, fish for Dan and pasta for me. While we ate, I brought Dan up to date.

"I'd like to help," he said. "I'll be over in Sonoma County, starting tomorrow. Some friends offered me the use of their house in Bodega Bay. I thought I'd take them up on it. Might as well get started on that book about hiking and camping on the Sonoma and Mendocino coasts. So I'll be up that way. Call me when you need me, any time."

"Thanks, I appreciate that. I'll keep you up to date on how things are going. It looks like I'll be up in Sonoma County a lot until we find Brian."

"You've got other cases here in the Bay Area," Dan said.

I nodded. "That means early mornings and late hours in the office."

After sharing a dessert we walked back to my house. He kissed me good night. "You look tired. Get some sleep."

"I will."

But I didn't. I went to bed and lay staring at the ceiling, fighting back tears and "what ifs," wondering what had happened to my brother.

TWELVE

HOW CAN THIS BE HAPPENING TO ME? HE THOUGHT.
It's a mistake. Surely they'll realize it's all a mistake. They'll let me
go.

His head ached, a dull, throbbing pain. Something wet on his
forehead, a damp towel, he realized. He opened his eyes but the
light was too bright, it hurt. He closed his eyes again and smelled
cigarette smoke.

They were talking. "I don't like it. Somebody's gonna be missing this guy."

"Don't sweat it. We'll be long gone."

After a while, they went outside.

He reached for his forehead, the spot where it hurt the most,
and realized that he was handcuffed to the bed railing. He lay on a
mattress covered with blue-and-white ticking, and his head was on
a pillow. With his free hand he moved the damp towel away from
his aching head. He stared at it, seeing streaks of blood.

Blood. How badly was he hurt?

He must have fallen asleep. When he woke up again, they had
returned. He heard them talking.

"Let me take a look. I want to see what a quarter of a million
dollars looks like."

THIRTEEN

EARLY MORNINGS AND LATE HOURS, AS I'D TOLD DAN
the previous night.

On Wednesday morning, I rose earlier than usual and had a
quick breakfast. Then I drove to my office, which is located in an
older building on Franklin Street in downtown Oakland. Despite

the fact that I'd cleared my calendar for my vacation, I still had a number of inquiries, via email and phone messages, from prospective clients. I responded to emails and returned phone calls. I wanted to devote as much time as possible to finding Brian. In some cases I put off meetings and appointments until the following week. In others, I simply said I wasn't available.

Back in my car, I headed across the Richmond–San Rafael Bridge and then north on U.S. 101, up to Sonoma County.

I wanted to talk with Detectives Griffin and Harris about the case of the body on the boat, and take a look at the autopsy report. The report would presumably answer some of my questions. When had the victim died? Who owned the boat? I needed all the information I could get.

Getting information out of the detectives, however, was like pulling hen's teeth.

The Investigations Bureau of the Sonoma County Sheriff's Office is located in the department's main building on Ventura Avenue, in the northern part of Santa Rosa. The large two-story building houses a number of departments and divisions. The deputy at the front entrance called Griffin, who came to escort me to his office. Harris wasn't in evidence, but Griffin took a seat at his desk, his hands steepled in front of him. I wouldn't want to play cards with this guy, I thought. He had a good poker face, smooth and bland underneath his blond hair. I knew why he was reluctant to share any information with me, and it wasn't just because I'm a private investigator.

"Your brother is a person of interest in this homicide," he said.

"Because his MedicAlert bracelet was found at the scene? If that's all you've got, it's not much."

"I think it's significant. How did the bracelet wind up with the corpse?"

"I can think of any number of scenarios," I said. "Starting with, my brother lost the bracelet somewhere, and your John Doe picked it up. That doesn't necessarily mean my brother shot John Doe. Have you had any luck identifying the body?"

He placed his hands flat on his desk. "Not so far. His description matches several missing persons in California and other states. Because his hands and feet were burned in the fire, we don't have much to go on in terms of fingerprints, palm prints, or footprints."

"Do you have an autopsy report yet? And can I look at it?"

Griffin took his time answering. "The report's not completed. When it is, I'll consider letting you look at it."

I tried another tack. "What about the boat? Who owns it?"

"His name is Lowell Rhine. We haven't talked with him yet."

The name sounded familiar, as though I'd heard it before, but I couldn't place it. I managed to pry one other detail out of Griffin. A witness who lived in a nearby cabin had seen an SUV near the dock before the explosion. The detectives were looking for the vehicle, but hadn't found it.

I felt frustrated as I left the sheriff's office. I was not, however, deterred by the unsatisfactory encounter with Griffin. If he wouldn't help me, I'd go around him, with the help of Sid, Grace and their contacts.

That morning's edition of the Santa Rosa *Press Democrat* was spread out on the dining room table at Aunt Caro's house, with my parents seated side-by-side at the table as they perused it. The front page story about the body was illustrated with an artist's drawing of the dead man. Below this was a box with an appeal to the public for information that might help identify him.

"I don't think this sketch looks like Brian at all." Mother reached for the mug in front of her, took a sip, and grimaced. "This coffee's cold."

"I'll get you a warm-up," I said.

She shook her head. "Thanks. I'll get it myself. I can't just sit here." She pushed out her chair and stood up, walking into Caro's kitchen, where a drip coffeemaker with a half-full glass carafe sat on the counter.

I pulled the newspaper toward me and read through the article. The reporter had ferreted out a few more details than Griffin had provided to me. The boat where the body had been found was called the *Esmeralda*. It was a fifty-foot wooden-hulled cabin cruiser manufactured by Chris-Craft, a well-known boatmaker.

The explosion and resulting fire had occurred at approximately one-fifteen A.M. on Sunday morning. According to fire investigators, the explosion and fire had most likely been caused by a propane leak in the boat's cabin. As to what had ignited the propane, they weren't saying. The article did say that the victim had been shot before the boat caught fire. There was nothing in the story that indicated who owned the boat, just that the burned-out hull had been hauled away for further investigation.

Aunt Caro came through the back door, carrying a colander full of tomatoes and cucumbers. "Jeri, how about some lunch? Just picked these veggies."

"You know, a tomato sandwich sounds really good." I sliced a few tomatoes and slathered some sourdough bread with mayonnaise.

I LEFT Santa Rosa after lunch and headed south to Petaluma, then took Lakeville Highway down to Newman's Roadhouse and Marina. The marina office was open. I stepped inside. The office was about half the size of the roadhouse. To my right was a collection of marine supplies, including hardware and cleaning supplies. In front of me was a short counter with a cash register, and behind this, a desk and a four-drawer filing cabinet. To my left was an interior door. I guessed it led to the bar next door.

A woman sat at the desk, sipping from a mug and reading a worn paperback novel, Agatha Christie's *Hickory Dickory Dock*. She was on the far side of fifty, her hair a mixture of gray and blond. As I entered the office, she put the paperback face down on the desk and got up from the chair, coming to the counter. She had hard lines around her eyes and mouth, but her expression was friendly as she smiled at me. "Hi, can I help you?"

"Is Mr. Newman around?" I asked.

"He's around," she said, "but not in the office at the moment."

"I have some questions about that explosion and fire early Sunday morning, when the boat burned."

"Are you with the insurance?"

"I do insurance work," I said, handing her one of my business cards. Let her think I'm investigating the claim on the boat. That's what the bartender in the roadhouse had assumed yesterday.

The woman looked at my card. "I'm Tracy Burgoyne. I help Walt run the marina and the roadhouse. Oh, that fire, what a mess. And scary. God, I thought the whole marina was going to go up."

Good, she was a talker. Such people were always helpful when I was investigating something.

"I understand it was a propane explosion. What time did it happen?"

"Before closing time. I think it was fifteen or twenty minutes after one. I'm not sure, wasn't looking at the clock." Tracy pointed a thumb at the door. "I was over at the bar, having a brew. And then, bang. I thought somebody dropped a bomb. A guy came running in, yelling there was a fire down at the north end of the marina, that one of the boats was burning. Somebody called the fire department and all the people who was in the bar and around the cottages and boats, they went running down to the dock where that boat was burning. They were using buckets and hoses, trying to put that thing out. It would have been a disaster if the other boats caught fire. There were three boats tied up at that dock, all of 'em belonging to the same guy."

Tracy paused and took a breath. I started to ask a question. Before I could speak, she went on telling me about the incident. "As it was, that boat burned real bad. And then, to top it off, the fire department guys found a man's body on the boat." She grimaced. "What a horrible way to go."

"Sounds like quite a mess."

"It was. A big section of that dock is gonna have to be replaced. That's where Walt is now. He's meeting with our insurance guy, down at the dock where it happened."

"How long had the boat been here?"

"I don't know for sure. It was before Rick..." She stopped and glanced back at the filing cabinet. "I'll look it up."

She pulled out the top drawer in the filing cabinet and removed a manila folder. She brought it back to the counter and opened the folder, leafing through several sheets. "Hmm, I don't see the agreement Walt has all the owners sign. He must have that paperwork with him."

I took a notebook and pen from my bag, and opened the notebook to the page where I'd written the name Detective Griffin had mentioned. "Let me verify the name of the boat's owner. I have it listed as Lowell Rhine. Is that correct?"

"Yeah," Tracy said. "Rhine, like that river in Germany. He's from San Rafael. Rick knew him, asked his dad to keep the boats here as a favor for the guy."

I wrote "San Rafael" next to Rhine's name. Again, I wondered where I'd heard Rhine's name before. At least now I knew he was from San Rafael.

"And you say Mr. Rhine has three boats berthed here?"

Tracy nodded. "Yeah, the one that burned, the *Esmeralda*, was the biggest, a fifty-foot cabin cruiser. It was a nice boat, a Chris-Craft. The others are cabin cruisers, too, but not as big. The *Silverado* is thirty-five feet, and the *Rosarita*, that's a forty-footer."

"You mentioned Rick. Who's that?"

"Walt's son," she said. "He died about six weeks ago, last week in June."

"I'm sorry to hear that."

"Yeah, well, it happens. What I started to say was, Rick and a friend of his brought those boats here about a week before Rick died." She thought for a moment. "That would have been the third week in June. That's when the boats got here."

"How did Rick die?"

"He wiped out on Highway One, north of Jenner. He skidded on the pavement and went off a cliff. They found his Harley at the bottom, but they never found a body." Tracy's mouth twisted into an ironic smile. "Knowing Rick, he was probably speeding. Live fast, die hard. That was Rick all over."

Highway 1—California's Coast Highway—is two lanes and sometimes quite narrow. It winds its way along the rocky coast, hugging the cliffs high above the Pacific Ocean. The stretch north of Jenner could be scary and unforgiving, in good weather and bad. Interesting that Rick Newman's body hadn't been found. But not unusual. If he'd been thrown into the surf when his bike went off the cliff, the body could have been washed out to sea.

"Rick must have been a young man," I said.

"Young enough. He was thirty-three, the oldest. Walt always favored Rick, took it real hard when he died."

"You said the oldest. Does Mr. Newman have another child?"

"Martha. She's a few years younger than Rick. She doesn't get along with her dad," Tracy said. "Walt's a rough cob, blue-collar, like me. Martha, she's artistic. Makes pottery. Here, this is one of her pieces. She gave it to me for Christmas. Real pretty, isn't it?"

Tracy turned back to the desk where she'd left her paperback mystery and picked up the pottery mug she'd been drinking from when I entered the office. She brought it to me. It looked a lot like the mug my brother had, though a different color. This one was glazed in green and blue with gold highlights.

"Yes, it's lovely." I took the mug from Tracy and examined it. There was an inch or so of coffee inside the mug. I raised it past eye level so I could see if the mug was signed on the bottom. It was, with a stamp that looked like a long, narrow leaf with a letter in the middle.

"Is that an 'M' for Martha?"

"No, it's a 'W' for Willow. That's what Martha calls herself now."

"Does she indeed." I set the mug on the counter. "She does good work. Is her pottery in any of the galleries around here?"

"Occidental," Tracy said, naming a small town in the forested coastal hills west of Sebastopol. "She lives there, too."

"You know a lot about the Newman family," I said.

Tracy smiled. "I don't just work here. Walt and me, well, we live together. I moved in about five years ago. Used to live here before that, in one of the cabins. I was working in the roadhouse, barmaid, cook. Still do a little bit of that, plus working the marina side."

"What about his wife, the children's mother?"

"Arlene? She died last year, had cancer. Her and Walt, they

divorced about ten or twelve years ago. It was right after Martha graduated from high school. Arlene remarried, a real nice guy named Steve Kennett. He lives in Cotati. He called us when Arlene got sick, to keep us posted. And when she died, he let us know about the funeral and all that."

"I suppose Rick and Martha went to Petaluma High School."

"Oh, sure. They rode the bus when they were younger. Then Rick got his motorcycle and Martha had her own car."

I didn't see any family photographs here in the marina office and I was itching to see what Martha, or Willow, looked like. And her deceased brother as well. If they'd gone to Petaluma High School, they probably had photos in the yearbook. Since Lance Coverdell was a Petaluma native, I wondered if he'd retained his PHS yearbooks, or if he'd known the Newman siblings in high school.

"I guess the marina's doing well," I said. "Looks like most of the slips are full."

"Oh, yeah, we got good prices, real competitive, you know, compared to those marinas in town. And we're downriver, closer to the bay. Walt's hoping to buy some land, just south of here. That way we can build more docks and spruce up the place." She looked past me and smiled. "Here's Walt now."

I turned and looked at Walt Newman, owner of Newman's Marina and Roadhouse. He was in his late sixties, I guessed, about six feet tall, with a face that looked lived-in, bags under his brown eyes and a network of wrinkles and freckles decorating his skin. He had a beer gut above the belt of his faded jeans. His hair had once been a sandy brown and I could see some of that color amid the gray that did a poor job of covering his bald spots. Right now he had a face as stormy as a thundercloud.

"What did the insurance guy say?" Tracy asked.

"God damn it," Walt Newman said. "Passel of trouble, nothing but trouble."

Tracy frowned. "Trouble about what?"

"The insurance. That damned high deductible. Gonna have to eat a big chunk of cash on the repairs to the dock. And Rhine called. He's sending somebody to pick up the other two boats. So now we're out the berthing fees for all three."

"That's rough, coming right now," Tracy said. "We could sure use the money from those berthing fees. And we need to get that dock fixed as soon as we can."

He scowled at her. "I know that. Damn it, never rains but it pours."

Tracy glanced at me. "Oh, Walt, this lady's here to see you."

Newman walked past me, around the counter's end, to the desk on the other side. He scowled at me and said in a gruff voice, "Who are you and what do you want?"

I guessed I didn't look much like a prospective customer. Or maybe Newman was this brusque with everyone who walked through the door. I took out one of my business cards. "My name's Jeri Howard."

He stared at the card. "Private eye, huh. It figures. Are you one of those damn tree huggers that's trying to shut me down?"

"No, I'm not."

"Then what the hell do you want?"

"I have some questions about the fire."

"Talk to the fire department." He crumpled my card and tossed it into the wastebasket. Then he walked to the door that separated the marina office from the roadhouse. He wrenched it open and went through it, slamming the door in his wake.

"I'm sorry about that," Tracy said. "He's really in a bad mood, has been since the fire. I guess it's gonna cost a bunch to repair that burned dock, and the high deductible we had on the insurance doesn't help. Plus, Mr. Rhine's gonna take those two boats. That and the boat that burned, that was a couple thousand bucks a month in fees, money we won't have now."

"That remark about tree huggers," I asked. "What's that all about?"

"The land Walt wants to buy, he's up against some environmental group that wants the same parcel. For wetlands, I guess. And they complain about the marina, say it's dirty, a hazard. I suppose they'll be using the fire against us, as ammo. But the fire wasn't our fault. Propane leak, that's what the firemen said. It happens if folks aren't careful with that stuff."

"Thanks for your help, Tracy. You have my card. If you think of anything else, let me know."

"Nice talking with you." Tracy turned back to the desk, settling onto the chair, and picked up her paperback mystery.

FOURTEEN

I WALKED TO THE NORTH END OF THE MARINA, TO cabin twelve near the dock where the boat had burned. Today there was a blue Mazda hatchback parked outside. The front door was open. I looked in through a screen door and saw a small, cluttered living room, with a kitchen beyond. I called a greeting and knocked. A middle-aged man wearing khakis and a green T-shirt stepped out of the kitchen, carrying a plate with a sandwich and some pickles.

"Chet Olsen?" I asked.

He set the plate on an ottoman and ran a hand through thinning blond hair as he approached the door. "Yeah?"

"I'd like to ask you a few questions about the fire on Sunday morning. Your cabin here, it's closest to the site."

He frowned. "I already talked to the cops."

"I haven't seen those witness statements yet," I said. And I might not, unless Sid, or Joe Kelso, was able to get some information from the Sonoma County detectives. I held out a business card. "I'm a private investigator. I understand you saw a vehicle in this area, just before the boat caught fire. Do you remember anything about the vehicle, make, model, color?"

He shrugged. Then he opened the screen door and stepped outside, reaching for my card. He examined it and looked up at me. "That SUV I saw, it was silver, I think. Or white. Light-colored, anyway. I couldn't tell you what kind it was. Mid-sized, I guess. It was parked over there." He pointed to a fence and a cluster of bushes that apparently defined the marina's northern boundary. "I couldn't see very clearly. It was dark. And I'd had a bit to drink. I was at a party on one of the other boats and I'd just come home."

"I understand. Did you see any other vehicles in the vicinity? Vehicles that you didn't recognize?"

He shook his head. "No. Most of my neighbors, I know what their cars look like. I heard a motorcycle really close, but with the roadhouse and the bikers who hang out there, that's pretty common."

"Getting back to the SUV, can you describe the driver?"

"There were two guys," Olsen said. "Didn't see which of them was driving. They made several trips from the SUV to the boat and back again. I figured they were loading up, getting ready to take the boat out. But I can't tell you what they looked like. I didn't get that good a look at them."

"Can you recall if they were young, old?"

"Younger than me, I guess."

"How long before the explosion was this?"

He thought about it. "Ten minutes, I guess. I left the party around one and walked down here. That's when I saw those guys and the SUV. I went into my cabin here. Took a leak, got ready for bed. And then, boom. I opened the front door and saw the fire, saw that SUV pulling out of here pretty fast. I put on my pants and shoes and came outside. A bunch of people came running from the bar and the other cabins. We were trying to put out the fire, but that boat was a goner. The fire department was still mopping up on Sunday, and then the cops came and hauled off the boat on Monday."

I probed further, but it appeared Chet Olsen had told me all he knew, or had seen. A mid-sized SUV, light in color, and it had left the scene very fast, driven by one of the men he had seen. The other man, presumably, was the corpse found on the boat.

Now that I knew Rhine was listed as the owner of three boats, I took more photos of the two cabin cruisers that were still tied up to the charred dock. Then I walked back to my car. Before I started the engine, I called Rita Lydecker's cell phone.

"Hi, Rita," I said when she answered. "I've learned that the owner of the boat that burned is named Lowell Rhine, and he's from San Rafael. That name sounds familiar. Does it ring any bells with you?"

"Sure as hell does," Rita said. "Lowell Rhine is an attorney. He's the lawyer that defended the guy who shot a local cop a couple of years ago. Got his client acquitted. Pissed off the San Rafael Police Department, and the Marin County DA's office."

"Now I remember." The case had been all over the Bay Area news outlets. "Rhine's client was a drug dealer, right?"

"Yeah. He represents a lot of drug dealers. This particular dealer shot the cop during a bust down in the Canal District. The officer survived, but he lost the use of his arm and retired on disability. Rhine got his client acquitted and the local authorities were not happy about that. I heard that the assistant DA who prosecuted assured everyone it was an open-and-shut case, but Rhine convinced the jury otherwise."

"What do you know about Rhine? Have you ever done any work for him?"

"He specializes in criminal defense," Rita said. "Works out of an office near the Civic Center here in San Rafael, but he takes cases all over the Bay Area. He handles a lot of drug charges and other stuff thrown in for good measure—DUI, traffic violations, assault, theft, domestic violence, and sometimes sex crimes. And yes, I did some investigative work for him a few years back. Just the one case. Let's just say, he and I had a personality conflict."

"How so?"

"You know lawyers," Rita said. "Some of them are nice people. Others are born with the arrogance gene, or they acquire it in law school. Rhine is definitely arrogant. Full of himself. He's slick and I've heard him called a shyster. Skates close to the legality line. He's good, though. He gets results. A lot of his clients are scumbags. Yes, I know they're innocent until proven guilty and entitled to a defense. Reasonable doubt and all that. Hell, I've worked a few defense cases in my day. But there have been quite a few of Rhine's clients who would be better off behind bars. And the rest of us would be better off if they were, that's for sure."

"Is he married?" I asked.

"Divorced from wife number two. Don't know anything about wife number one. I gather she was in the distant past. He was married to number two for about ten years and they had one child. Nasty divorce, from what I hear. Allegations of infidelity on both sides. Don't know if it was true about her, but him, yeah, he's a chaser. Always has some arm candy. I gather he had a girlfriend waiting in the wings, even before the divorce. Wife number two got custody of the kid, a big fancy house in Tiburon, and probably a very large pile of money. So now Rhine lives in San Rafael. Not sure where, but I can find out."

"Is Rhine a sailor?"

"That I don't know," Rita said. "Could be. I've never heard anything about him being a sailor, but he does have money, and he likes toys. Drives a fancy car. So I suppose a fancy boat would be just his style."

"According to someone who works at the marina, Rhine is listed as the owner of three boats that were berthed there, including the boat that burned. If he does like boats, why have three? Expensive toys. You've got to berth them somewhere and maintain them. And why keep the boats at an out-of-the-way marina in Sonoma County, when he lives in Marin County? There must be half a dozen marinas right there in San Rafael. Any one of them would be quicker and easier to get to than this place up here in Lakeville."

"Those are very good questions," Rita said. "Want me to look into it?"

"Yes, I'd appreciate that. Are you at a computer?"

"Sure. What do you need?"

"First give me Rhine's office address and phone number. I'll pay him a visit. Then I need a phone number for a man named Steve Kennett. I'm guessing it's spelled the way it sounds. He lives in Cotati." Kennett was Willow's stepfather and I wanted to talk with him.

"Can't be that many Kennetts in Cotati," Rita said. "The town ain't that big."

Rita provided me with Rhine's address and number. Then she

did a search for Steve Kennett's phone number. It didn't take her long to locate the listing. I jotted down the information, thanked her, and disconnected the call. My next phone call, to Kennett, got me voice mail. I didn't leave a message, planning to try again later.

Donna must have called while I was on the phone. Now I had a voice mail message from her. I listened to it. She'd checked around, following up on my earlier request about permits. Nothing showed up. Brian hadn't requested a permit for backcountry hiking in any of the state parks. Nor was there any record of his Jeep sighted at a state park.

Another dead end, I thought.

I made another phone call, this time to the law office of Lowell Rhine in San Rafael. The young woman who answered the phone told me Rhine was unavailable. I left my name and phone number, declining to give her the reason why I was calling. I'd go to his office instead, hoping to grab the attorney if he was in the building.

I started the car and left the marina parking lot, heading south on Lakeville Highway. At Highway 37, I drove west to U.S. 101, and then south through Novato to San Rafael. Lowell Rhine's law office was in a commercial suite on North San Pablo Road, across the street from the Marin County Civic Center, the futuristic building designed by Frank Lloyd Wright.

The building where Rhine had his office had been designed by a more mundane architect. Bland, boxy and three stories high, the walls were beige and the carpet was brown. Rhine's office was on the third floor. I went through the front door into a waiting room. Here the carpet was plusher, a lighter shade of brown, and the walls were decorated with photographs showing some of the local sights, including Mount Tamalpais, the Sausalito waterfront, the Marin headlands, and the Golden Gate Bridge.

At a desk in front of me was a receptionist. She wore a gray silk blouse and a short shirt, her legs crossed as she talked on the phone. Sitting in a chair on the right was a young man who looked like a gangbanger, baggy pants and a baseball cap worn backwards on his dark hair. He was talking on a cell phone, loudly.

When the receptionist ended the call she was on, she looked up at me. "May I help you?"

"Is Mr. Rhine available?"

"I'm sorry, he's with a client," she said. "Do you have an appointment?"

"No." I gave her one of my business cards.

"Oh, yes, you called earlier. If you'd just tell me what this is about."

"I'm working on a case. Mr. Rhine may have some information that would help me."

She looked somewhat irritated, taking her role as gatekeeper seriously. "If I could give him a hint, Ms. Howard."

"Certainly. Tell him it's about the *Esmeralda*. I would appreciate hearing from him as soon as possible."

"*Esmeralda*," she repeated, frowning. She wrote the word on a pink message slip and tore it off the pad. "I'm sure he'll be in touch."

I was sure he wouldn't, I thought.

The young man who been talking on his cell phone ended the call by yelling at whoever he was talking to. He swore and stuck the phone into one of his pockets, glaring at the receptionist. "How much longer I gotta wait?" he demanded.

She gave him a tight, frosty smile. "He's with another client. I'm sure he'll see you as soon as he's free."

FIFTEEN

I LEFT THE ATTORNEY'S OFFICE AND WENT OUT TO MY car. I headed north again, back to Petaluma. I wanted another look at the coffee mug I'd seen at my brother's house yesterday. I also needed to talk with my sister-in-law about a few things.

When I got to Petaluma, I took the exit for East Washington Street and drove to the rented house where Brian and Sheila lived. She met me at the door. "Come on back to the kitchen. I'm fixing a snack for the kids."

As we went through the dining room, I didn't see the oversized pottery mug on the desk where it had been yesterday. I followed Sheila into the kitchen. I spotted the mug, with its reddish-purple glaze, upside down in a dish drainer next to the sink. I walked over and examined the bottom. The mug had the same signature stamp that I'd seen earlier on Tracy's blue mug at Newman's Marina. I realized now that the long, narrow symbol was a willow leaf, with the letter "W" in the middle.

"How about some lemonade?" Sheila asked.

I turned from the sink. "I'll get it myself, if you'll tell me where the glasses are."

"Sure. Pitcher in the fridge, glasses up there." She pointed at one of the cabinets. I opened it and took out four glasses, filling them with ice and lemonade.

Sheila went back to work at the counter, with a knife and a cutting board, coring and slicing apples. She arranged them on a plate, then sliced some cheddar cheese, and added an assortment of carrots, celery, and crackers. When she finished, she went to the dining room. I heard her call to the children, who were out in the backyard. When they came inside, they bubbled over with news about local wildlife.

"We saw a raccoon," Amy cried. "It was trying to get into the trash can."

"Yeah," Sheila said. "I had to put a bungee cord around that lid, so the little devils can't get in."

"We got squirrels, Aunt Jeri," Todd said. "I saw three of them, in that big tree in the backyard. I'll show you where."

"Mom says we can get peanuts at the store to feed the squirrels," Amy added.

"They'll dig holes and bury them," I said. "Squirrels like to do that."

"They forget where the nuts are and trees sprout," Todd said. "That's what Dad told me."

"Peanuts growing in the backyard, that's all we need." Sheila set the plate in the middle of the kitchen table. "Eat up, and then you can show Aunt Jeri where you saw the squirrels."

We talked about squirrels and birds as we ate the snacks, then

Sheila offered homemade peanut butter cookies. "Baked this morning."

I took a cookie, broke off a piece, and put it in my mouth. "Mmm, just the way I like them, chewy in the middle."

The children each took a cookie and looked at me. "Can we go see squirrels now?" Todd asked.

"I'll be out in a little while. I need to talk with your mom first." I waited a moment as Todd and Amy headed out the back door. "They seem less subdued today. Are they doing all right?"

She shrugged. "They still want to know where their father is. So do I." She put the remaining snacks into a container and put it in the refrigerator. "Have you found out anything new?"

"I had a talk with Lance Coverdell yesterday afternoon. He mentioned that Brian was upset about an incident last spring, involving one of his students in Sonoma. Had Brian said anything to you about that?"

Sheila shut the refrigerator door. She sat down at the table and reached for a cookie. "No, I don't remember anything specific. What happened?"

"Lance says the student tried to commit suicide."

"What?" Shock rounded Sheila's mouth into an O. "Brian never said anything about that. And I don't remember reading anything about it in the paper, or hearing anything on the news. Of course, if the student didn't die, the authorities or the family might have hushed it up. But if something like that had happened, Brian would have talked about it. Where's Lance getting this information?"

"He says Brian told him."

Sheila looked dubious. "Have you checked out the story?"

"Not yet, but I'm going to." Once again, I wondered if Lance had made up the story. Or embellished it. Or for that matter, misinterpreted something Brian had said. But it could be, as Sheila and I had discussed yesterday, that Brian hadn't mentioned anything about the suicide attempt—or his planned change of job—to Sheila because she was distracted by her father's illness.

"I'll follow up on this," I said. "I'll need the names of some of his fellow teachers, people he was close to. I'll contact them to see if I can find out anything."

"There's one I remember. Nancy Parsons. I met her at a couple of school functions. She's been teaching at Brian's school in Sonoma for ages." Sheila got up and left the kitchen. She returned a moment later with an address book. She sat down again and opened the book, turned the pages to the *P*s. "Here it is."

Next to Nancy Parsons's name was a phone number, no address. I wrote down the number. Then I closed the book. "I'll call her later."

"Did you find out anything else?" Sheila asked.

"Do you know a woman named Martha Newman?"

Sheila thought for a moment, then shook her head. "No, I don't."

"She's a potter. She made that mug that Brian bought at the craft fair last spring."

"And this is important, because?" Sheila asked.

"She calls herself Willow. She must be the person who wrote the note to Brian."

"And they met for coffee several times." Sheila broke the cookie into pieces and then set them aside. "I thought…"

"You thought Willow was Becca. Why?" Sheila didn't answer. I pressed further. "I know you don't like Becca. That was clear when I talked with you yesterday. It's got to be more than her being full of herself. But something else is going on between the two of you. Why do you dislike her so much?"

"It goes back to when we were in college," Sheila said. "Brian and I dated our junior and senior years. Going steady, I guess you could call it. Do they still use that term? Anyway, we did break up for a time the summer before our senior year. I was at home in Firebaugh. Brian and Becca were both in summer school. And Becca moved in on him. He was seeing her before we got back together."

"That was a long time ago. You and Brian have been married ten years. You have two children. You're still upset with Becca about that?" Why was Sheila so insecure?

Sheila sighed. "I know it sounds crazy to hold a grudge. But I guess I've always felt...well, Becca's so elegant and glamorous. She's the rich girl from the Bay Area and I'm the hick from the Central Valley. It isn't logical. But she makes me feel that way. She acts like she's bored with Lance and she could just move in on Brian again. The way she puts her hand on his arm and leans toward him. Sometimes I think she's trying to take him away from me."

"That's not going to happen," I said.

"Or has it already?" Sheila shot back. "You don't know. Maybe Becca and Brian are using this Willow as a go-between. Even if they're not, who is this Willow person and where does she get off writing to my husband? None of this makes any sense."

"Sheila, I know you're upset, but the possibility of Brian having an affair wouldn't explain the MedicAlert bracelet on the boat."

"With a corpse," she finished. "Oh, God, listen to me." Tears leaked from her eyes and she put her head down on her hands and cried.

"You've got to hold it together," I told her. "I know it's hard, but you have to do it."

She sat upright and wiped tears from her face. "I had to call the principal of his new school this morning and say that Brian can't keep his appointment. I didn't know what to say when the man asked why. I told him some story about Brian being sick. What am I going to do if Brian doesn't come home? I'm a stay-at-home mom. Without Brian's salary... We have some savings, but...I'd have to go back to work, and child care for the kids..."

"Don't worry about that now. You're getting ahead of yourself. Let's focus on finding out what happened to Brian. Now, I've learned a thing or two. Willow—Martha Newman—is the daughter of the man who owns Newman's Marina down in Lakeville. That's the place where the boat and the body were found."

Interest sparked in Sheila's eyes. "You think there's a connection?"

"Yes, I do."

"Newman's Marina," Sheila said. "I read something about that in the newspaper. Some land use controversy."

I nodded. "Mr. Newman wants to buy a parcel south of his current location, so he can expand. The local environmental groups are fighting it, because they want to preserve the land. Yesterday, while I was in the real estate office talking with Lance, Becca came in. She was talking about Newman's Marina. Evidently she's involved in the fight against the marina's expansion plans. She told me the marina is a big polluter, the kind of stuff you get when you have boats, paint, solvents, all of those with a potential to get spilled into the Petaluma River. Plus, there's a bar next to the marina. It seems to be a biker hangout. Though when I was out there it didn't look any worse than some of the bars I've been in."

"So where does Willow factor into all of this?" Sheila asked.

"I asked both Lance and Becca if they knew anyone named Willow. Becca said she didn't, but I'm sure she wasn't telling the truth."

Sheila made a rude noise. "If Becca's fighting Newman's expansion plans, and Willow is Newman's daughter, you can bet Becca knows it. So she's lying to you."

"That's what I figure. The question is why. I'll have a talk with her later this afternoon. Is she a stay-at-home mom?"

"So to speak," Sheila said. "Becca's got her fingers in a lot of pies. She volunteers for all sorts of organizations, especially the environmental ones. But she's at home more often now, while her daughter, Lucy, is out of school."

"Where do the Coverdells live?"

"On B Street near Sixth. They invited us over for dinner right after we moved here." Sheila gave me the address. "The house is in the middle of the block, one of those ornate Victorians with bright colors, yellow with purple trim. You can't miss it. There's an orange climbing rose on one side of the front door."

"I'll head over there. But first, I need to let the kids show me the squirrels."

I helped myself to another peanut butter cookie. Then I went outside to the backyard, for a conversation about squirrels and other critters.

SIXTEEN

THE COVERDELLS' HOUSE WAS ON THE EDGE OF THE
historic district of downtown Petaluma, a collection of homes and
other buildings constructed between the 1860s and the 1920s. The
house was built in the Victorian style known as "Stick," which had a
decorative grid of raised boards called "stick work" overlaying the
clapboards. It had a steep gabled roof and a boxy bay window on the
left of the front door. The exterior paint was indeed a bright sun-
shiny yellow, with trim in a dark purple as well as a lighter mauve.
To the right of the small porch, a high trellis supported the climbing rose, its petals deep orange verging on red. A driveway to the
right of the climbing rose led back to a detached garage. Two cars
were parked in the drive, a late model light blue Prius hatchback,
evidently Becca's car, and behind this, a red Honda Civic.

I found a parking space on the same side of the street as the
house and shut off the engine. I had just opened my car door when
the front door opened. Becca stepped onto the porch, followed by
another woman and two young girls. I recognized the blond girl
from the photo on her father's desk. This was Lucy, the Coverdells'
daughter. The other woman and the second little girl looked like
mother and daughter, both short with dark hair. The four of them
stood on the porch for another minute, talking. Then the dark-
haired woman and the two girls went down the front steps, heading for the Honda.

Becca stood at the front door, watching them drive off. Then
she stepped into the house briefly and came out again, her large
white shoulder bag swinging at her side. She shut the front door
and locked it, slipping the keys into her shoulder bag as she walked
down the steps. She turned at the sidewalk and walked along B
Street, heading toward downtown. I got out of my car and followed her. The melon-colored shirt she wore was easy to keep
in view. Was she going to Lance's office? No, she wasn't. When
she reached South Petaluma Boulevard, she turned north and

meandered slowly along this downtown main drag, window shopping mostly, but occasionally going into stores.

Midway down the block between Western and Washington avenues, she passed Putnam Plaza Park, near the Petaluma Pie Company where I'd met Donna for pie and coffee on Tuesday. Becca walked past the little park. A few doors down she turned left and walked into the Della Fattoria bakery and café. The sign in the front window said the café was open for lunch until four. It was just after three. But Becca wasn't having lunch. Instead she stepped up to the counter that ran along one wall, chatting with the man behind the counter as she selected a loaf of bread and several other items. She paid him and put her purchases into a nylon shopping bag that she pulled from her purse.

When Becca left the bakery, she reached into the bag and took out a cupcake decorated with swirls of dark chocolate frosting. She pulled off one side of the paper wrapping and took a bite. I recognized the look that passed over her face—chocolate-sugar-rush nirvana.

Then she set out in the direction she had come. I waylaid her a few steps past the bakery. "Hello, Becca."

She looked at me, startled. "Jeri. What a surprise to see you."

"I have a few questions for you."

Her face turned wary. "About what?"

"Willow. Her real name is Martha Newman. She's Walt Newman's daughter. But you already knew that. So why did you tell me you didn't know who Willow is?"

"I wasn't sure," she said, hedging.

"I'm not buying that." I gestured in the direction of the little park. "Have a seat and finish your cupcake. You and I are going to have a conversation."

Becca stared back at me. Then she sighed. "I can't really tell you very much."

"Tell me what you know."

There was a fountain in the center of the park. Becca took a seat on the concrete rim, trailing her fingers through the water. "Willow is a potter. She's very talented. At least I think so. I met her last year at a gallery in Occidental. I bought one of her pieces, a bowl."

"Are you friends?"

"Casual acquaintances, hardly friends. I see her from time to time, at that gallery. Or here in town. Sometimes we have coffee. But it's a spur-of-the-moment thing." Becca took another bite of her cupcake and wiped a streak of chocolate frosting from her mouth.

"When did you find out she was Walt Newman's daughter?"

"Sometime during the spring. That's when this issue over the marina expansion came up. Willow said something in passing, about her father. And I realized the connection. I was hoping it would prove useful, that she'd give me some information that we could use to stop the marina expansion plans."

"How did that work?"

"It didn't," Becca said. "Willow's estranged from her father, has been for some time. And from her older brother as well. My impression was that the old man favored the brother over Willow, and that was the reason for the bad feeling between them. But the brother's dead now. She said he was killed in a traffic accident."

"What about Lance?" I asked.

"What about him?" Becca looked alarmed. "He doesn't know Willow."

"He might. Lance grew up in Petaluma, went to school here. The brother's name was Rick. He was about Lance's age, and Willow's just a couple of years younger. So Lance may know them from school."

"You'll have to ask him that. I really have to get home. Lucy's due back from her outing and I need to be there."

"Not so fast. Willow and Brian. Did she ever mention how she knows him?"

Becca sighed. "She met him sometime last spring, when he bought a mug from her at a craft fair. She was attracted to him."

"She told you that?"

"Yes. She said she'd met this schoolteacher in Sonoma, and he was married, but she thought he was such a nice guy. I asked her what his name was. She said Brian. I figured out it was the Brian we knew. Then maybe a month later, she mentioned that she'd had coffee with him. Just by chance, she said. I told her then she should back off. But I guess she didn't." Becca licked frosting from the top of the cupcake, then she put it back in the paper bag. "I did see them having coffee a few weeks ago, at a place just up the street. I wondered about that."

"Wondered about what?"

"Whether they were having a fling. She really likes him."

Sheila was wondering the same thing, after finding the note Willow had sent to Brian. "She sent him a card, like the ones you had in your purse yesterday."

"I got those at Hestia Gallery in Occidental, the one that carries Willow's work. I didn't know she was going to write to him."

"How did she get his address?"

Becca sighed. "The last time she and I got together for coffee, Willow brought up the subject and I mentioned that Brian and Sheila were moving into our rental house here in Petaluma. She knows the house because another friend of hers rented it from us a couple of years. Telling her that Brian was moving into that house was a boneheaded move on my part. I told her she shouldn't have any contact with him. I knew Sheila would just be furious."

"She is. For a while she thought you were Willow."

"Me?" Becca looked stunned. "We're all friends. We have been since college. Except... Did Sheila say something to you about me and Brian?"

"As a matter of fact, she did."

"I knew it. She's jealous. It was years ago, for God's sake."

"So tell me about it."

"We had a fling. I didn't know Sheila then. I'd met Brian through Lance. Brian and Sheila had a disagreement at the end of our junior year. She wanted to get married, he wanted to wait until they graduated. They broke up and she went home to Firebaugh. I was in summer school and so was Brian. Lance was off doing an internship. He and I weren't dating exclusively anyway. Brian asked me out and one thing led to another. The fall semester started and Brian and Sheila got back together. End of story."

"Is it?"

She glared at me. "As far as I'm concerned. But Sheila never forgot. Sometimes she gives me the evil eye. Thinks I'm out to steal her man. Well, I'm not. I'm fine with the one I've got." She stood up, poised for flight. "I have to go home."

"Not until you tell me where Willow lives."

"Occidental. She rents a cottage there, not far from the gallery. Although she was making plans to move to a bigger place, the last time I talked with her."

"When was that?"

"It's been weeks."

"And you're sure you don't have a phone number for her?"

Becca shook her head. "I don't. It's just a casual relationship. Honestly, I really do have to go now."

I let her escape down Petaluma Boulevard. I wasn't sure I believed her when she said she didn't know Willow's phone number.

I doubled back to Della Fattoria and looked at the cupcake offerings. I spotted one that looked particularly delectable and pointed. I ordered some coffee and sat down to eat my mid-afternoon treat. The cupcake was every bit as good as it looked.

Then I walked down to Lance's office on Second Street. I was in luck. He was in.

"Any news on finding Brian?" Lance asked. "I keep hoping he'll call."

"He hasn't. I'm following some leads. I have more questions for you."

"Sure. How can I help?"

"When I was here yesterday, I asked you and Becca whether you knew a woman who calls herself Willow. I've recently learned that her real name is Martha Newman."

"Walt Newman's daughter? Really? I had no idea." Lance gave me a lopsided smile. "I knew Martha in high school. Not well, but I knew who she was. It's a big school, and she was a sophomore when I was a senior."

"And her brother, Rick?"

Lance nodded. "Oh, sure. Rick was in the same class I was.

We didn't have a whole lot in common. He barely graduated and he didn't go to college, although Martha did. She went to Sonoma State University, over in Rohnert Park."

"What can you tell me about Rick?"

"He's dead now. It happened just a few weeks ago. His motorcycle skidded off a cliff on the Coast Highway. That's all I know about the accident, just what I read in the paper. Rick was something of a hell-raising biker dude, even back in high school. He had several run-ins with the law as a juvenile. Drugs and fighting, according to the grapevine."

"What about his record as an adult?"

Lance thought for a moment. "I went off to college in Davis after we graduated from high school, but I heard things. Rick was growing marijuana and selling it. He got busted once when he was in his early twenties and spent some time in jail."

"Here in Sonoma County?"

"Yes, I believe so. But it could have been Mendocino County. I heard he lived up there for a while. But according to the newspaper, he was living in San Rafael when he died."

"What did Rick look like?"

Lance smiled. "It's been a long time since I've seen him."

"You haven't seen him since you graduated from high school?"

"Not that I recall."

"Give it a try. Hair color, eyes?"

Lance frowned, as though he was trying to conjure up Rick Newman's face. "Eyes, beats me. Hair…sandy, dirty blond, whatever you'd call that. Just an ordinary guy, nothing unusual." His face brightened. "Say, I've got an idea. I have all my old high school yearbooks at home. We can go over there and have a look."

"Good idea. I left my car on the other side of Petaluma Boulevard." I didn't tell him it was parked just down the street from his house.

"We'll take mine," he said. "I live a few blocks from here. I could walk to work, but being in the real estate business, I use my car all day."

Lance and I left the building. A few minutes later, Lance

parked his Prius in his driveway. We went up the steps to the front door and he unlocked it.

The Coverdells' daughter, Lucy, was home from her earlier outing. Now she was in the living room, draped over an armchair reading a book. "Hi, Dad," she said, giving me a curious glance.

Becca appeared in the doorway leading to the kitchen. "You're home early. Want a glass of wine?" Then she stopped and glared at me, still smarting from our recent interview. "What is she doing here?"

Lance looked taken aback at her rudeness. "What's the matter?" She didn't answer. He shrugged. "I'm going to show Jeri some yearbooks from high school. I will take that glass of wine. Jeri, how about you?"

"No, thanks, just the yearbooks."

Lance took me down the hall to the bedroom he used as a home office. My own high school yearbooks were in a box at the top of a closet. Lance's yearbooks were stored in a similar fashion, in a banker's box at the back of a closet, barricaded by a plastic tub containing wrapping paper and ribbons. He pulled out a yearbook decorated with a big *P* on the front cover. "Here it is. This is the year I graduated. I'll be in the kitchen if you need me."

I flipped through the pages of the yearbook, finding the senior class photos. I looked for Lance's photograph and found a younger version of the older man who'd gone to the kitchen to soothe his wife's ruffled feathers. I turned pages again, looking for Rick Newman's picture. When I found it, I studied his features. Something had been tugging at me since I found out about Rick. Now that I saw what he looked like in high school, that thought took on more importance.

The high school photo of Rick Newman resembled my brother, Brian, as he had looked in high school. Age the man in the photograph, and he might look the way my brother looked now. He might also look like the man whose body had been found on the boat.

But Rick was dead. His motorcycle went off the Coast Highway back in June. The bike had been found at the bottom of a cliff. But Rick's body hadn't. Everyone assumed the body had washed out to sea.

So Rick Newman was dead.

Or was he?

SEVENTEEN

WHAT IF? IT WAS A LINE OF QUESTIONING WORTH pursuing.

I leafed farther back through the photos, past the juniors, looking through the sophomore class until I found a picture of Martha Newman, aka Willow. She looked very young, not surprising since she would have been fifteen or sixteen years old when the photo was taken. She had a wistful, tentative smile on her round face. Her hair was dark, falling to her shoulders in unruly curls, and she hadn't dressed up the day the class pictures were taken. I didn't find any other photos of her in the yearbook, but I did find two more photos of Rick Newman, candid pictures instead of the senior class studio portrait.

I used my cell phone camera to take photos of the pictures I'd found of Rick and Martha Newman. Then I replaced the yearbook in the box, left the office, and walked up the hall to the living room. Lance was there with his daughter, talking with her about her day.

"Did you find what you needed?" He set down his wineglass and walked me to the front door.

"Yes, thanks."

"Let me know if you hear anything from Brian."

"I will."

My car had been sitting in the afternoon sun for a couple of hours now, and it felt like an oven. I rolled down the windows and removed the top from the stainless steel bottle of water I kept in the front seat. The water was warm by now, but it was still wet. I took a couple of drinks and capped the bottle. Then I dug in my bag for the notebook where I'd written the phone number for Steven Kennett, Willow's stepfather. This time I got Mr. Kennett himself. He agreed to talk with me later this afternoon and gave me directions to his home in Cotati.

I started the car and drove east, getting on the freeway headed north. When I reached Santa Rosa I took the Highway 12 exit west, then angled to the northwest on Occidental Road, which cut to the north of Sebastopol. This winding two-lane highway led through gentle, rolling terrain dotted with houses and farms, then into a landscape of tall coastal redwoods that covered the hills.

Occidental is a small town of about a thousand people. It dates back to the eighteen-seventies. At one time it was a stop on the North Pacific Coast railroad that went all the way to Sausalito, in Marin County. It was a timber town, with half a dozen sawmills. Nowadays Occidental is known for its restaurants, shops and art galleries, and its location on the scenic Bohemian Highway, which runs from Highway 12 north to the Russian River.

I turned left, off Occidental Road onto Bohemian Highway, and drove slowly through the middle of the town. I spotted Hestia Gallery in a stretch of shops near the Howard Station Café. I pulled into a parking spot.

Ceramic pots near the gallery's front door held an assortment of petunias, pansies, marigolds, and zinnias. In the front window, I saw a sign explaining that Hestia was the Ancient Greek goddess of architecture and domesticity. Her symbol was the hearth and its fire, and I saw a drawing of both at the bottom of the sign.

I entered the gallery and walked through the front section. On the wall to the right, about twenty feet from the door, was an L-shaped glass-enclosed display case holding jewelry and other small items. At the corner of the L was a cash register and a holder with business cards. Several postcards decorated the counter, advertising art shows and fairs. I glanced through these and saw one advertising the upcoming Gravenstein Apple Fair in Sebastopol.

The hearth-and-fire logo was repeated on business cards,

which showed the gallery's address and phone number, and a name, Avie Northrup. I guessed this was the silver-haired woman who was behind the display case, talking with a customer who was looking at several pairs of earrings.

I circled the front section of the gallery, glancing at the wares made by local artists. In a basket near the door, I saw several packets of note cards with birds on the front, the same cards Becca had had in her bag the day before. One of these had the scene of the yellow-rumped warbler, the card Willow sent to my brother. I picked up a packet and looked at the back, checking the name of the artist. Then my eye was drawn upward, to a small watercolor done by the same artist. It showed a male Anna's hummingbird, and the artist had caught the iridescence of the bird's red-pink head and neck, a contrast with its gray-green body.

Dad would like that, I thought. And he had a birthday coming up.

I turned to examine the wall opposite the counter. Here were shelves displaying an assortment of pottery. Many of the pieces were functional items, cups, dishes, vases, bowls, and small pots.

I spotted a large green mug, similar to the one my brother had purchased from Willow. I picked it up and turned it over, seeing the distinctive willow-leaf mark with the "W" inside. Next to this was a vase in the same purplish red shade as Brian's mug, then a set of three blue bowls, each a bit larger than the other. The piece I really liked was an asymmetrical platter in shades of green. I turned it over and looked at the price tag. It was steep, but not unusual for the quality of the work. I set the platter back on the shelf.

At the end of the long shelf I saw a three-ring binder with a cover that read POTTERY BY WILLOW. I picked it up and opened it. The binder contained photographs of Willow's larger and more artistic pieces. She made hand-thrown dishes in sets of six, and they sold for a price in the four figures. There were more platters like the one I'd been looking at. If a customer wanted a larger piece, Willow could be commissioned to make something to order, such as birdbaths and garden statuary.

The prices I saw listed in the binder were a revelation. I looked through the pictures of work Willow had already done and figured she must be making a living at it. At the back of the book was a sheet that indicated her work could be purchased here, at Hestia Gallery, or through her website. I took my notebook from my bag and jotted down the website URL, so I could look at it later.

The customer at the display case selected a pair of earrings. The silver-haired woman rang up the purchase. Then, as the customer departed the gallery, the woman approached me. She was short and sturdy, clad in a pair of blue slacks with a light blue shirt and comfortable low-heeled shoes.

"Good afternoon. May I help you?"

"What can you tell me about this potter, Willow?" I set the binder back on the shelf.

"Willow does beautiful work. She's local, lives here in the Occidental area. We're the only gallery that sells her pottery, although she sometimes goes to art fairs."

Like the fair in Sonoma, where my brother bought the mug. I took a business card from my bag and handed it to her. "My name's Jeri Howard."

"Avie Northrup," she said, examining the card. "I'm the owner. What's this about?"

"I'm working on a missing persons case. I'd like to talk with Willow. I believe she may have some information that would help me find this person. I understand she lives here in Occidental. Could you put me in touch with her?"

Avie Northrup thought a moment before answering. "She did live in town until recently, but she's moved. I have a phone number for her. But I can't give it out, of course. You understand, she likes her privacy. I suppose the best way to get in touch with her is to send her an email message through her website."

"I plan to do that. It would be helpful if you'd call her and ask her to get in touch with me. The matter is urgent."

"I will. Though sometimes she's not good about returning calls." The gallery owner turned slightly, then stopped. "I just thought of something. The gallery will be having a booth at the apple fair in Sebastopol this coming weekend. Willow promised to bring in some small items for the fair. She said she might drop by the gallery, either tomorrow or Friday. If she doesn't call you back, maybe you can catch her here."

"Thanks. I appreciate your help."

I turned and walked toward the front door, past a middle-aged couple who had just entered. Outside the gallery, I stopped and glanced back through the front window. Avie Northrup greeted the couple. Then she stepped back behind the counter and picked up the telephone.

EIGHTEEN

I LEFT OCCIDENTAL BY ANOTHER ROUTE, HEADING east on Graton Road. The little town of Graton was known for apples, with orchards and processing plants. It was more than a hundred years old, situated in a lovely valley, its hills and meadows a mixture of oaks and grasslands. Before I reached the town, I turned into the gravel driveway that led to a two-story Victorian farmhouse surrounded by orchards full of apple trees. My cousin Pat lives here, with her husband, Bruce Foxworth, and her mother, Aunt Dulcie, the younger sister of my grandmother Jerusha, Dad's mother.

Aunt Dulcie is now well into her nineties. Her husband, Fred, who died several years ago, had been a career Air Force officer. Pat and her siblings grew up on Air Force bases all over the United States and overseas. That's where she met Bruce, a Graton native, who had also been an officer. When Bruce retired after thirty years in the service, he wanted to come back home and grow apples. So here they were, surrounded by apple trees, many of them loaded with fruit. The trees closest to the house were Gravensteins, an early August apple famed for its flavor. Many consider the Gravenstein the best pie apple. I certainly do, and I was hoping my cousin would give me some.

I parked next to a late-model Ford sedan I didn't recognize, and got out of my car. Mabel, the Foxworths' floppy-eared dog, greeted me, barking a couple of times. Then she gave my feet and legs an enthusiastic sniff. I knelt and scratched her behind the ears and she groaned with pleasure. I straightened and headed around the back of the house, where the patio looked out at the coastal hills to the west. I had a feeling I'd find Pat and Bruce here, enjoying a glass of wine in the late-afternoon sunshine.

I was right, they were here, seated around a glass-topped table, with a third person, an elderly woman with a head of tight gray curls. They each had glasses, and there was an open bottle of Pinot Noir on the table.

"I thought I heard someone drive up," Pat said, rising from her chair to greet me with a hug. She was short and slim, with salt-and-pepper curls.

Bruce laughed. "Mabel was snoozing. Then she got up and went round to the front of the house. That's a dead giveaway that someone drove up." He got up and hugged me as well. He was tall and lean, looking sun-browned. He gestured toward the elderly woman. "Jeri, this is my Aunt Glad. Jeri is Pat's cousin."

"Jeri Howard," I said, offering my hand.

"Gladys Tate," the woman said, shaking hands. "Though Bruce always calls me Glad. Has ever since he was a little boy. Bruce's dad was my brother. How are you related to Pat?"

"Pat and my father are cousins. Aunt Dulcie, Pat's mom, and my grandmother Jerusha were sisters. How is Dulcie?" I asked Pat.

"She's fine, having a nap right now." Pat motioned to me. "Come into the kitchen while I get another glass." Once we'd entered the big kitchen at the back of the house, Pat turned to me, a serious expression on her face. "I'm glad you stopped by. I was going to call you. I talked with your father earlier today. He told me Brian's missing."

I nodded. "Yes. Evidently he left home on Friday and was supposed to return on Sunday, but he didn't." I left out the part about the body on the boat.

"I told your dad, and now I'm telling you," Pat said. "I'm sure I saw Brian's old Jeep in Graton on Friday."

"You did? When?"

"Late morning. I'd been to a meeting at the Community Hall downtown. I was just leaving, getting ready to cross Graton Road to where I'd parked my car. I saw a red Jeep heading west, driven by a man, though I didn't get a good look at him. He was alone, and the Jeep had a dent on the passenger side door. The reason I noticed it is because Brian's Jeep has a dent just like that."

I pictured my brother's Jeep Wrangler, its red paint faded and lots of miles on the odometer. "The Jeep didn't have a dent the last time I saw it. Of course, that's several months ago."

"It was recent damage," Pat said. "I saw the Jeep when we had that Fourth of July barbeque at Caro's house. I asked Brian about it, and he said someone had backed into the door when he and Sheila were up in Yosemite in June. It was minor, he said, and he was going to hammer the dent out himself, but he just hadn't gotten around to it."

"It could have been any Jeep with a dent," I said, thinking out loud, "but... thanks, Pat, I don't have many leads to go on. You should call Detective Colman at the Petaluma Police Department. She's handling the missing persons case. I've got her card in my purse."

Pat took a wineglass from a cupboard and handed it to me. "Sure, I'll call right away. Anything I can do to help. It's just not like your brother to vanish like that."

"No, it isn't." I thought about what Pat had said. The man in the Jeep Pat had seen was driving west on Graton Road, in the direction of Occidental. Which was where Willow lived, or had until recently.

We went back out to the patio and Bruce poured wine into my glass. I pulled out the card for Detective Colman and handed it to Pat. She went back into the house to make the call.

I took a seat next to Gladys Tate, who said, "As I was saying, I used to be able to pump good water from my well, but I can't anymore. I am so annoyed I could just spit."

"Is there something wrong with your well?" I asked, taking a sip of the Pinot.

"Yes," she said tartly. "That blankety-blank winery that bought the parcel above my land. They sank a well that went deeper than mine. My well has gone dry. Instead of water, I'm getting dirt and clods. Now I've got to buy my water."

"That's terrible. Is it a big problem around here?"

Bruce nodded "Oh, yes. Water's always an issue in California. Particularly in a dry year, like this one."

Pat rejoined us, handing the card back to me, with a nod saying that she'd talked with Detective Colman about seeing Brian's Jeep. I tucked the card into my bag.

"It's the wineries," Gladys said. "They've taken over. Soon there won't be any apple orchards left. When I was growing up, this county was covered with apple orchards. All sorts of varieties, not those tasteless lumps you get in the grocery stores. Not that I buy apples in the store when I have an orchard full of trees right in back of my house."

Bruce took a sip of his wine. "I'm like Aunt Glad, I can remember when there were acres of apples and several processing plants. Each year there's more land taken out of production. And the only processing plant left is the one here in Graton. I read an article a couple of years ago that said Sonoma County is down from thirteen thousand acres of apple orchards to three thousand. I'll bet the acreage has dropped since then. Now the biggest apple-growing area in California is down in the San Joaquin Valley."

"China's gotten into growing apples in a big way," Pat added. "They don't ship apples to the United States, but the Chinese do sell apple juice concentrate here, for a lot less money than ours. That's why the apple processing business here has dried up and people are tearing out orchards."

"I had no idea." I looked out at the orchard. "I come up here every fall to get apples right out of your orchard."

"And I'm planning to give you a bag before you leave," Pat said. "We're retired. We're growing apples because we want to, not so we can make a living." She waved a hand at the trees. "Take those Gravensteins out there. The best apple in the world, in my opinion. Sweet, tart, juicy. Best for pie and best for juice. But they ripen early, they don't store well, and they don't travel well. So what you get in the stores are those tasteless lumps, as Aunt Glad calls them. Usually Red Delicious, which is a misnomer if I ever heard one."

"A Red Delicious is okay, right off the tree," Bruce said. "But I'll take a Gravenstein any day. Or a Rome Beauty or Pippin."

"A Northern Spy," Pat said.

"I'm partial to a Rhode Island Greening myself," Gladys said. "There are so many varieties. Now, the Walkers down the road grow twenty-seven varieties, some that most people have never heard of."

"You can grow anything here in Graton," Pat said.

Gladys nodded in agreement. "Apples, pears, and those folks over on Sullivan Road grow those Asian pears. Now, when I was a girl, we used to grow hops, too. I remember the hop-picking. We've got such nice weather, with good water."

"Right here in Graton we have best aquifer in the county," Bruce said. "A geologist friend of mine called it the Wilson Grove formation, sandstone. It's a sandy loam. You can sink a well and it will produce. Farther west, toward Occidental, you get what they call metamorphic terrain, where you only get water out of fractures."

"I don't know what formation my place is on," Gladys said. "All I know is, my well used to produce, and now it doesn't. All because of that winery sucking up all the water."

"So the wine grapes are where the money is," I said.

"Right. You can get a couple of thousand dollars for a ton of grapes and less than two hundred for apples. So farmers are digging out the trees and putting in grapes." Bruce gestured toward the bottle on the table. "Pinot Noir is what they grow here, mostly. Other varieties in other parts of the county."

"Sad to see things change," Gladys said. "But at my age I've seen a lot of changes."

Yes, change was constant, I thought, sipping my Pinot Noir. The Miwok Indians had lived here, not that long ago, then the Spanish had moved in with their land grants, taking big tracts of land for ranches. In the late nineteenth century, it was immigrants from the East Coast and the Midwest who came to this area, putting in orchards and farms, people whose family, like Bruce and his aunt, had lived here for several generations.

I noticed something at the far edge of the patio, in the middle of a garden patch planted with flowers. I pointed at the small birdbath, in a familiar shade of reddish purple. "That's new."

"I got that a month or so ago," Pat said, as a dark-eyed junco landed on the birdbath and began splashing in the water. "It was in a gallery in Occidental and it caught my eye."

It most definitely caught my eye as well. It looked just like the birdbath I'd seen in the book of photographs at Hestia Gallery.

"I've seen the potter's work before," I said. "She calls herself Willow, though her real name is Martha Newman."

"Martha? Is that Walt Newman's daughter?" Gladys asked. "The man that owns the marina and bar down in Lakeville?"

"Yes. Do you know her?"

"I know of her." Gladys looked at Bruce. "Her mother was Arlene Hargis, Pete's daughter. We're related on my mother's side. Mama was an Eklund, and Arlene's mother was a Stenberg. They were cousins, Swedes from Minnesota. I don't know what possessed Arlene to marry that Newman fellow. He's an odd bird. They had two children, Martha and a boy a few years older. The marriage lasted longer than I thought it would, but eventually Arlene divorced Walt. She married a nice fellow named Kennett, and lived in Cotati. She died last summer, cancer, I think. And Pete died in January. I wonder what will happen to his ranch."

"Ranch?" I asked. "Where is it?"

"What you'd call a farm, we call a ranch." Pat waved her arm, encompassing the apple orchard. "So here we are on the Foxworth ranch."

"And the Hargis ranch is west of here," Bruce said, "about midway between Graton and Occidental. About a hundred acres, half of it in apples. As for what's going to happen to the ranch, Pete left it to his grandchildren."

"Martha and the boy," Gladys said. "What was his name? Richard, that's it. But he's dead. Some sort of accident. It happened recently, last month or two. So the ranch belongs to Martha. If she's making pots, I doubt she's going to farm it. Probably sell out to some winery."

Bruce nodded. "She's gotten several offers for the land."

I finished the last of the Pinot in my glass, remembering what the gallery owner had said about Willow moving recently.

Then Bruce confirmed what I'd been thinking. "She moved into the house, built a kiln, and turned the barn into a workroom. Sounds like she plans to stay there."

NINETEEN

PAT INVITED ME TO STAY FOR DINNER, BUT I TURNED down the offer. I had a late-afternoon appointment in Cotati, with Steven Kennett, Willow's stepfather.

I spent some time talking with Aunt Dulcie, who got up from her nap and made her way out to the patio for a glass of wine. She looked much the same as she had when I'd last seen her, a couple of months ago. She was in her nineties, and I suspected she'd live to be a hundred. Of course, that's what I'd hoped with my own grandmother. We never know what life has in store, or when death will take those we love.

I left Pat's house with a large bag of Gravensteins and a jar of homemade apple butter. When I reached the end of the gravel drive, I consulted my watch. I had an hour before my appointment with Kennett. So I turned left and drove west on Graton Road again, slowing and looking at road signs and mailboxes. Finally I saw a mailbox marked "Hargis," and a small sign that read, HARGIS RANCH ROAD. PRIVATE PROPERTY.

A gravel road led up a slope past an orchard where apples littered the ground. Bruce's aunt had said Peter Hargis, the owner of the ranch, had died after Christmas, so there was no one to pick these August-ripening Gravensteins, or the other varieties farther up the slope, where trees were filled with fruit.

My slow progress on the gravel road was stopped by a locked

gate. This was as far as I could go. Some thirty yards away, through the trees, I saw a one-story house that looked as though it had been built in the nineteen-fifties. Visible behind the house was a barn roof.

According to Bruce, Willow had recently moved from Occidental to this house on the property left to her by her grandfather. Though the property had been left jointly to Willow and her brother, Rick, his death in June would complicate the inheritance. He had probably died intestate, without a will.

If he was dead at all. The fact that his body hadn't been found after the motorcycle accident nagged at me.

There were no vehicles parked near the house, so presumably Willow wasn't there. I turned my car around and headed back down to Graton Road. I drove back through town, then headed south on Highway 116, through Sebastopol toward the small town of Cotati, located where 116 met Highway 101.

Cotati is a small town to the south of Santa Rosa and Rohnert Park, where Sonoma State University is located. I found Steven Kennett's house easily, on a quiet street on the east side of town. It was a well-kept one-story, wood frame ranch-style house, its front yard landscaped with native plants and grasses. I turned into the driveway and parked behind a Chevrolet.

The front porch was a small concrete rectangle decorated with a clay pot planted with succulents. The front door was covered by a bronze steel screen door. When I rang the bell, I heard a dog barking inside the house, the sound getting closer as the dog ran to the door.

The front door opened. A man peered out through the steel mesh. I guessed his age as late sixties or early seventies. He was about six feet tall, with short white hair and hazel eyes in a tanned, creased face that spoke of a life lived outdoors. He wore faded blue jeans and an orange T-shirt.

The dog crowding in next to him was a Rottweiler, big with heavy shoulders and a sleek coat of black and mahogany. He barked at me and the man said, "Rowdy, sit." The dog sat and looked at me, alert.

"Mr. Kennett, I'm Jeri Howard. We spoke on the phone."

He nodded. "You said you're a private investigator."

"Yes." Earlier he'd agreed to talk with me, but now I wondered if he had changed his mind.

"Okay," he said. "Come on into the house. Don't worry about the dog. He's well-trained. Just let him get a good sniff."

Kennett opened the security door and motioned me inside. I stepped into the entry hall and held out my hand, palm up, taking it on faith that Rowdy wouldn't take a bite out of my fingers. The Rottweiler gave me a thorough inspection with his large wet nose, starting with my hand and my arm. Then he moved to the legs of my slacks, which no doubt had Mabel's hair all over them, as well of that of my two cats.

"I was at my cousin's house earlier," I said. "She has a dog. And I have cats."

"That's probably what he smells. I have a cat, too, so he's used to them."

Rowdy decided I was all right and wagged his tail. I ventured an ear scratch and he enjoyed that.

"You want a cup of coffee?" Kennett asked.

"Yes, thanks."

I followed him as he walked through a living room–dining room combination. The living room contained several old china cabinets full of glass and silver, while the dining area containing a round oak table and matching chairs. Both rooms looked as though they weren't used very often. The kitchen at the back of the house was spacious and certainly more lived-in, with a round table covered in yellow Formica. The kitchen opened onto a family room. A sliding glass door and screen led out to a patio with chairs and beyond that, a backyard with a vegetable garden and an apple tree loaded with ripening fruit. The door was open, admitting a slight breeze. Just in front of the screen, a big black-and-white tomcat was stretched out on his side on the beige tile floor, soaking up the late-afternoon sun. The cat opened one eye, looked at me, and then settled back into his nap.

Kennett stepped over to the kitchen counter, reaching for a stainless steel thermal carafe. He poured each of us a mug of coffee. "You take anything in it?"

"Black is fine."

He handed me one mug. I took a sip of the strong brew, while he doctored his own coffee with half-and-half from a carton in the nearby refrigerator. Then he led the way to the family room. A large-screen TV stood on a low stand against the wall opposite the kitchen, with a worn leather recliner and a sofa grouped in front of the TV. Shelves on either side of the TV contained books, photographs, and various objects, including an unusual pottery piece, three vases joined with a single bottom. I walked over and looked at it.

"That's one of my stepdaughter's pots," Kennett said. "Martha. Or Willow. That's what she calls herself."

"I thought it might be."

Kennett pointed at a framed photograph on one of the shelves. "That's Arlene. She died in July of last year. So it's been just over a year. Cancer. My first wife died of cancer, too."

"I'm sorry for your loss." The passage of time since the death didn't make any difference. It was always a loss when someone you love died. And this man had lost two wives to the disease.

I examined the picture of the late Mrs. Arlene Kennett. It showed a pleasant-looking woman in her sixties, her short brown hair threaded with streaks of silver. Laugh lines crinkled the corners of her hazel eyes.

"We were married over ten years." Kennett picked up the photograph and ran his work-calloused fingers over the frame. "Arlene and Walt got divorced the summer after Willow graduated from high school. I met Arlene about a year after that. My wife had been gone for about five years then, and my kids—I have three—were grown and out of the house. So...Arlene and I got married. We had a good run. I just didn't expect to lose her this soon."

"Do you have photographs of your stepchildren, Rick and Willow?" I asked.

"Sure." Kennett reached for another framed photo on the shelf. "This one was taken at Christmas, a couple of years ago, before Arlene was diagnosed with cancer."

The color photograph showed Mrs. Kennett, with her children

on either side. I could see a Christmas tree in the background, and the older woman was wearing a red sweater decorated with white snowflakes. Willow, on her mother's left, looked a lot like Arlene, hazel eyes, and the same brown hair, though worn longer, tied back with a colorful red-and-green scarf that matched the red-and-green checked top she wore.

Rick Newman, posed on his mother's right, wore a black sweatshirt with a Harley-Davidson logo. He had been in his early thirties when the picture was taken. Once again I was struck by his resemblance to my brother Brian. His hair was sandy-colored and didn't have the strawberry-blond hints that my brother's hair had. Rick wore his hair long, curling around the ears, just like the dead man in the morgue. His eyes were blue, almost the same shade as Brian's eyes.

I couldn't shake the feeling that Rick hadn't died in the motor-cycle accident, that he was still alive. Or was that his body in the Sonoma County morgue?

"Thanks," I said, handing the photo back to Kennett. He put it back on the shelf and motioned me to take a seat. I moved to the sofa, while he took the recliner.

The black-and-white cat got up from his sprawl and stretched. Then he strolled over to the recliner. With one easy movement he jumped into Kennett's lap. "Hey, there, Mojo," Kennett said, stroking the cat's head. Mojo purred and kneaded Kennett's leg, then circled and settled down for another nap.

"I wasn't sure I should talk with you," Kennett said. "But I'm curious. You told me you have some questions about my wife's children."

"Their names came up in connection with a missing persons case," I said.

"Does this have something to do with Rick?"

"Why do you ask?"

"It's a hell of a thing," Kennett said. "Arlene died last summer, her dad died in January, and Rick died in June. They say things come in threes. The reason I asked if this is about Rick is be-cause... Well, he was a wild one, always in trouble. Arlene always worried about him, though he didn't come around much while she was alive. When she died, he didn't come around at all. Willow visits now and then."

"What can you tell me about Walt Newman, your wife's first husband?"

"Don't know why Arlene ever married him. They were as different as chalk and cheese. Walt's a character. So was his father."

"You knew his father?"

"Heard stories about him, from Arlene and other people," Kennett said. "Old Man Newman is gone now, fifteen years or more. Walt's lived there in Lakeville his whole life."

"I understand there is some controversy about his plans to expand the marina."

Kennett nodded. "Read about that in the paper, and Willow told me about it, too. There's a parcel of land on the river just south of the marina. The guy that farmed it died. His family put the land on the market. Walt wants to buy it and build more slips. But the local environmental groups are kicking up something fierce. They want that parcel for wetlands. Never mind that it's been farmed for years. I guess they want to restore it."

Kennett took another swallow of coffee. "Then there's the roadhouse. It's popular with bikers, and things can get lively down there. A lot of people don't like that. Every now and then there's talk about pulling his liquor license. But nothing ever comes of it. Besides, the roadhouse has been there for years. During Prohibition, they say booze was coming up the Petaluma River by boat. The rum-runners would land at the marina and the roadhouse would distribute the liquor." He chuckled. "I've heard some tales about that roadhouse."

I laughed. "I'm sure you're right."

"This land thing came up earlier this year," Kennett said. "Now Walt's tussling with the environmentalists over that. And the latest thing is that there was a fire out there on Saturday night. A boat blew up, propane leak, according to the news, and some fellow was killed."

"I met a woman at the marina, Tracy Burgoyne. At first I

thought she was an employee. Then she implied that she was involved with Walt."

"She's his girlfriend," Kennett said. "Although at our age it seems strange to talk about girlfriends. She and Walt have been living together for several years. He has a house there at the marina."

"I imagine Mr. Newman was really upset about his son's death."

"He sure was." Kennett glanced at the photographs on the nearby shelf. "I know I would be if any of my kids died. You just don't expect to outlive your children. Much as I miss Arlene, I'm glad she was spared that."

"When did Rick die, exactly? And how did it happen?"

"The last week in June, on a Thursday," Kennett said. "It was odd, that accident. Rick and a friend of his—Harry Vann—were up north of Jenner, headed south on Highway One. If you've ever driven that highway, you know what it's like, even on a good day."

"I have driven it, and I do know. That road's very twisty, and narrow in places. What was odd about the accident?"

"That Rick should have an accident on a day like that," Kennett said. "It was a really nice day, sunny and clear. No rain in June, of course, and there wasn't any fog at that time of the afternoon. Highway One can be deadly when the weather's bad, but the weather was fine. Still, I suppose Rick was speeding. He had a habit of doing that. Anyway, Rick's motorcycle skidded on a curve and he went off a cliff. His buddy Harry was behind him and saw Rick go over the edge. Harry pulled off the road and tried to get down to help Rick, but it was too steep." Kennett shook his head, stroking the cat on his lap.

"Harry told me Rick wasn't moving, just lying there by the bike, right there at the surf line, and there were some big waves hammering the shoreline. He couldn't get a signal on his cell phone—no surprise, the cell reception's bad on the coast. So Harry got back on his bike and went down to Jenner. Time he got back with some help, the Harley was still there, at the bottom of the

cliff, but Rick's body was gone. It must have washed out to sea.
Walt was really broken up about it, still is, of course, since it's only
been six or seven weeks since it happened. Rick was Walt's favorite. I suppose fathers shouldn't have favorites, but Walt always
favored Rick."

"What about Willow? Was she close to her brother?"

Kennett shrugged. "I wouldn't say close. You know brothers
and sisters."

Yes, I knew about brothers and sisters. There were times,
when we were growing up, that I'd wanted to bounce Brian off a
wall. But still, he was my brother, family. Now all I wanted to do
was find him and make sure he was safe.

"They grew up together and went their separate ways," Kennett said. "Rick never went to college and Willow did. Rick was in
trouble with the law, over and over again, went from job to job.
Willow's never had so much as a parking ticket. They had their
differences. Sometimes they got along, and sometimes they didn't.
But Willow was pretty upset when we heard the news about Rick.
No closure, you know, not having a body. They haven't had a me-
morial service yet. I guess Walt's not ready to go there."

"You have three children from your first marriage. Did they
know Rick and Willow before you married Arlene?"

He shook his head. "No. My children are older, in their forties, all of them married with kids of their own. Rick would have
been thirty-four this year. Willow's three years younger, so she's
thirty-one. She and Rick went to school in Petaluma, and my kids
grew up here in Cotati, went to high school in Rohnert Park."

"What else can you tell me about Willow? Was she always artistic?"

"I think so, from what Arlene said. Willow studied art up at
Sonoma State. She lived here with me and Arlene for a time, until
she found a place of her own closer to campus. After she graduated, she went to work at a gallery in Santa Rosa. She did her
pottery on the side. Over the years she's worked hard. These days
she sells her stuff out of that gallery over in Occidental. She lived
there until recently, had a little house in the main part of town."

"I understand she's moved to her grandfather's place."

"The apple ranch," Kennett said, rubbing the cat's ears. "Now, that's a situation. I don't know what's going to happen there."

I took another sip of my coffee, then set it aside. "Why do you say that?"

"That place is about a hundred acres, up there between Graton and Occidental. A little over half of it, about sixty acres, is apple orchards. The rest is pretty rugged, steep and forested. If Arlene had lived, she would have inherited it. After Arlene died, Pete changed his will and left the land to Rick and Willow. They were arguing about what to do with it. Rick wanted to sell the whole thing. That didn't surprise me. He always needed money. And they would have made a lot of money selling that land. Willow told me she's been approached by two different wineries. That's where the money is these days. They're buying up land right and left, ripping out apple trees, and planting grapes. She doesn't want to sell any of it. But she might have to."

"How so?"

"Economic reality," Kennett said. "It's hard for Willow to make a living doing what she does. When she was just starting, she worked at all sorts of jobs, like that first one in the gallery, doing whatever she could to pay the rent. She started off making small pieces, cups and vases and bowls, that sort of thing. She'd sell them at arts and crafts fairs, almost every weekend, spring, summer and fall. It got old, she said, hauling pottery around from place to place. Plus, you've got the gas, the time, wear and tear on the car. Then she started selling her work at that gallery in Occidental, and she didn't have to go to the fairs as often. She's managing on what she makes with her pottery and a little money her mother left her."

"But it's not a whole lot of money?"

"No. For Willow, that land takes off some of the financial pressure and gives her a chance to do what she loves to do."

"But Rick wanted to sell. That's pressure of a different sort."

"Yes, it was. Up until Rick died, she was thinking she'd have to buy him out, so he'd get some money and quit pushing her to sell the place outright. But she didn't know how she was going to afford that."

"Rick's dead now, so presumably Willow owns the place free and clear."

"I don't know how it all sorts out in terms of the legalities," Kennett said. "Rick's presumed dead, because the body wasn't found. But yes, Willow figures the place is hers to do with as she sees fit. She moved into the old house in July, right after Rick died. And she built herself an outdoor kiln. She's using the barn for a workroom."

"So she's living rent free. As you say, that should alleviate some of her financial difficulties."

"Right. But there's property taxes with a place like the ranch," Kennett said. "It's a bigger place so that's more to spend on utilities. There's a well and a septic system to maintain. And that old house sure needs some fixing up. Besides, there are the apples, all those trees. She's not going to farm the place. I don't know that she can afford to hire somebody to do it for her. It's not worth the money spent to harvest apples these days. The apple growing industry around here is going downhill. People are tearing out orchards right and left."

"Yes, I've heard that. My cousin and her husband over in Graton grow apples. So what is Willow going to do?"

"She hasn't decided. She may sell some of the acreage and keep a portion for herself. That would probably be the most sensible thing to do. Those winery offers are real tempting. She told me how much they're offering. But Willow would like to see the land used for apples. So would a lot of the preservationists here in the west county."

So members of the Newman family were involved in two issues surrounding land use here in Sonoma County—Walt with his plans to expand the marina, and Willow contemplating what to do with the apple ranch she'd inherited.

"I'd really like to talk with Willow," I said.

"How does this figure into your missing persons case?" he asked.

"Willow has had some correspondence with the man who's missing. I'd like to see if she knows anything that might help me find him." I steered the subject back to Rick. "You said Rick was always in trouble. What kind of trouble?"

"Drugs," Kennett said. "Using, growing and selling, all the way back to when he was in high school. He did some jail time in the county lockup. Last year he got busted for selling pot, but he was acquitted."

"What sort of work did he do?"

Kennett frowned. "Rick never could hold a job for long. He did a little of this, a little of that. Sometimes he worked for Walt down at the marina. He did know his way around boats and motorcycles. Harry Vann, Rick's friend, he and his sister have a motorcycle repair shop in Santa Rosa. Rick worked for them off and on."

"By the way, who was Rick's attorney, the one he had when he was acquitted of that most recent drug charge?"

Kennett thought for a moment. "What was his name? Oh, I remember. Same name as that river in Germany. Mr. Rhine."

TWENTY

I LEFT COTATI AND GOT ON THE FREEWAY, HEADING north to Santa Rosa. As I drove, I mulled over the information I'd gleaned during my conversation with Steven Kennett. Both he and Tracy Burgoyne told me there had been a witness to Rick Newman's accident. Now I needed more information on Rick's friend Harry Vann, who had been there when Rick's motorcycle went off the cliff at the end of June.

And where did Lowell Rhine figure into all of this? The defense lawyer from San Rafael supposedly owned the boats at Newman's Marina, including the one that burned. I had wondered why he had berthed the boats at such a remote location. Now I'd learned that he'd represented Rick on a drug charge last year.

I passed a slow-moving truck, then used my hands-free headset to call Rita Lydecker's cell phone. "I dropped by Lowell Rhine's office earlier this afternoon, but I couldn't get past the receptionist. I left my card and a message to call me. Said it was about the *Esmeralda*. I don't think he'll call, so I'll have to catch up with him. Did you find out if Rhine is a sailor?"

Rita laughed. "Mr. Rhine likes fancy cars, fancy threads, good wine, and gourmet restaurants. But as far as I can determine, he is not into boats."

"Yet I was told he owns those three boats berthed at the Lakeville marina," I said. "I heard Walt Newman himself say that Rhine had called to make arrangements to have the two remaining boats moved. Rhine's name must be on the paperwork involving those boats."

"So he's a boat owner in name only," Rita said. "I can think of some scenarios that might explain that."

"So can I." My exit into Santa Rosa was coming up. I signaled a turn and slowed as I left the freeway. "Suppose Rhine was keeping the boats for someone? A client who was facing some jail time or fines and didn't want the boat listed as an asset. Or…could be, Rhine's name is listed as the owner to keep the boats from being impounded. That would explain keeping the boat in an out-of-the-way location."

"We could do a boat history search," Rita said. "It would help if we had a hull number."

Rita was right. With the *Esmeralda*'s twelve-digit hull identification number, we could trace the boat's history. A report would tell us the make and model of the boat, its age, and let us know whether the boat had been involved in any incidents such as a collision or a grounding, or whether it had a history of storm damage. Such a report would also tell us if the boat had ever been seized for any reason.

The number is usually found on the boat's stern, but also on various documents such as the boat's title, registration, and insurance documents. I would have to see if I could get the hull identification number from the tight-mouthed Sonoma county detectives—or maybe Tracy Burgoyne at Newman's Marina.

"I'll get a hull number for the *Esmeralda*," I said. "While I was at the marina yesterday and today, I took pictures of the other two boats. They're still tied up at the same dock where the *Esmeralda* burned. I'd like to get boat histories on those boats while we're at it. The pictures I took have the names and hull numbers. The shots are on my cell phone camera. I'll drop by your place on my way home and we can get started."

"I'm thinking about the possibility of the boat being impounded," Rita said. "I have a contact at the Coast Guard station in Sausalito. I'll check with him to see if I can find out if the boat was ever impounded in the past."

"Good idea." I stopped at a red light. "I'm in Santa Rosa now, but I can stop by San Rafael on my way home."

"Come to my house. I'm completely moved out of the office now." Rita gave me her address and we ended the call.

The light turned green. I went through the intersection, then turned and drove through city streets to Aunt Caro's house.

"Your mother's lying down," my aunt said when she answered the door. "Tim's in the backyard. Any news?"

"No. But a lot of questions."

"I figured. There's a pitcher of iced tea in the fridge." Caro sounded distracted, but I understood. She was working on another one of her dense historical novels, notes and papers spread out around her as she stretched out on the living room sofa with her laptop. That was her favorite place to work, but usually she was there alone, or with Uncle Neil. It must have been difficult for her to focus on her work with two unexpected houseguests—my parents—and a family crisis in the offing.

I left her in the living room, my bag on the counter separating the family room from the kitchen, and retrieved my cell phone and notepad from my bag. I called Nancy Parsons, Brian's former coworker in Sonoma, but she wasn't home. I left my name and number, and disconnected the call.

In the kitchen, I opened a cabinet, took out a glass and put lots of ice in it. I was really warm and my cotton shirt was sticking to me. I helped myself to some tea from the pitcher in the refrigerator. Then I went out the back door to the patio.

Dad was stretched on a chaise longue, a book in his hands and a glass on a nearby table. As I approached, it looked as though he too was napping. His head was tilted to one side on the pillow, and his eyes were closed. I mapped the wrinkles on his face and the silver threads in his thinning hair. Then his eyes opened. "Do you have any news?" he asked.

I pulled up a chair and sat down. "Nothing specific." The iced tea tasted good. I drank half the glass and then set it on the nearby table. "Listen, Dad. I want you to think back to your conversations with Brian over the past few months. Did he ever say anything about incidents at the school where he was teaching in Sonoma? Maybe something involving one of his students?"

Dad shifted to a more upright position and set the book on the table. "He didn't care for the principal who took over his school, after the other one died. I know that was a problem. Clash of styles, I suppose. It happens. I think that's why he was interested in changing schools."

He looked thoughtful as he reached for his glass and took a sip. "I was surprised, though, about the move from Sonoma to Petaluma. It seemed so sudden. But he must have been thinking about it for a while. As for something involving one of his students, he did mention... When was it?" Dad paused and drummed his fingers on the side of the glass. "It was after spring break, so it must have been April. Brian said he was concerned about a boy who was being bullied. He didn't think the principal was taking it seriously."

Bullying. That could have led to the boy trying to kill himself. Bullying had received a lot of news coverage over the past few years, and there had been suicides. Who knew how many suicide attempts had gone unreported?

"Did Brian say anything else? Did he plan on talking to the principal or someone else in the school administration?"

"No. After mentioning it that one time, he didn't say anything further about it. So I don't know if he talked with anyone about the situation. I'd forgotten about it till now. Why do you ask?"

"Something Lance Coverdell told me. You remember Lance?"

"Of course. Brian's friend. He was best man at the wedding. What did he say?"

"I have to check and make sure this really happened," I said. "But it's possible, given what you've said about the student being bullied." I recapped my conversation with Lance, the part about the student who'd attempted suicide.

Dad shook his head. "That's terrible. Yes, I can see your brother being upset if one of his students tried to kill himself. But he didn't say anything to me, other than mentioning the bullying. It might not even be the same student."

"I thought of that. Sheila gave me the name of one of Brian's fellow teachers in Sonoma. I hope to set up a time to talk with her."

I went back into the house for a refill on my iced tea. It was after five, according to the clock on the kitchen wall. Caro came up behind me. "Don't even think about getting on the freeway at this hour. Rush hour traffic's a mess. Wait till after dinner."

"Done writing for the day?" I asked.

She gave me a wry grin. "I have reached a bump in the plot road, so I'll contemplate a detour while I rustle up some grub. Something cold. It's so hot I don't want to turn on the oven."

My mother walked into the kitchen from the bedrooms down the hall. "I'm the chef. I'll fix dinner."

"Did you get any sleep?" Caro asked.

Mother shook her head. "No. Tossed and turned, thinking about things. It's better that I keep busy." She opened the refrigerator and assessed the contents. "Now what do I have to work with? Here's that leftover chicken we grilled yesterday. I'll make a big salad. And there's the rest of that plum tart we got at the bakery."

Mother pulled the container of chicken out of the fridge and set it on the counter. She reached into the refrigerator again, piling up plastic bags full of fresh fruits and vegetables. She reached for a cutting board and knife and began pulling the chicken off the bone and chopping it into pieces. Caro rinsed and drained a head of romaine lettuce. I set the table and went outside to tell Dad dinner would soon be ready.

Back in the house, I reached for my cell phone, stepping into the now-vacant living room as I redialed Nancy Parsons' number.

This time the phone was answered by a woman's voice. As she said "Hello," I heard a man's voice and a barking dog in the background.

"Nancy Parsons?"

"That's me. Who's this?"

"Jeri Howard. I'm Brian Howard's sister."

"Oh, hey, you left me a message. I was going to call you later. You're the private investigator. Brian's mentioned you." There was the hint of a chuckle in her voice. "I hope you're not calling because you're on a case."

"I'm afraid I am," I said. "Brian is missing."

"Good lord," she said, all trace of humor gone. "When? How? I mean, how awful."

"That's the way I feel. Ms. Parsons, I wonder if I could talk with you about Brian."

"I'd be happy to, except I'm due at my in-laws' for dinner in ten minutes. I'm free tomorrow morning. How about ten o'clock?"

"That works for me. I can come to Sonoma, if you'll pick a place."

She suggested a café and bake shop not far from the historic plaza in downtown Sonoma. "The coffee's good and they have yummy pastries. Not that I need any." The chuckle was back in her voice. "I'm on the pleasingly plump side."

"I never pass up a good pastry. How will I recognize you?"

"Short, round, salt-and-pepper hair. And you?"

"Tall, reddish hair. I'll see you there."

I sat down and ate dinner with my family. Mother had worked wonders with the supplies she had to hand, constructing a salad full of chunks of chicken mixed with lettuce and other vegetables, almonds, sliced peaches and figs, all of this sprinkled with pungent blue cheese from the Cowgirl Creamery and drizzled with a homemade vinaigrette. We finished off a loaf of kalamata olive bread and the plum tart as well.

Before I left Caro's house, I took the front page of that morning's newspaper, with the artist's sketch of the dead man. Then I said my good-byes and got on the road, heading south. Traffic was definitely lighter at that time of the evening. I was tired after my day driving around Sonoma County, but I had one more stop to make, at Rita's house.

I left Santa Rosa and its environs, heading over the hills into Petaluma. As I reached the outskirts, I called Sid, my ex-husband.

"I was thinking about you. I heard from Joe Kelso," he said, mentioning his former partner who was now chief of police in Cloverdale. "I called him yesterday and he got in touch with those two detectives at the Sonoma County Sheriff's Office."

"Did he get any information from them?"

"You're right, they definitely think Brian is a person of interest in the homicide. The sooner you can find him, the better."

"I know. But so far I'm not having any luck finding him." I banged my hand against the steering wheel. "Have they identified the body?"

"No," Sid said. "They're hoping the sketch that was in the newspaper will help. Joe got copies of documents and photos. He scanned and emailed those to me, and I'll send them to you. Joe says he should have a copy of the autopsy report as soon as it's available."

"Is there anything in those documents relating to the boat? As in, who owns it? And a hull identification number? Rita Lydecker and I are going to run a boat history."

"I think so." Sid was silent for a moment as he looked at the papers. "Yeah. Here's a paper that says the boat is owned by Lowell Rhine, San Rafael. As for a hull ID, hmm... Wait, here's a picture of the boat after they pulled it out of the water. I can just make out the plate on the back. Got a pen?"

I had a small notepad and pen affixed to the dashboard of my Toyota. I reached for the pen and wrote down the number as he read it off. "Thanks," I told Sid. "I'll look forward to seeing what Joe sent you."

I ended the call as I approached Novato. So Lowell Rhine of San Rafael did in fact own the *Esmeralda*. Officially. But the attorney was not a sailor, according to Rita. The more I found out, the more questions I had.

I called Rhine's office and got voice mail. I disconnected the call and frowned at the traffic on the freeway. I'll catch up with you, Mr. Rhine. Sooner or later, but I will.

TWENTY-ONE

RITA LYDECKER LIVED IN THE TERRA LINDA SECTION of San Rafael, north of downtown and west of Highway 101. I had never been to her home before, but was interested to see that it was an Eichler house, built in the years after World War II, by Bay Area developer Joseph Eichler. The house was typical of many of the Eichlers I'd been in, with its low-sloping A-framed roof and small front windows. Rita's house had an atrium, an open-air entrance foyer. Inside were floor-to-ceiling glass windows and exposed post-and-beam construction. The floors were concrete slab with radiant heating, and Rita had covered them with colorful oriental rugs. The house had the usual open floor plan, with sliding doors for the rooms and closets.

"Nice Eichler," I said.

"Yeah. I've always liked the style. I guess they call it California Modern. I bought the place after my first divorce." Rita led the way to the back of the house, pausing at the door that led to the kitchen. "Had dinner?"

"Yes, I ate something at my aunt's house."

"Have some wine, then."

I shook my head. "Better not. I'm driving and I'm tired enough as it is. I have a feeling a glass of wine would put me to sleep."

"I'll have some, then." Rita detoured to the kitchen and poured some Chardonnay into a glass, then motioned me to follow her to a back bedroom that she'd converted into an office.

The room was crowded with cardboard boxes. She was still in the process of putting away the files she'd moved from her old office downtown. Her desk was in the middle of the room, with a laptop and mouse. Next to these were a small printer and a phone. Rita took the chair behind the desk. There was another chair in the corner of the room. I moved a box off the seat and pulled the chair close to the desk.

I took out my cell phone and accessed the photos I'd taken of the two remaining boats tied up at the dock where the *Esmeralda* had burned. The pictures showed the hull identification numbers, as well as the boat names, the *Rosarita* and the *Silverado*.

"Plus, I have the hull number for the *Esmeralda*," I told her. "By way of Sid, my ex, and a friend of ours who's in Sonoma County law enforcement."

"Great. I put a call in to my Coast Guard source, but he hasn't called me back yet. Let's see what we can find out about the history of that boat."

She took a sip of her wine and set the glass on the desk. On her laptop she went to a website specializing in boat histories. She put in the hull identification number for the *Esmeralda* and clicked the "Submit" button. Then she went through the process again for the other two boats.

"In my experience it will take some time to get back a report," she said. "And we're looking for three. In the meantime…" She reached for several sheets of paper in the paper tray of her printer. "I did some Internet searches on Rhine and boats to see what came up. I didn't find anything about this particular boat, but here's a case that sounds interesting."

I looked at the papers, printouts from several newspaper websites, involving one of Rhine's current cases. The attorney was representing a man from Oakland whose car had been seized by the Drug Enforcement Agency. The DEA agents said the vehicle had been used to transport drugs, but the owner denied this. Rhine was claiming this was an illegal forfeiture of his client's property. The article said that Rhine had used the argument successfully in the past, utilizing some recent changes in the forfeiture laws. In doing so, he'd helped several people regain their property—not just cars, but boats as well. But none of the boats were listed by name.

"Yes, this is interesting," I said. "Makes me wonder if those boats in Lakeville were ever seized."

"We'll know more when we get those boat histories," Rita said. "We'll have to wait until then."

I LEFT RITA'S HOUSE AND HEADED THROUGH SAN Rafael, then east over the bridge to Richmond. But I didn't go home. I spent another hour in my downtown Oakland office, checking email, responding to phone messages, and working on Brian's case. I had received Sid's email forwarding the information he'd gotten from Joe Kelso, which Joe in turn had obtained from the Sonoma County Sheriff's Department.

I printed out the documents and photos. Then I looked through the photographs of the scene, showing the *Esmeralda* after the fire had been put out. Here was the picture Sid had mentioned, with the plate affixed to the stern of the boat and the hull identification number clearly visible. Other photos showed the badly damaged cabin cruiser. It looked as though the fire had been confined to the cabin but the exterior deck had been damaged as well, as had the dock in the vicinity of the boat.

I set the pictures aside and read through copies of the witness statements from the people at the marina, taken after the Lakeville Volunteer Fire Department had extinguished the blaze on the boat and the body had been found. I'd already talked with Tracy Burgoyne, Chet Olsen, and several of the people in the bar. None of the statements added much to what I'd already learned from talking with people. They hadn't been paying any notice to the cabin cruiser tied up at the north end of Newman's Marina—until the propane explosion and fire caught their attention.

I put the witness statements aside and looked through the other documents. I didn't see anything that indicated that the detectives had talked with Lowell Rhine, the ostensible owner of the *Esmeralda*. The detectives were looking for the light-colored SUV that Chet Olsen had seen leaving the marina right after the explosion. But they hadn't found it yet.

The cell phone records from Brian's account indicated that his cell phone had not been used since last Friday, the day he evidently left home and disappeared. A copy of some notes from the detectives' investigation told me that they'd found no sign of Brian's red Jeep Wrangler, although it was possible that Cousin Pat had seen it in Graton on Friday.

I picked up the phone and called Joe Kelso, Sid's old partner, who had traded the mean streets of Oakland for the more bucolic environs of Cloverdale, the northernmost town in Sonoma County. He answered the phone on the second ring.

"Jeri Howard, as I live and breathe. How the hell are you? When are you coming up to see us? Can I tempt you with barbecue? I built myself a smoker in the back yard, and I have a rack of ribs in that baby as we speak."

"Sounds wonderful. Listen, I called to thank you for talking with the Sonoma County detectives and getting that information on the case."

"Hell, no problem. Couldn't believe it when Sid called me and told me your kid brother had gone missing. Anything I can do to help, just ask. Those two county detectives, Al Griffin and Stan Harris, I've worked with them before. They're good people, and good investigators."

"I'm sure they are," I said. "Problem is, their case is a murder, whoever killed the man on the boat. Brian's missing persons case is something else entirely. And I must say the Petaluma police officer who's handling that, Marcy Colman, is more closemouthed than Griffin. That's why I asked Sid for help, and am asking you as well. Griffin made it plain that he and Harris consider Brian a person of interest in the murder."

"Could he be?" Joe asked, talking like the cop he was. "I mean, I understand where you're coming from, you're Brian's sister. But I also understand where Griffin's head is, too. Your brother's bracelet was found at the crime scene."

"I don't know. I've turned that around in my head ever since this thing broke. I just can't see my kid brother killing anyone. Of course, I can't see him pulling a disappearing act either. Here's what I've found out so far."

Joe listened while I brought him up to date on my investigation. "You don't think he's bailed on his marriage," he asked. "Run off with this woman, Willow?"

"No. Even if he is on the outs with his wife, he just wouldn't do this. Certainly not to his kids. My brother's a responsible person. He's the kind of guy who shows up fifteen minutes early for appointments and calls to let you know if he's running late." I shook my head, even though Joe couldn't see me.

"No, Brian wouldn't vanish like this. Something else is going on. Somehow it's tied up with that dead man on the boat. All I can think of is that he's been taken and held against his will. Or…" I sighed as I voiced the darkest thought that nagged at me during my waking hours as well as the past two nights. "Or he's had an accident and he's lying dead at the bottom of a cliff."

"Okay," Joe said. "I'll keep nosing around. We're all Sonoma County law enforcement, same family, different branches. Maybe the Petaluma cop, Colman, will talk with me."

"She certainly didn't want to talk with me," I said, recalling my short and unsatisfactory conversation with Detective Colman. "Speaking of people lying dead at the bottom of a cliff, there's something else that troubles me. The last week in June, a man named Rick Newman had a motorcycle accident on Highway One. The way I heard it, his motorcycle skidded and went off a cliff. It happened somewhere north of Jenner, I'm not exactly sure where. The motorcycle was found, but Newman's body wasn't. The theory is that the body was washed out to sea. I'm thinking Newman's death would have been a county investigation."

"Probably," Joe said. "That happens all the time. Bodies not being found, I mean. Somebody goes climbing on the rocks and a sneaker wave washes them off the shore. Sounds like when this guy went off the cliff, he landed in the surf. So this traffic accident is important, because?"

"I've seen a recent photo of Rick Newman," I said. "He looks a lot like that body I saw in the county morgue. He also looks a lot like my brother."

Joe gave a long, low whistle. "Really? Okay, I'll see what I can find out about that, too."

"According to my sources, Newman has a police record dating back to his high school days," I added. "And just to make things more interesting, Willow's real name is Martha Newman. She's Rick Newman's younger sister."

"I'm on it," Joe said.

"Thanks, Joe. I really appreciate your help."

After Joe hung up, I thought about calling my friend Cassie Taylor, then decided against it. She's an attorney and her office is down the hall from mine. But she wasn't in her office, and hadn't been since the first of August. Cassie was on maternity leave. She and her husband, Eric, were expecting their first child, due at the end of August. Cassie had decided to take the whole month off to get ready for the new arrival.

I turned back to my computer and initiated a background check on Harry Vann, Rick Newman's friend. I also looked up whatever I could find on the motorcycle accident back in June. There wasn't much. I found a couple of short articles and printed them out. The accident had occurred on a Thursday, around three o'clock in the afternoon, according to Vann, the only witness. I was hoping Joe Kelso could get more information on the accident.

Now I turned my attention to Willow. While looking at the three-ring binder containing photos of her pottery in the gallery in Occidental, I'd noted the URL of her website. Now I went looking for it. I typed in the web address and waited for the site to load.

The banner at the top of the page read POTTERY BY WILLOW. On the first page of the site, I saw photographs of Willow's pottery. There were the utilitarian pieces, like the coffee mug my brother had purchased from her at the Sonoma craft fair. Other pieces included bowls, vases, dishes, and small pots. Then there were more artistic works. Here was a photo of the piece that had caught my eye in the gallery, the oddly shaped platter in shades of green.

I clicked on one of the tabs at the top of the website. The next page that loaded contained a photograph of Willow, a three-quarters view of her at work. She was dressed in plain blue slacks and a lavender T-shirt, working at her potter's wheel, head inclined, expression thoughtful as her fingers shaped a lump of clay into a pot.

Willow had a link called "Available Pieces," with a "Buy Now" button below the photographs. She also had her own storefronts on eBay and Etsy. This, plus the pieces she had in the gallery, and the custom pieces she did. Once again I wondered if she sold enough pottery to make a living at it. From what her stepfather said, she might very well have to sell a portion of the land that was left to her by her grandfather—if in fact she had clear title to it. Rick's death a few months earlier raised some questions.

I did an Internet search on Lowell Rhine. I wanted to see what the attorney looked like. I clinked on a link and found myself on his law firm's website. Here was a posed head-and-shoulders shot that showed Rhine in a dark gray suit and pale blue shirt, wearing a red-and-gray striped tie and a large diamond tie pin. He looked to be in his forties, with brown hair and eyes that looked light blue in the photograph. I backed out of the website into the results of my Internet search, and clicked on some more images. These were shots dating back to the high-profile case Rhine had been involved in a few years ago, when he'd defended the drug dealer who'd shot the cop. The photos were taken at a distance, rather than the close-up on his website, and they showed Rhine to be tall and thin.

My cell phone rang. It was Dan. I answered the call. "I tried your house," he said, "but you're not there."

"I'm in the office." I leaned back in my chair.

"It's after nine," he said. "And knowing you, you've been at it since early this morning. You're not going to be any good if you don't get some sleep."

"I'm not sleeping very well, that's the trouble." I'd had a restless night again, playing various scenarios in my head, only to wake feeling wrung out. "I just worry about Brian."

"I know."

"Are you in Bodega Bay?" I asked.

"Yes, I drove up this morning and got settled at my friends' house. I hiked the Bodega Head Trail this afternoon and took lots of photos. Tomorrow I'm going to check out some trails near Sebastopol. I know you'll be up in Sonoma County again tomorrow. I could meet you somewhere, for coffee or lunch."

"I'd like that. I'll call you. Now I'm going to take your advice and go home."

After I said good-bye to Dan, I shut down the computer and locked my office. When I got home, I fed the cats and fell into bed.

I was so tired I thought I might sleep better. But I didn't. Unanswered questions and worry about my brother roiled my mind.

TWENTY-THREE

IT TOOK ABOUT AN HOUR TO GET WHERE THEY WERE going. It was late when they turned off the road, the dark countryside pierced by lights. He was in the backseat, his hands cuffed behind him. The vehicle bumped down a gravel road, turned, backed up. They got out and opened the rear door, unloading gear and supplies. Earlier he'd heard them talking about a boat. This must be where it was docked.

He heard music in the distance, punctuated by the roar of engines. Motorcycles, from the sound of it. He turned his head, trying to see, wincing because it still hurt. He sat up in the seat and looked back. A boat loomed, a big cabin cruiser. They were leaving. They said they would leave him here. Soon this nightmare would be over.

He heard another engine, then saw movement, someone walking this way. The new arrival walked past the vehicle, toward the boat. Then raised voices, arguing.

The gunshot sounded incredibly loud. Then there was an explosion. He stared back at the boat, enveloped in flames.

TWENTY-FOUR

I GOT UP EARLY ON THURSDAY MORNING, NO MORE rested than I'd been last night. I breakfasted on coffee and an English muffin before leaving the house. My first stop was my office where, as I had the day before, I checked my email and phone messages. One email came from Rita. She told me that she hadn't yet received the boat history on the *Esmeralda* and the other two boats, but she'd let me know as soon as it came in.

The background check on Harry Vann hadn't come back yet, but I looked up the address of Vann's Motorcycle Shop. It was on Guerneville Road, west of Santa Rosa.

I shut down my computer and was headed for the door, ready to drive to Sonoma for my meeting with Nancy Parsons. My cell phone rang. I stopped, my hand on the doorknob. The readout told me the call came from the Petaluma Police Department.

"We found your brother's Jeep," Detective Colman said.

"Where?"

"An old quarry west of Forestville," she said. "Somebody dumped it there in the past few days. The guy who found it says the Jeep wasn't there when he left work on Friday. The place where it was found is on a side road that isn't used often."

"Any prints?"

"The vehicle had been wiped down pretty good," Colman said. "But we did find a few prints, all of them your brother's."

"He's been abducted," I said.

"Or he dumped the Jeep himself," she countered.

"What about his cell phone?" I asked.

"The cell phone company says the last signal they had from it was on Friday, in the area between Forestville and Santa Rosa. But there's no signal now. It's probably out of juice."

We ended the call. I was frustrated by Colman's attitude. She was still clinging to the theory that Brian had left on his own.

I closed and locked my office and went down to the lot where

I parked my car. I took Interstate 80 across the Carquinez Bridge, driving through Vallejo, and then headed west on Highway 37, along the marshy upper reaches of San Pablo Bay. Highway 121 north took me into Sonoma.

The Sonoma Valley had long been populated by California's Native American tribes. They called it the Valley of the Moon, a term still used today. The town of Sonoma was founded when California was Spanish territory, and its mission, San Francisco Solano, was built in 1823, after Mexico won its independence from Spain. Sonoma was also the site of the Bear Flag Revolt, when a group of rebels raised a flag in June 1846 and proclaimed independence from Mexico and started a short-lived country called the California Republic. The Bear Flag soon gave way to the Stars and Stripes with the Mexican–American War, and California became a United States territory.

These days, Sonoma was known for wine, as it should be. Despite the popularity and publicity accorded to the Napa Valley, just over the Mayacamas Mountains to the east, Sonoma and its own valley were historically the birthplace of the California winemaking industry, dating back to the days when the mission had its own vineyards. In fact, as I parked near the town's historic downtown plaza, I saw posters advertising the upcoming Valley of the Moon Vintage Festival, which takes place each year on the last weekend of September.

It was cooler this morning, but the forecast was for more heat. I strolled around the plaza and located the café and bake shop where I was to meet Nancy Parsons at ten o'clock. It was a few minutes before ten, so I went to the counter to survey the yummy pastries she'd mentioned. They did indeed look enticing. Which one to have? It was a tough decision, but I finally narrowed it down to a *pain au raisin*, a spiral of flaky pastry liberally studded with plump raisins. When my turn came at the counter, I ordered a latte to go with the pastry and carried my purchases to a nearby table. With a fork, I cut a piece of the pastry and lifted it to my mouth. Mmm, good choice.

As I sipped my latte, a woman of about forty walked into

the café, wearing sandals, khaki capri pants and a blue T-shirt on her short, rounded frame, her salt-and-pepper hair brushing her shoulders. She glanced around the café as though looking for someone and I made eye contact. She crossed to the table where I sat. "Jeri Howard?"

"Yes." I waved a hand toward the counter. "Can I get you anything?"

"Oh, thanks, I'd love a cappuccino. And a chocolate croissant. My weakness. Hey, there's chocolate and there's everything else."

I laughed. "My sentiments exactly. Although you see I got seduced by something else."

She examined my pastry. "Oh, that one's good, too."

Nancy sat down at the table while I stepped up to the counter and ordered. I returned a moment later and set the cup and croissant in front of her.

"I appreciate your meeting me," I said, sitting down across from her.

"Anything I can do to help. I was so shocked when you told me Brian was missing. What happened?"

She ate a few bites of her croissant while I gave her an edited version of events. "I'm following up on something Brian told a friend. He also mentioned it to my father. Brian was upset over something that happened to one of his students, a boy who tried to kill himself after being bullied."

"Ah, that." Nancy wiped chocolate from her fingers. Then she sipped her cappuccino and licked a bit of foam from her lips. "Anything I tell you is strictly off the record. I bet you hear that a lot, in your line of work."

"Yes, I do. And this would be for my use only. I'm interested in Brian's state of mind. I'm not even sure this has anything to do with his disappearance, but I'm exploring every avenue."

"It may not have anything to do with Brian disappearing," Nancy said, "but I'm sure it has something to do with him changing jobs. That asshole McManus."

"Who's that? The principal?"

"Yes." She sighed, took another bite of her croissant, washing it down with more coffee. "It's all been hushed up, you see. Never happened, not the school's fault, et cetera. Just because McManus didn't take the bullying seriously and he doesn't want any record of anything happening on his watch. It didn't happen at school or there would have been some official repercussions."

"So what did happen?" I cut off another wedge of my pastry and raised the fork to my lips.

"A lot of what I know is hearsay, but I'll tell you anyway. The kid's an eighth-grader. I understand he comes from a very conservative, strict, religious family. I'm sure he's gay and conflicted as hell about it."

"That spells trouble." I sipped my latte.

"You got that right. These kids are middle-schoolers, twelve and thirteen, and some of them are emotionally quite young. They pick up on any differences, any student who's different from the herd. In this case, a bunch of boys were bullying this particular kid, calling him the usual names. It escalated during the school year. I don't know when Brian first picked up on it, but sometime around the last part of April, he said something to the principal about the kid being hassled. McManus pretty much ignored it."

"Can he do that? I thought there were measures in place to deal with bullying in the schools."

"There are supposed to be. It's a serious problem and it's gotten lots of media coverage. But McManus blew it off. He should have his ass in the wringer for that, but it's not gonna happen. His excuse is that he couldn't really do anything because the complaint hadn't come from the student himself. It was just Brian's opinion, you see. I know Brian talked to the kid. But later that week, the kid got hit by a car."

"Traffic accident?" I reached for my coffee. "I thought it was a suicide attempt."

Nancy waved a piece of croissant at me. "Officially, it's a traffic accident. Unofficially—well, make that the school grapevine—the boy deliberately ran out in front of the car that hit him. The driver said he never saw the kid until he was in front of the car.

Another witness said it looked like the kid did it on purpose. So who knows?"

"That muddles it," I said. "If the boy had taken a fistful of sleeping pills, there would have been an investigation, some official record."

Nancy nodded. "But in this case, the police called it an accident. Kid versus car and the kid was seriously injured. Brian was sure it was a suicide attempt, due to the bullying. He told me so and confronted McManus about it. I gather there was quite an argument in the principal's office. It wasn't long after that Brian confided in me that he was looking for another job. I didn't think he'd find one this soon, but when that position opened up in Petaluma, he jumped on it."

After Nancy left, I finished my pastry and coffee and thought about what she had told me. It was interesting and it certainly gave evidence of Brian's state of mind at the end of the last school year.

But did it have anything to do with my brother's disappearance? I didn't think so. Nor did I think there was any point in talking with the principal. From what Nancy had told me, he was in denial that anything had happened.

TWENTY-FIVE

I LEFT SONOMA AND HEADED NORTH ON HIGHWAY 12, past the small town of Glen Ellen, where Oakland-born writer Jack London had a ranch here in his beloved Valley of the Moon. The ranch is now the site of the Jack London State Historical Park. Farther north, the highway begins a slow curve to the west, passing Annadel State Park and heading into Santa Rosa. I drove through the city and continued west on Guerneville Road.

I located Vann's Motorcycle Shop on the north side of the two-lane road, where the urban landscape began to give way to the country. I slowed and pulled into the paved parking lot. A bronze

Hyundai hatchback was parked in front. I pulled up behind the hatchback and parked, reaching for my stainless steel water bottle. Today was shaping up to be as hot as yesterday, and it wasn't even noon yet.

Then I got out of the car and walked toward the one-story building. It was painted a utilitarian gray. As I approached it, the small office was on the left side and a single service bay on the right. The metal door that closed off the bay had been raised and I could see inside. The far wall held a collection of large red metal toolboxes and several workbenches. A small microwave oven perched on the end of one of the workbenches, and next to this was a small refrigerator. Inside the bay were three motorcycles in various stages of repair, but I didn't see a mechanic at work.

I walked into the office. A plastic fan attached to the wall stirred the air around, but it wasn't doing much to alleviate the heat. The walls were green, decorated with posters of motorcycles tacked to the walls with nails. A calendar featured a blonde in a bikini stretched out on a Harley. A door to my right went through to the service bay.

The office had a short counter, covered with an untidy pile of magazines and parts catalogs. To one side of this, in the middle of the room, was a scarred wooden desk with a tattered desk blotter. At one corner of the desk was a glass ashtray containing several cigarette butts. It looked as though whoever had smoked them was rolling his own. The butts were unfiltered.

A woman in denim shorts and a bright pink tank top leaned against the desk, her back to me. Her dark brown hair was caught up in an untidy bun secured with a pink plastic clip. She was talking on a cell phone, holding it to her ear with her right hand.

"I don't know where he is. How many times do I have to say it?" Her voice sounded angry as she punctuated the air with her left hand. "Yes, I'll call you. I said I would, and I will." She listened to whoever was on the other end of the line. Then she held out the phone and thumbed a button, ending the call.

"Son of a bitch," she said.

"Problems?"

She straightened and turned, startled to see me. She was in her late twenties or early thirties, I guessed, tanned and well muscled, with a round, full-lipped face and multiple earrings in both ear lobes. A pink rosebud tattoo decorated her right shoulder. Her long fingernails were the same shade of pink, decorated with something glittery.

"You could say that." She gave me a rueful smile as she tucked the cell phone into the pocket of her shorts. Then she reached across the desk for a can of Diet Coke, tipped it to her mouth, and swallowed. "Can I help you?"

"I'm looking for Harry Vann."

She laughed, but there wasn't much humor in it. "You too? So am I. So's that guy that just called. I don't know where Harry is. I haven't seen him since Saturday. And when I do, I'm gonna give him a piece of my mind."

"That's interesting," I said, thinking of the fire at Newman's Marina early Sunday morning.

"Interesting, hell. It's a pain in the ass." She fiddled with an errant strand of hair. "Harry's supposed to open up the shop at eight o'clock Monday morning. He didn't show up. I haven't seen him all week, and it's Thursday now. That's four freaking days. And the customers are freaking out. They can't get Harry on his phone here, or his cell phone. He must have it turned off or it needs a charge. So now they're calling me, like that jerk on the phone just now, wanting to know when his bike's gonna be done. I don't know what to tell people."

"Why are they calling you?"

"I'm a partner." She grimaced. "My name's on the lease anyway. I'm Carla Vann, Harry's sister. Anyway, since Harry did his disappearing act, I've been coming down here every day, fielding phone calls and dealing with paperwork. Around here, I do everything except fix bikes. Harry and Scott do that."

"I didn't see anyone in the shop when I drove up," I said.

"Scott went to pick up some parts we ordered." She looked past me as a blue-and-white Chevy Tahoe drove up and parked outside the service bay. A slender, dark-haired young man got out of the driver's seat. "There he is now."

Scott walked into the office, looking like a choir boy gone bad. He was in his mid-twenties, I guessed, with a sulky expression on his face and hard brown eyes. He wore heavy work boots, faded jeans decorated with grease stains, and a yellow sleeveless T-shirt that showed an array of tattoos on both arms. His brown hair was long and curly. He gave me a once-over, as though wondering who I was and what I was doing there.

"Did you get everything?" Carla asked.

"Yeah. Here's the paperwork." He handed her several sheets of paper. Then he turned and went outside, without waiting for a reply.

Carla looked at the top sheet of paper he handed her, then set it on the desk. Reading upside down, I could see that the young man had signed the bottom with the name "Scott Cruz."

Scott had opened the back of the Tahoe. Now he removed several large cardboard cartons from the truck bed, stacking them on the concrete floor near the door that led from the office to the service bay.

"Have you reported Harry missing?" I asked.

Carla looked at me as though she hadn't considered it. "No. I figure Harry's just gone off somewhere. I checked his house. It looks like he packed some things. So he's taking a break. He's done it before. He usually tells me, though. Calls me up and says, hey, sis, I'm going away for a few days, can you handle the shop? You know, that kind of thing."

"But not this time?"

Carla shook her head. "Not a word. Anyway, that's my problem, not yours. How can I help you? Are you a customer?" I shook my head. "Didn't think so. You don't look like the motorcycle-riding type."

"No, I'm not. I want to talk with Harry about another matter. My name's Jeri Howard. I'm a private investigator." I handed over one of my business cards.

I glanced to my right. Scott was just the other side of the door that separated the office from the service bay. He had a pocket knife in his right hand, using it to slit open one of the cartons. But he didn't seem to be focused on unpacking the supplies. I suspected he was listening to my conversation with Carla, with more than casual interest.

She looked at my card and frowned. "A private eye? Really?"

"I have some questions about an accident that happened the last week in June. A man named Rick Newman was killed. I understand Harry was a witness."

"What's this about, insurance?" Carla flicked her fingernails against my business card. Then she propped the card against the rim of the glass ashtray.

"I'm just tying up some loose ends." It suited me to let her think my interest was due to an insurance matter.

My words seemed to bother Scott, though. His right hand, holding the knife, stopped briefly. Then he closed the knife, tucked it in his back pocket, and began taking parts out of the cartons.

"All I can tell you is what Harry told me." Carla took another swallow of her Diet Coke. "He and Rick had been up to Fort Ross."

I knew the place, located about twelve miles north of Jenner. Fort Ross was the site of a Russian settlement on the California coast. The fort had been established in 1812, a distant outpost of the czar's empire, home to a number of Russians and California Indians, until abandoned in 1842. It is now a state park, with displays in the historic old buildings.

The motorcycle accident had occurred on a Thursday afternoon. I had wondered about the timing, on a weekday. It had seemed odd to me that Harry, who with his sister owned this motorcycle repair business, would take time off on a Thursday go to Fort Ross with his buddy Rick. However, Carla had just told me that Harry was in the habit of taking off from time to time.

That was a plus about being self-employed, I knew, since I was a sole practitioner with my own business. I could leave the office whenever I liked—as long as the work got done. If the work didn't get done, the bills didn't get paid.

As for Rick, it appeared he hadn't had a steady job. Instead he'd worked at times for his father at the marina, and sometimes here at the motorcycle shop.

"So Harry and Rick were on their way back from Fort Ross,"

I said, prompting her to continue. "And Rick went off the road. But it was June, no rain, no fog, or so I heard. Were they going too fast?"

"Probably. Rick did like to push that Harley to the limit." Carla finished her Diet Coke and tossed the can into a cardboard carton on the floor next to the desk. "Harry said Rick was in front. They went around a curve. Rick's bike slid and kept going, off the cliff. Harry tried to get down to Rick, but he couldn't. He said it was way too steep and he couldn't see a way down. So he got on his bike and went to Jenner for help. When he got back with some deputies, Rick was gone. I mean, his body was gone. Washed out to sea."

"What kind of car does Harry drive?" I asked. "And what color is it?"

"A silver Ford Escape," Carla said. "Why?"

I glanced to my right. Scott was still hovering near the door that led to the shop. He had a frown on his face. Was it due to my question about Harry's vehicle?

He saw me looking at him and dropped his gaze. He took his knife from his pocket and broke down the empty cardboard cartons, stacking them against the wall near the door. Then he disappeared from view.

I was suspicious of Scott Cruz. It was the way he looked at me. The way he pretended indifference but listened in on my conversations with Carla Vann waved a red flag.

"Tell me about Scott," I said.

Carla shrugged. "He's just a kid that works for us. Mechanics come and go. Rick used to work here, too. Scott's been here, oh, I guess Harry hired him right before Christmas. I think he met Scott at the roadhouse, you know, that place Rick's dad owns. He lives right here, in that little green house the other side of the shop. We own that, and we give him a break on the rent."

I reached into my bag, looking for the artist's sketch of the dead man found on the boat. I didn't know what Harry Vann looked like. But the fact that his sister hadn't seen him since Saturday had set off alarm bells.

Before I could get the sketch out of my bag, a loud rumble

heralded the arrival of two Harleys, ridden by two men in motorcycle leathers. Carla walked into the service bay to greet them as
they parked their bikes. I followed, watching from the doorway.
Scott was kneeling on the concrete floor at the back of the shop,
working on a torn-down Harley, various parts scattered around
him. He set down a wrench and reached for a nearby plastic liter
of Pepsi. He uncapped it and took a drink.

"Hey, Duke," Carla said, addressing the larger of the two men,
a burly fellow with a graying ponytail. She turned to the smaller
man. "Good to see you, Robbie. How's it going?"

Duke enveloped Carla in a hug. "Yo, Carla. Where the hell's
Harry? I been calling his cell phone and he don't pick up. Call
goes straight to voice mail."

Carla shrugged, spreading her arms, palms up. "Your guess is
as good as mine. You find out where Harry is, you tell me."

"He take off again?" Robbie laughed. "I remember that time
he went up to Laytonville for a few days, didn't tell anybody. You
were mad at him."

"Well, I'm not too happy with him now," Carla said. "I've been
holding the fort all week and I sure wish he'd show up, or at least
call."

Robbie walked over to Scott. "Hey, man, you get that part?"

Scott had been watching me, his expression wary as he took
another drink of Pepsi. Now he stood and spoke to Robbie. His
voice seemed friendly, but his face didn't reveal much. "Yeah, I
just picked it up. Everything's cool. Give me till the end of the day
and I'll have this baby up and running."

"No problem," Robbie said.

Carla bantered with Duke, then her cell phone rang. She
pulled it from her pocket. "Hey, maybe it's Harry—finally." Then
she looked at the display. "Nope, it's Mom. Oh, hell, what time is
it? I'm supposed to pick her up at the dentist." She pushed a button on the phone and said, "Hi, Mom. I'm sorry, I know I'm late.
I got caught up in something here at the shop. Be there in ten
minutes."

She ended the call. "Scott, I have to get Mom. I'll be back as
soon as I take her home."

"I'll be here." Scott turned his attention back to the bike he was working on. Duke and Robbie said good-bye to Carla and got back on their motorcycles, heading out of the parking lot toward Santa Rosa.

Carla looked at me as though she was surprised I was still there. "Sorry, gotta go. Mom doesn't drive, her eyes are real bad. So I have to chauffeur her around."

"I understand." I'll come back later, I thought. I wanted to show Carla the picture of the man who died on the boat. And I wanted to find out more about Scott Cruz.

Carla retrieved her handbag from a desk drawer, left the office, and got into her Hyundai hatchback. I walked toward my Toyota, glancing at the house where Scott lived. It was small, a cottage really, some twenty yards to the east of the shop. Painted a pale shade of green, it looked as though it needed some upkeep.

I got into my car and unscrewed the top of my water bottle. As I tipped it back to take a drink, I saw something on the right, in my peripheral vision. Scott had entered the office from the service bay. He reached for something on the desk. The phone? No, it was the business card I'd given Carla, propped up against the ashtray. He examined it, then tucked it into his back pocket.

Scott certainly seemed interested in my conversation with Carla—and my card. Why?

TWENTY-SIX

I TOOK ANOTHER DRINK OF WATER AND PUT THE CAP on the bottle. Then I started my car and headed out of the parking lot. I waited for several cars to pass before turning west onto Guerneville Road. I used my headset and called Rita Lydecker.

"Hi, Rita. I'm calling to ask for another favor. See what you can find out about a guy named Scott Cruz. He's in his mid-twen-

ties, looks like a real bad boy. He works as a mechanic at Vann's
Motorcycle Shop in Santa Rosa. I'd be interested to know what
else he's been up to in this lifetime."

"Sure thing," Rita said. "I'll email you when I get some results.
In the meantime, I got the boat history report on the *Esmeralda*.
I'll email that to you, too, but as long as I'm on the phone, I'll give
you the short version. Lowell Rhine's not the owner."

"I'm not surprised to hear that." I slowed as I approached an
intersection, where a pickup truck made a running stop and then
pulled out in front of me. "Rhine must be stashing the boats for
someone else."

"That's my guess," Rita said. "Here's the scoop. The owner of
the *Esmeralda*—and the other two boats—is a man named Enrique Lopez. He's a U.S. citizen, lives in Santa Cruz. Last year, the
Coast Guard seized the *Esmeralda* down by Moss Landing. The
boat was full of bales of marijuana. Lopez was transporting pot
from Mexico to the States."

"Why the hell do we need to import pot from Mexico?" I asked.
"We've got plenty of marijuana growing right here in Northern
California. From what I hear, the locals are building greenhouses
and running generators for indoor grows. I see garden shops up
here with signs advertising 'indoor gardening supplies.' Believe
me, it ain't tomatoes they're growing."

"Supply and demand," Rita said. "It's big business. Used to
be, the pot growers in Northern California were small-timers,
mom-and-pop operations planting fifty to a hundred plants. Now
those people are being pushed out by the big commercial growers.
Where there's money, there's competition, so now the Mexican
cartels want a piece of the action. They're loading bales of pot
onto boats and running them up the California coast. Sooner or
later the state is just going to have to legalize the stuff so we can
regulate it."

"I'm sure that will happen eventually." The pickup truck in
front of me stopped suddenly and I hit my brakes. Then the truck
turned left onto a gravel road. I eased my foot off the brake and
onto the accelerator. "So if the *Esmeralda* was seized by the Coast

Guard, how did it wind up at Newman's Marina in Lakeville, with Rhine listed as the owner?"

"Lopez is Rhine's client," Rita said. "Rhine got the boat back from the Coast Guard, due to some changes in the forfeiture laws. And he got Lopez a light sentence, some jail time and probation. My guess is, Rhine stashed all three of the boats in Lakeville because it's out of the way. Once Lopez is off probation, he can get his boats back and resume his smuggling activities."

"Except one of his boats is a burned-out wreck, with a body aboard, that's getting all sorts of attention from the Sonoma County detectives."

"And a couple of private eyes." Rita chuckled. "That's you and me, girlfriend."

"Thanks for all your help," I said. "I'll look forward to seeing that report, and hearing whatever you can dig up on Scott Cruz."

I ended the call and continued driving west on Guerneville Road. By now it was past noon and my stomach was growling. It had been a while since that pastry I'd eaten in Sonoma.

I called Dan's cell phone. "Got time for a quick lunch?" I asked.

"Yes. Where are you?"

"Just left Santa Rosa, heading for Occidental. How about you?"

"I'm in Sebastopol," Dan said. "I just finished hiking the trails at Ragle Ranch Park and now I'm heading for Graton, to check out the West County Regional Trail."

"Graton's perfect. There's a place downtown that's good, called the Underwood Bistro. I'll meet you there, probably in twenty minutes."

"Great. I'll get a table."

Guerneville Road intersected with Highway 116 above Graton. I turned south, then headed west on Graton Road. The Underwood Bar and Bistro was in a one-story wooden building, the exterior walls painted a dark red. The restaurant was kitty-corner from the Community Hall that Cousin Pat had been leaving last Friday morning, when she saw Brian's Jeep—or one that looked a lot like it. I parked and walked across the street. Inside the restaurant had polished wood floors and dark wainscoting, with red plush upholstery on some of the seats. A long wooden bar ran down one side of the front section.

Dan had secured a table for two, near the bar. He stood up, looking good in khakis and a green shirt. He put his arms around me. I felt his lips brush my hair.

"How are you?" he asked.

"I'm tired. I didn't sleep very well last night." I rested my head on his shoulder for a moment. Then we separated and he pulled out the chair for me.

"I'm glad you could meet me. I've been wanting to see you."

I smiled. "You saw me Tuesday night."

He took my hand. "That was two days ago."

The server stopped by our table, asking if we'd like anything to drink. Dan ordered a beer. No alcohol for me, though. I stuck with iced tea. I examined the menu, debating between a sandwich and a salad. When the server came back with our beverages, I ordered a Cobb salad. Dan, who'd been hiking all morning, opted for a burger.

"Have to keep my strength up," he said with a smile. "Although the hike I took this morning at Ragle Ranch was an easy one. They're getting ready for the apple festival."

"Yes, I know. That's Saturday and Sunday."

"This afternoon I'm going to hike the West County Trail. I can pick it up on Occidental Road and hike to Forestville. It's about four miles round-trip, on the old rail line that connected Petaluma and Santa Rosa with Sebastopol and Forestville. There's a Rails-to-Trails system that's going to be about thirteen miles long when it's completed."

"I'm glad they've repurposed the old rail right-of-way," I said. "Where are you going tomorrow?"

Dan looked up as the server delivered our food. He doctored his burger with mustard and catsup. "Guerneville, I think. Armstrong Redwoods and Austin Creek are contiguous, and there are lots of trails to explore."

"I know. There was a brochure on Brian's desk. That's one of the places he was researching, for day trips or camping, I suppose." I forked up a mouthful of salad.

"There's a campground at Austin Creek, called Bullfrog Pond." Dan picked up his burger. "But at this time of year, and close to a weekend, all the campsites get booked up. Maybe he decided to do day trips, and something happened."

"I can't shake the feeling that there's more to it than that. An accident while hiking doesn't explain why Brian's bracelet turned up with the dead man on the burned boat." I paused. "I got a call from the Petaluma detective, Colman, this morning. They found Brian's Jeep on the grounds of an old quarry up by Forestville."

"There are several quarries up there, just west of town."

"No prints, except Brian's. Whoever left the Jeep there had wiped it. Of course, Colman is still convinced that Brian took off, staged his own disappearance. But Dan, I'm sure someone's taken him. Why, I don't know, but finding the Jeep that way just underscores it. I've got to find him."

"You will," Dan said. "I'm sure of it."

We talked a while longer about my efforts to find my brother, then I changed the subject. "How's Bodega Bay?"

"My friends' house is really nice. It has a view of Bodega Harbor. They're going to be gone about three weeks. Once you find your brother and all this is settled," he added, "I hope you'll come over and spend a few days with me."

I nodded, my fork paused over my salad. "Sounds great. I'd like that."

TWENTY-SEVEN

DAN AND I SHARED A CHOCOLATE TORTE FOR DESSERT. We paid the lunch check and went outside, where he kissed me good-bye. Then we separated, heading for our respective cars.

I took Graton Road west, driving out of the little town into the countryside beyond. Just as I passed the turnoff leading to Cousin Pat's house, my cell phone rang. When I answered it, I heard Joe Kelso's voice.

"I've been looking into that accident back in June," he said, after we'd exchanged greetings. "The one involving Rick Newman. I got the file from a friend of mine in county law enforcement. There's nothing to suggest that it was anything but an accident. But I can see why you're suspicious."

"How so?" I crossed the bridge over Purrington Creek and headed into a curve.

"Hard to put my finger on it," Joe said. "But my gut tells me something's off. Why did this guy's motorcycle go off the road? It was a sunny day in June."

"Yes, that's the way it hit me. So I'm left with the theory that maybe, just maybe, Rick Newman isn't dead, but he wants people to think he is. And if that's the case, why?"

"Don't know," Joe said. "I took a look at this guy's record. Drug offenses, the most recent one possession for sale. Some breaking-and-entering, a couple of fights, the occasional drunk-and-disorderly. He did jail time for several of those. But his record is small-time stuff, nothing big or flashy. Maybe he got himself involved in something that got out of hand and he decided to disappear. I'll keep looking."

"Thanks, Joe."

I ended the call, then slowed my Toyota as the car in front of me signaled and then made a left turn into a driveway. The road leading to the Hargis ranch was coming up in another mile or so. As I approached that intersection, I saw a blue sedan stopped there, waiting to make a turn onto Graton Road. I passed the car. The blinker was on, signaling a right turn, and the driver was a woman. She had dark hair tied back with a scarf. After I passed, the blue car turned, heading the same direction I was.

I kept the car in sight in my rearview mirror. At the first opportunity, I pulled off the road in front of several mailboxes. The driver didn't look at me as the blue car passed, but I looked at her closely. I was pretty sure the driver was Willow, and I guessed she was going to the gallery in Occidental.

I pulled back onto the road, following her. When we reached Occidental, she turned left on Main Street, driving slowly through the town's small commercial district. She parked in front of Hestia Gallery. I pulled into a space nearby and got out of my Toyota.

The woman got out of her car. She was dressed for the hot weather in her Teva sandals and khaki shorts. She wore a gauzy flowered cotton shirt in purple and blue, the colors matching the scarf she'd used to tie back her hair. Her handbag was made of purple quilted cotton, the strap slung across her shoulder. She walked around to the back of the blue car, a fairly new Honda Accord hybrid. She opened the trunk and took out a large carton, carrying it toward the front door of the gallery. I was there to hold open the door.

"Thanks," she said in a pleasant, low voice.

I followed her inside and hung around the shelves near the display of Willow's pottery. I noticed that the green platter I liked so much was still there. She set the carton on the floor near the counter. There were several customers inside the gallery, and Avie Northrup was ringing up a sale.

When she had finished with the customer, the gallery owner turned to the woman. "Hi, Willow, good to see you. It's a gorgeous day."

"Hi, Avie. Yes, it's beautiful. Hot, though." Willow pointed to the box at her feet. "I brought you some things to take to the apple fair this weekend. Small pieces—mugs, vases, bowls, plates, the usual. Where do you want it?"

"Great. Thanks for bringing it in. I'm sure we'll sell lots of art at the booth. Put the box in the storeroom." The gallery owner waved toward the back of the shop. "We're taking everything over to Ragle Ranch Park early Saturday morning. Are you planning to stop by the fair?"

"I might," Willow said. "I'm not sure what I'll be doing on Saturday."

She picked up the carton again and walked toward the rear

of the gallery. Another customer stepped up to the counter and asked to see a piece of jewelry in one of the cases. As Avie leaned down to open the case, I followed Willow back to the storeroom. She set the carton on a bench, opened the flaps at the top and took out a newspaper-wrapped bundle. She removed the newspaper, revealing a large coffee mug, similar to the one she'd sold Brian. This one was cobalt blue, chased here and there with an iridescent rust.

"Nice piece," I said. "I like the color."

Willow smiled at me, a friendly expression on her face. "It's for the Gravenstein Apple Fair on Saturday. The gallery's going to have a booth. Interested in buying it? I'm sure Avie will sell it to you now, rather than wait for the fair."

"Right now I'm more interested in conversation. I'm Jeri Howard, Brian's sister."

Willow's hazel eyes widened and took on a deer-in-the-headlights expression. She opened her mouth and then closed it again. She rewrapped the mug and put it inside the carton. "I don't know where Brian is."

"But you do know something. How did you know he was missing?"

"Becca told me. She called me, well, called my cell phone and left a message."

So Becca had been lying—once again—when she told me she didn't have a phone number for Willow.

"We need to talk," I said.

Willow nodded. "I know. Let's get something to drink."

We left the gallery and walked a few doors down the street to the Howard Station Café. As hot as it was, coffee didn't sound good. Willow ordered iced tea, and I opted for lemonade. When I took a sip, it was good, a nice balance between tart and sweet. We took our drinks out to the café's front porch. Willow sipped her tea in silence. I waited for her to say something.

Finally she spoke. "There isn't anything going on between me and Brian. Even though Becca thinks there is. Brian and I are just friends, that's all."

So you say, I thought, examining her face. There might not be anything going on between her and my brother, but I had a feeling Willow wished there was.

"I am less concerned about your relationship with my brother than I am with what you know that will help me find him."

"I told Brian he could use the cabin," Willow said.

I straightened and leaned toward her. "What cabin? Where?"

"On the ranch. My grandfather died earlier this year and left the land to me and my brother, Rick. They used the cabin when they went hunting, Rick, Dad and Grandpa. There are wild pigs up there in the hills, and deer and wild turkeys, too."

"Why did you offer Brian the cabin?"

"He wanted to get away for a few days," she said. "I ran into him a week ago, at Andy's Market north of Sebastopol. He'd been on a day hike up here. He said he wanted to get away, but he hadn't been able to find a campsite at short notice, because they were booked. He said he was planning to stay home in Petaluma and do day hikes at places here in the area. I said he could use the cabin. It would be okay because I was going away. I left Friday morning and went up to Mendocino. I got back yesterday afternoon."

"When did Brian go up to the cabin?" I asked.

"Friday, I guess. I saw him at the market on Thursday afternoon. We talked about it and he said that sounded like a great idea. I was planning to leave on my trip early Friday, so I gave him my extra key to the gate. He said he'd pack up his gear and go up to the cabin sometime Friday morning. That's the last time I saw him or talked with him."

I nodded. What Willow was telling me fit with the information I'd gotten from my cousin Pat. She was right, she had seen Brian's Jeep in Graton last Friday.

"Brian left a note for his wife saying he was going away for a few days and would be back on Sunday. He never came home."

"She must be frantic," Willow said. "But Brian isn't at the cabin. I went up there as soon as I got back yesterday and checked my messages. You see, I didn't check the voice mail on my cell phone while I was away, not until I got home. That's when I got the message from Becca saying that Brian was missing. She thought maybe we'd run off together. That's Becca for you. She's such a drama queen. She reads more into me and Brian having coffee than there really is. By the way, I don't think Becca likes Sheila much. But I wouldn't do anything to jeopardize Brian's marriage. He and I are just friends."

"You said that. So Brian's not at the cabin. Did you see anything that indicates he was ever there?"

"I don't know. I just drove up there yesterday when I got back and heard Becca's message. I went up again this morning. I didn't see his Jeep, and the cabin was empty."

I finished my lemonade and set down the glass. "I want to take a look. Maybe I can see something you didn't."

Willow nodded. "Okay. That makes sense. You're the private eye, you can look at it with different eyes."

We went back to our cars and I followed her out of Occidental, onto Graton Road. When we reached Hargis Ranch Road, we turned left onto the gravel road. We drove up a gentle slope past the orchard I'd seen on my earlier visit, where windfall apples littered the ground under the trees. When we got to the gate, Willow got out of her Honda and unlocked it. She went through and I followed. She locked the gate again, and we drove up a gently curving hill, through more apple trees, these heavy with ripening fruit. She turned off the gravel road onto a half circle drive in front of the one-story, wood-framed house. It was painted white with blue trim, and it had a wide front porch with an old-fashioned swing hanging from the porch rafters, the kind of swing where one could sit and rock, looking down into the valley with its rolling hills and stands of trees. To the south of the house I saw the brick kiln that Willow had built for herself when she moved into the house. Behind this was the barn she used as a work space.

Willow parked her car in the drive and got out. She walked to my Toyota and spoke to me through the open window. "The road gets really narrow. We'd better take one car up there."

"Good idea." I unlocked the passenger door. She got in. I

drove back onto the gravel road and continued driving uphill. We went through another orchard with trees full of green apples. Then the road curved and led into a forest of pine and oak trees. "It's rugged country up here."

"Yes. My great-grandfather used to log up here. Occidental was a timber town, you know." She sighed, a wistful sound. "I miss Grandpa. And my mother. She died last summer. Then Rick died in June, just a few weeks ago. Now that Rick's gone, I'm not sure what I'm going to do with all this land. It's almost a hundred acres. I'm happy to have the house, after living in a rental for so many years. I built a kiln and I turned the barn into a workshop. I'm so glad to have that, now that I'm doing well with my pottery."

"A hundred acres is a lot of land." I slowed as the car bounced over some ruts. "And a lot of it in orchards, from the look of it."

"I don't know what to do," Willow said. "You saw all the apples on the ground. Things have been neglected since Grandpa died. I've had offers from two wineries. It's very tempting. They're offering a lot of money. They want to tear out the trees and plant grapes."

The road narrowed, trees closing in on us. "Yes, that's happening all over the area."

"Becca's after me to turn them down. The wineries use so much water and so many orchards are being torn out. But I'm no farmer. Even if I was, people are getting out of apples as a crop. They're not getting very much for apples, and lots of money for wine grapes. I'm up in the air about the whole thing." Willow waved at the thick forest around us. "I was thinking about preserving this part of the land as open space. I wonder if it could be a county park, with hiking trails. There's a creek up here by the cabin.'"

"That's a thought," I said. "But access would be a problem. People would have to drive past the house."

"This road goes farther. It winds around to the north and west, and connects with Green Valley Road. So people could have access that way. But the road would have to be improved, either way. That's the cabin, up there." Willow pointed as we rounded a curve. Ahead was the creek she'd mentioned. I drove slowly over a bridge with no railings, my tires rumbling on the rough wooden planks, and we entered a small clearing.

The cabin looked to be about twelve feet square, with a small porch in front of the door. Off to the right I saw an old wooden outhouse. I parked my Toyota and got out, looking around me. There were no cars here now, save my own, but I saw tracks on the dirt and grass in front of the cabin, indicating the recent presence of several vehicles. Willow had said she'd driven her own car up here, both yesterday and today. What about the other vehicles? Was one of them Brian's Jeep?

I walked toward the cabin, noticing cigarette butts on the dirt near the porch. I opened the door and stepped inside. The cabin was a large single room, with no other entrance than this one. There were uncovered windows on all four walls. Directly in front of me was a rectangular table made of lightweight aluminum and two metal folding chairs. The table surface held a grease stain and an empty tuna can that had been used as an ashtray. Next to the table, several wooden fruit crates had been stacked on their sides to create shelves. These were empty, except for a few flakes of something that looked like cereal and a scattering of ground coffee, salt, and pepper.

Someone had been here, though how long ago I couldn't tell. And that someone smoked. It wasn't Brian. Smoking was a habit that neither of us had picked up.

To my left, I saw two single mattresses, the kind covered with blue-and-white ticking. The mattresses rested on two old iron bedsteads, with knobs at the head and foot. The bedsteads were painted white, but the paint was flaking, showing black metal underneath. There was a rough wooden stool between the beds and another wooden fruit crate on the back wall, the other side of the second bed.

I moved closer and looked at the mattresses. There was a stain on the mattress on the near bed, a rust-colored stain I examined. Then I backed away and noticed a similar stain on one of the knobs at the foot of the bed. Dried blood, I thought. Not unexpected in a cabin that had been used by hunters. But how recently had the bed knob and the mattress acquired the bloodstains?

"Did your brother smoke?" I asked Willow, who had followed me inside the cabin.

"Yes, he did, started when he was a kid." She looked around and saw the can filled with cigarette butts. "He must have been up here before he died."

"That's a lot of butts," I said.

"Rick's friend Harry used to come up here, too. He's a smoker."

"When was the last time you came here to the cabin, before yesterday when you came looking for Brian?"

Willow thought about it for a moment. "It was after Grandpa died, which was in January, but before Rick died in June. So I was up here sometime in the late spring, sometime after the rains stopped. That road gets to be a mess when it storms, and in a really wet year the creek floods over the bridge."

I paced around the cabin, looking in corners. Then I spotted something shiny on the floor near the front door. I bent down and picked it up, holding it in the palm of my hand. It was a tiny link to a bracelet, and I was betting it had come off Brian's MedicAlert bracelet.

I tucked the link into my pocket. Then I turned and looked at the can full of cigarette butts on the table.

"What kind of cigarettes did Rick and Harry smoke?"

Willow frowned. "Rick? Marlboros, I think. Harry always rolls his own, though."

So Harry's cigarette butts would be unfiltered, just like the butts I'd seen in the ashtray at Vann's Motorcycle Shop. I picked up the tuna fish can and gave it a shake, shifting the contents. There were two kinds of cigarette butts in the can. Two smokers had been in the cabin, and I figured they'd been here recently, in the past few weeks.

Once again I thought about Rick's motorcycle accident, the one where his body had supposedly washed out to sea from the bottom of that cliff. And the more I thought about it, the more certain I was that Rick Newman was alive. Unless he'd been the man whose body I'd seen in the Sonoma County Morgue a few days ago.

I reached into my bag for the picture I'd torn from the Santa Rosa *Press Democrat*, the artist's sketch of the man who'd died on the boat. I handed it to Willow.

She looked at me, curious. Then she looked down at the picture. Her eyes widened.

"Oh, my God. That's Harry Vann."

TWENTY-EIGHT

WILLOW, STUNNED AND SILENT, FOLLOWED ME OUT of the cabin. We got into my car. I turned it around in the clearing and drove back down the gravel road to the house. When we arrived, we both got out. She unlocked the front door and we went inside.

The house was comfortable, but old and lived-in, needing some updates and repairs. The furniture was a mix of Willow's things, which looked more contemporary, and old pieces that had belonged to Willow's grandfather, like the bow-fronted china cabinet with its glass shelves and Blue Willow china, and the faded chintz sofa covered in colorful quilted pillows. The beige carpeting in the living room and hallway was worn in places, and the faded linoleum floor in the big kitchen was coming up in one corner. The appliances were white, the refrigerator a large, bulky side-by-side that made a lot of noise. Next to the fridge was a gas range, an old O'Keefe & Merritt four-burner that was similar to the one my grandmother had in her house.

Willow set her bag on the counter and opened the refrigerator. She poured iced tea into two glasses and set them on a scarred oak table that held a solitary placemat. We both pulled out chairs and sat down.

"The man in the picture—Harry—are you saying he's dead?"
Willow asked.

I nodded. "His body was found Saturday night on a boat
that burned at your father's marina. He wasn't killed by the fire,
though. He was shot."

"How do you know all this? And what does it have to do with
Brian being missing?"

"Brian's MedicAlert bracelet."

Willow nodded. "Yes, I saw that he wears one. I asked him
about it and he told me he's allergic to penicillin."

"The bracelet was found on the boat, near the body. The band
was broken. Because of that, the Sonoma County detectives who
are investigating the case thought the body might be Brian, since
Sheila reported him missing. I went to the morgue on Tuesday
morning to look at the body."

"Oh, how horrible for you to have to do that," she said. "But
it wasn't Brian."

"No, I could see that right away. But why was the bracelet
there on the boat?" I reached into my pocket and pulled out the
link I'd found on the cabin floor. "I think this is a link to Brian's
bracelet. If it is, that means he was at the cabin."

Willow took a sip of her tea. "But how did Brian's bracelet
get to a boat at Dad's marina? What in the world was Harry doing
there? Whose boat was it?"

"According to Tracy, your father's friend, the boat that burned,
and two others berthed at the marina, belong to a man named
Lowell Rhine."

Willow shook her head. "I don't know anyone named... Wait
a minute. Rhine, did you say? Rick was in trouble a year or so ago,
facing more jail time. His lawyer's name was Rhine."

"The same man, I believe. He lives in San Rafael."

"Why would he berth his boat in Lakeville?" she asked. "Boats,
I mean. You said there were three, including the one that burned.
There are all sorts of marinas in San Rafael, if that's where Rhine
lives." She stopped and snapped her fingers. "Unless Rick talked
him into it, or talked Dad into giving him a deal on the berthing
fees."

That was my theory. I steered the conversation back to the man in the sketch. "When I saw the body in the morgue, I didn't know who it was. Then I wondered if it might be Rick."

"Rick's dead." Even as she said the words, Willow looked as though she was trying to convince herself that he was.

"Are you sure about that?"

She stared at me. The deer-in-the-headlights look was back again. "I thought maybe, when they didn't find a body... Yes, I have to say I wondered if Rick and Harry had cooked up something. It's just like Rick to fake his own death. To get away from whatever idiotic mess he was in. He's always been involved in a mess, his whole life, ever since he was a kid." She sighed and shook her head. "Damn it, if Rick's not dead, that tears it."

"It certainly complicates your life. Your grandfather left this land to both of you. What did Rick want to do with it?

Willow put her face in her hands. Then she dropped them, laying her palms flat on the table. "He wanted to turn it into a pot plantation. There's a lot of marijuana growing up here in Sonoma County. Like Mendocino County. It's a big industry. Sooner or later the state will legalize it, I suppose."

She swallowed more tea. "Rick had...has this friend, Tony. I don't know the guy's last name, or where he lives. Tony grows pot on a large scale, Rick said, and he moved his operations to this part of the county after getting busted last year at another location. Seems he was growing pot in a state park and he got caught."

That sounded like the case Donna had worked on, I thought. Could it be the same one? "Was this other location in Sonoma County?"

"I don't know," Willow said. "I'm just telling you what Rick told me. When Grandpa died and we inherited the land, Rick came up with this cockamamie scheme to go into partnership with Tony, using this land. Rick said the farm was ideal for growing pot. They could hide the plants up in the forest, and there's a water source, with the creek running through. He was going to turn the barn into a processing plant of some sort."

"How did you feel about that?"

"I told him he was crazy. I told him, no way in hell. It's illegal, and those pot farmers just destroy the landscape with all the herbicides and fertilizers they use. We argued about it. I told him if he planted any marijuana up here I'd turn him in. He was really pissed off about that." Willow shook her head, her dark curls moving around her face. "Then Rick died. I thought the land was mine, free and clear. So I moved into the house and built my kiln. It would just screw up my life to have him back in the picture."

It would certainly screw up the title to the land. "How did Rick meet Harry?"

"In jail. How did Rick meet anyone?" Willow rolled her eyes. "They met six or seven years ago. They were both doing stretches for drug-related offenses. Which is why the lease on the motorcycle shop is in Carla's name instead of Harry's. My ne'er-do-well brother, in trouble from the minute he could walk. Or ride a bike. Truth be told, he and I didn't get along very well. He was the bad boy and I was the good kid. And who's my father's favorite? Rick, of course." She sounded bitter. "Dad was so upset when we got the news that Rick was dead. He wouldn't react that way if I died."

"When was the last time you saw Rick?"

Willow got up from the table and walked to the counter to retrieve her shoulder bag. She pulled out a small datebook and opened it, pointing at a Sunday in early June. "Dad's birthday. We took him out for brunch." Then she indicated the last Thursday of the month. "This was the day Rick had the motorcycle accident. Supposedly."

"How did you find out about the accident? Did the authorities contact you?"

"Harry called me," Willow said. "He told me what happened. He wanted me to go to Lakeville and break the news to Dad. Like I said, Dad was really upset, taking it hard. As for me, all I could think was, now I won't have to worry, the land belongs to me."

"Did you suspect that Rick might not be dead?"

"Not until now." She shook her head. "What in the world was he thinking? He must have gotten into something bad, so deep he couldn't get out, so he decided to escape."

Escape. The word echoed through my mind. Escape on a

boat? The cabin cruiser that had burned had been used to transport marijuana from Mexico to the United States, according to the boat history. It could certainly go the other way, taking Rick and possibly Harry down to Mexico.

"What do you know about Harry and Carla?"

Willow shrugged. "Harry, not much. He's got a record for drugs and some alcohol-related stuff, fighting, and so forth, just like Rick. Carla's all right. A little rough around the edges, but I like her."

So did I. Now I was going back to Vann's Motorcycle Shop to tell Carla that her brother, Harry, was most likely dead, shot to death on Saturday night at Newman's Marina.

TWENTY-NINE

"YOU WERE GOING TO LET ME GO. JUST LET ME GO." HE pleaded with the man at the wheel as the vehicle raced away from the burning boat.

The driver had a gun. He pointed it.

"Shut the fuck up. I gotta think."

The driver sped up the gravel road and jerked the wheel, turning onto the highway. Sirens and flashing lights signaled the coming of the fire department. The driver didn't say anything else, driving with one hand on the wheel, the other gripping the gun. He didn't know what time it was.

The driver just kept driving. It seemed as though they'd been moving for hours. He fell asleep, then he woke up again, confused. They must be in another state by now.

But they weren't. As the sun began to rise, he raised his head and looked out, seeing a few landmarks he recognized.

The driver pulled off the road and pointed the gun at the prisoner in the backseat. "Get down."

He obeyed, scrunching down on the seat, but staying high enough to get a sense of where they were.

The driver guided the vehicle back onto the road. He drove into a town, sleepy and deserted in the early morning hours.

The driver made a turn, heading out of the town, away from buildings and houses, into the countryside. Then he slowed and turned off the pavement onto a dirt road, the vehicle bouncing over ruts as it headed up a hill and into a curve. Then the driver stopped.

Several armed men surrounded the vehicle.

THIRTY

WILLOW TOLD ME THAT THE ROAD LEADING TO THE cabin kept going, intersecting with Green Valley Road. I left the Hargis ranch, drove back toward Graton, then cut to the north on Sullivan Road. A left turn took me west, onto Green Valley Road, which ultimately met Highway 116 between Forestville and Guerneville. I drove slowly, looking for the road Willow had described.

I spotted it just past a curve, on the left side of the road, a narrow gravel track barred by a gate, similar to the one near Willow's house. At the first opportunity I made a U-turn and drove back to the gate, parking where the two roads met. I got out and walked around to examine the gate. It was secured with a padlock and the road beyond had thick stands of pines and oaks on either side. I saw broken branches indicating that vehicles had passed this way. Then I looked at the gate and saw a spot where something, probably a vehicle, had scraped against the gate while it was open. I examined it more closely.

Red paint, a dull red, just like the paint on Brian's Jeep.

I got back in my car and pulled out my map of Sonoma County. The quarry where the Jeep had been abandoned was west of Forestville, not far from here.

I started the engine and drove back the way I'd come, heading east on Green Valley Road. North of Graton I crossed Highway

116 and continued east on Guerneville Road. My cell phone rang and I hit the button on my headset to answer it.

"Scott Cruz has a record," Rita Lydecker said.

"I'm not surprised. What did he do?"

"Assault with a deadly, over in Vallejo, his home town. Cruz has a juvenile record, too, but that's sealed."

"Serious charge, assault with a deadly weapon. Who did he beat up?"

"Got into a fight with some guy in a bar and went after him with a tire iron. Beat the crap out of him."

"Who was the defense attorney?" Had it by chance been Lowell Rhine? But maybe the San Rafael attorney was too high-powered for the likes of Scott Cruz.

"Public defender. Scott did time in the Solano County jail. About a year after he got out, he moved to Sonoma County. Worked in a couple of motorcycle shops, one in Petaluma and the place near Santa Rosa where he works now."

"You do good work," I said.

"Thanks. Any closer to finding your brother?"

"So far I'm coming up blank. But I know where he's been." I gave Rita an overview of my conversation with Willow. I told her where Brian's Jeep had been found, and about the red paint I'd discovered on the gate at the other end of Hargis Ranch Road.

"It looks to me like Rick Newman faked his own death, with the help of his buddy Harry Vann. I don't know why yet, but my guess is Rick got involved in something that he couldn't handle. It looks like he was hiding out at the cabin on his grandfather's property and planned to take the boat to get away. Brian went up to the 'empty' cabin, thinking he was going to stay there while doing some hikes in this part of the county. And..." I let her fill in the blanks. "Now Harry Vann is dead and Rick's on the run. My guess is that he has another bolt-hole, with a friend of his named Tony, who has a pot plantation somewhere. But I don't have a last name and I don't have a location."

"We can start with Sonoma County," Rita said. "I'll put out some feelers."

"I will, too," I said. We ended the conversation. I was moving into the outskirts of Santa Rosa. In the distance I saw Vann's Motorcycle Shop. I slowed and pulled over to the side of the road to make another phone call.

Donna answered her cell phone on the second ring. "Hi, Jeri. Any news?"

"Hi, cuz. I'm making progress, piecing together what happened. I have a question for you. It's about something you said when we talked a couple of days ago. You busted a grower last year, for planting marijuana on public land, at Annadel State Park."

"That's right," Donna said. "He had a big plantation on private land west of Oakmont. He expanded over the park boundaries and we caught him."

"You also said he got away with a slap on the wrist, because he had a slick lawyer. What was the grower's name, and who was the lawyer?"

"I don't remember, but I can sure find out. Where are you now?"

"Outskirts of Santa Rosa. I have to talk with someone there."

"I'm in Cazadero, following up on that poaching case. I'll make some calls and get some information on the pot grower and get back to you. We're both in Sonoma County at the moment. Maybe we can meet up."

"That would be great. I'll be in touch." My next moves would depend on my upcoming conversation with Carla Vann.

I disconnected the call and pulled back on the highway. Carla Vann's Hyundai hatchback was parked at the motorcycle shop. I didn't see the blue-and-white Tahoe Scott Cruz had been driving. Scott wasn't in the service bay when I drove into the lot and parked. There was a large Harley-Davidson in the bay, in the middle of repairs, I guessed, from the parts and tools strewn on the floor and the nearby workbench.

Carla sat at the desk, a pile of papers in front of her, and another can of Diet Coke at the ready. She had emptied the ashtray into the wastebasket and set it on the counter. When I walked into the office, she looked up. "You're back. Got more questions?"

"I need to talk with you, Carla. Where's Scott?"

"He went to grab some food. Should be back soon."

I reached into my bag and took out the newspaper illus-
tration of the man who'd died on the boat. "Take a look at this
picture."

She frowned and took the sketch from me. Holding it with
both hands, she looked it over, a growing sense of disquiet evident
on her face. "This looks a lot like Harry. What's the deal? Where
did you get this picture?"

"It's from an article in the Santa Rosa *Press Democrat* yesterday. Early Sunday morning, there was a fire on a boat out at
Newman's Marina. When the fire was put out, the firemen found
a body on board. This is an artist's sketch of that man."

Carla's face went white. "What? Oh, my God. You're telling
me Harry's dead?"

"It's possible."

Carla looked at the sketch and shook her head. "No. No, it
can't be. You're wrong."

"You should at least check it out. Call the detectives at the
Sonoma County Sheriff's Department. Their names are Griffin
and Harris. They can give you more details." I took out one of the
cards, Harris's, and jotted Griffin's name on it as well. I handed
the card to Carla. Her fingers closed over it and tears leaked from
her eyes.

"This man, he died… It was an accident, right?"

I shook my head. "No. The dead man was shot."

Now she looked stunned. "Oh, my God. If it really is Harry…
How… What am I gonna tell Mom?"

I couldn't answer that question. Whatever she told her mother, it would be difficult to relay this unwelcome news. I thought
of my own mother—and father—waiting at Aunt Caro's house for
any news about Brian's disappearance.

Now Carla had a few more questions of her own. "Newman's
Marina. What happened? If it's Harry, and I'm not saying it is,
what the hell was he doing down at the marina?"

"I think he was with Rick."

Carla shook her head, looking baffled. "What are you talking
about? Rick's dead."

"Maybe not. They never found a body."

She stopped and considered this for a moment, hands clench-
ing, then opening. "That would explain…"

"What would it explain?"

Carla looked wary. Then she opened up. "Harry was cooking
up some scheme. I knew it, I could feel it, ever since Rick's accident in June. I don't know what, but Harry was keyed up, wired.
He was definitely up to something."

Up to something, I wondered, as in helping Rick get away on
the boat? Or had Harry been planning to go with Rick?

"How well did you know Rick?"

"He worked here, repairing bikes. That was off and on. And…"
Carla looked sad. "Well, I used to go out with him, a couple of
years back. But that relationship was over. I liked the guy, but he's
not what you'd call reliable. I gotta stay away from those bad boys.
But there's something about them. Rick could be really charming
when he wanted to be."

The blue-and-white Tahoe pulled into the parking lot, and
Scott got out, carrying a pizza box and a liter of Pepsi. He went
into the service bay without glancing into the office.

Carla got up from the desk and went into the bay, carrying the
artist's sketch. I followed her. Scott had set the pizza box on one of
the work benches. He had the lid open and was lifting a slice laden
with pepperoni and sausage from the box.

He didn't look pleased to see me again. "What's up?" he asked.

Carla stumbled over the words. "I just found out… It could
be…oh, hell, maybe Harry's dead."

Scott dropped the pizza slice back into the box. "What makes
you think that?"

Carla showed him the sketch. "This picture. It looks like Harry, doesn't it?"

Scott wiped the tomato sauce from his fingers with a wad of
napkins, squinting his brown eyes at the sketch. He shrugged.
"Could be him, I guess."

"This person got shot down at Newman's on Sunday morning," Carla said.

Scott reached for the Pepsi and opened the bottle, taking a
drink. "No shit."

No interest, I thought. Scott Cruz's reaction to the possible death of his employer was flat, unemotional, without curiosity. I saw none of the emotion that Carla was expressing, with her facial expressions, her voice, her tears. Some people are more shut down, showing little or no emotion. Maybe Scott was one of those people. Or maybe there was another reason. Scott's reaction, or lack of it, made me wonder if he already knew Harry Vann was dead. I also wanted to know where Scott had been early Sunday morning when everything went down at Newman's Marina.

Carla turned, heading back toward the office. "I gotta go. I gotta make some calls. And tell Mom."

"Sure thing. I gotta finish this bike. I'll close up at five, like I always do." Scott took another long drink from the bottle of Pepsi. Then he reached for another slice of pizza.

I left when Carla did. She got into her hatchback and drove off, heading east in the direction of Santa Rosa. I drove out of the parking lot heading west, then I made a U-turn and pulled to the side of the road at a spot where the motorcycle shop was clearly visible.

Inside the service bay, Scott Cruz wasn't eating his pizza, nor was he working on the Harley. He was pacing back and forth, talking on a cell phone. He ended the call and jammed the phone into the back pocket of his jeans. Then he went to a control box on the side wall of the bay and lowered the metal door, closing off the bay. A moment later he came out of the office and locked the door.

I glanced at my watch. A quarter to four. So much for closing up at five.

THIRTY-ONE

SCOTT GOT INTO HIS TAHOE AND STARTED THE EN-gine. He turned east onto Guerneville Road. I followed him into Santa Rosa. At U.S. 101, he got onto the freeway, heading south.

He drove fast but I kept up with him. When we got to Petaluma, he took the exit for Lakeville Highway and headed east.

Was he going to the marina down in Lakeville?

No, he wasn't. Just past South McDowell Boulevard, the Tahoe turned right into the lot of a small strip mall and parked in front of a Starbucks.

Long way to go for a cup of coffee, I thought. I pulled my Toyota into a spot where I could see both the Tahoe and the coffee shop.

But Scott didn't go inside. He got out of his Tahoe and looked around the parking lot. Then he leaned against the hood and lit up a cigarette. He stood there, watching the entrance to the parking lot. He was waiting for someone.

I kept an eye on Scott as I pulled out my cell phone and Detective Griffin's business card. Griffin wasn't available, but I left a voice mail message, telling him the dead man was most likely Harry Vann, and that he'd be getting a call from Harry's sister, Carla.

A moment after I disconnected the call, my phone rang. I glanced at the number. It was Donna. I answered the call.

"The grower I arrested last year," she said, "the one that walked, his name's Anthony Busto. The slick lawyer was a guy named Rhine."

"Thanks. That clarifies a few things." I'd been keeping an eye on Scott, slouched against the hood of his Tahoe as he smoked his cigarette and tossed the butt to the pavement. Now he straightened and looked toward the parking lot entrance. Whoever he was meeting had arrived.

"Listen, I've got to go. I'm tailing someone and it's about to get interesting."

"Call me later," Donna said, and hung up.

A silver BMW pulled into the lot and parked at the end of a row of cars. Scott walked toward it as a tall man in a business suit unfolded himself from the driver's side.

I recognized him from the pictures I'd seen on the Internet. Lowell Rhine.

What business did Scott Cruz have with the defense lawyer?

Obviously the kind of business that couldn't be conducted in the attorney's San Rafael office.

The two men went inside the Starbucks. I followed. They queued up to order drinks, plain coffee for Scott, a cappuccino for Rhine, who paid for the drinks. When they got their coffees, I took my turn and ordered an iced latte. They found a table near the back. I got my latte and sat down at a nearby table, making sure Scott's back was to me. I didn't want him to see me, but his attention was on Rhine.

The conversation between the two men was conducted in low tones, so I couldn't make out the words. But I was close enough to watch their body language. In an exchange between the motorcycle mechanic and the attorney, Rhine dominated the conversation, punctuating his words with quick hand gestures. And Scott didn't like what he was hearing.

I got out my cell phone, pretending to take a call. I snapped a couple of photos of the two men, hoping the noise in the coffee shop would mask the sound of the shutter. Insurance of a different sort, I thought, just in case I needed something to hold over Rhine's head. I tucked the phone in my bag and picked up a discarded copy of that morning's *San Francisco Chronicle*.

The exchange grew more heated. Then Scott pushed back his chair and stood up. I raised the newspaper to shield my face as Scott left the coffee shop.

Rhine took another sip of his cappuccino, a frown on his face. At this distance, he looked older than the photo on his website. The attorney was in his forties, I guessed, edging toward fifty. His brown hair had threads of gray, and there were lines around his pale blue eyes. Over a white shirt, he wore a light gray suit. It looked expensive, tailored to fit him. Just as in the website photo, he wore a large diamond-and-gold pin anchoring his red striped tie.

Rhine shoved back his chair and stood to leave. I got up, too, blocking his exit. He looked down at me, his blue eyes hooded, waiting for me to move. I didn't. Instead I handed him one of my business cards.

"I'm Jeri Howard, Mr. Rhine. You haven't returned my phone call."

He looked at my card through narrowed eyes. Then he tucked it into his jacket pocket. His voice was deep and resonant, just the voice for a trial lawyer. "You were calling about?"

"A boat called the *Esmeralda*."

Rhine pursed his lips and narrowed his eyes. "In what connection?"

"The *Esmeralda* burned on Sunday morning, at Newman's Marina in Lakeville. After the fire was put out, a body was found onboard. You're listed as the owner of that boat, and two others berthed at the marina. But you're not."

"What has this got to do with a private investigator from Oakland?"

"I appreciate a good stall as much as the next person, Mr. Rhine. But this private investigator's not going away. My associate and I generated boat histories on all three vessels berthed by you at Newman's Marina. They're owned by a man named Enrique Lopez, one of your clients."

Rhine didn't react. He had a good poker face.

"The smaller boats are clean," I said, "But the history on the *Esmeralda* says it was seized once before, for running drugs from Mexico to the United States. You got the boat back due to the most recent changes in the forfeiture laws."

"You're thorough," Rhine said.

"Yes, I am."

"You still haven't told me why you're interested."

"I'm working on a missing persons case."

"Do you think the body on the boat is your missing person?"

"The body on the boat is Harry Vann." That didn't get a response from Rhine, but my next words did. "You knew that already. It was supposed to be Rick Newman. My guess is, Scott Cruz pulled the trigger. The question I have at this point is whether he was acting on his own, or whether he was following your orders."

Rhine's frown had deepened as I spoke. Now he gave me a

look that was supposed to flash-freeze me. It might have worked on a witness in a courtroom, but this afternoon it wasn't working on me.

The attorney's mouth tightened. Then he gestured at the table he'd just vacated. "Let's sit down and finish our coffee, Ms. Howard."

"Certainly, Mr. Rhine." I set my iced latte on the table and pulled out the chair Scott had vacated. Rhine sat down in front of his cappuccino. "Ball's in your court," I told him.

"I'm not in the practice of ordering hits," he said.

"Glad to hear it, counselor. That would get you disbarred for sure. Though I do think the California Bar Association would take a dim view of your actions in hiding Mr. Lopez's boats. And conspiring with Scott Cruz to do whatever Scott's doing."

"I'm not conspiring with Scott Cruz to do anything," Rhine said.

"So Scott's taking the initiative, acting on his own?"

Rhine took a sip of his cappuccino and drummed his fingers on the table. "Is this conversation off the record?"

I leaned forward. "Nothing's off the record, Mr. Rhine. I will do anything I have to do to find my missing person. If that includes making you uncomfortable, or bringing certain of your activities to the attention of the sheriff's department or the bar association, I will do it. Are we clear on that?"

For a second, he looked startled. Then he masked it. "Clear enough. All right, what do you know?"

"I know you defended Rick Newman on a drug charge last year. You got him off. Then he started working for you, doing errands. I know Enrique Lopez owns the boats. You stashed them at Newman's Marina, probably on Rick's suggestion. I know Rick's not dead. He and his buddy Harry staged the motorcycle accident to make it look like he was. I think Rick and Harry were going to take the *Esmeralda* and get away, to Mexico, I assume. The question is why?"

Rhine's mouth quirked in what might have passed for a smile. "You're good at guessing. What's your theory?"

"My theory?" I sipped the latte. "Rick took something that didn't belong to him. A large sum of money."

Rhine drummed his fingers again. "Very good theory. The term 'large sum' is relative. But large enough. A quarter of a million dollars."

That sounded plenty large to me. It would have been catnip to Rick.

"What did Rick do?"

"He took the cash, which belongs to a client of mine. The client wants it back."

"Bad enough to kill Rick?"

"I'm not going to answer that," Rhine said.

"Suit yourself. How did Rick get his hands on the money?"

Now Rhine looked annoyed, with himself, it seemed. "As you say, I employed Rick to do various errands for me. In June, I sent him up the coast to fetch the cash from the client, who has a house up there. The cash was in a locked aluminum briefcase. Instead of bringing it back to my office, Rick stole it."

"Stole it how? And how did you find out about it?"

"Rick and Harry staged the accident on his way back from the client's house. I called the client that evening when Rick didn't return with the briefcase. The client told me what time Rick had left, and said he'd had a friend with him. I guessed that it was Harry. So I tracked Harry down. Harry told me Rick had skidded off the highway and over a cliff. Although the motorcycle was found at the bottom of the cliff, the aluminum briefcase containing the cash was not. Harry claimed the briefcase was at the surf line with Rick's body, and that both the body and briefcase must have been washed out to sea."

"Did you believe Harry?"

"I wasn't sure," Rhine said. "The police report on the accident was straightforward. But I couldn't shake the feeling that Rick had stolen the money and was hiding out somewhere."

"So how does Scott fit into all of this? As far as I can tell you've never represented him. Scott got really nervous when I paid a visit to Vann's Motorcycle Shop today. So nervous that I decided to follow him here. Why are you meeting him?"

"I decided to keep an eye on Harry. And Scott works for Harry. Eventually Harry said something out of turn, about Rick and the money. Scott figured out that Rick was still alive, hiding up in the hills somewhere, plotting the escape on the boat."

"So Scott contacted you."

Rhine was drumming his fingers again. When he realized it he stopped and reached for his cappuccino. "He did. Scott offered to retrieve the money, for a price. We discussed the matter and... Things didn't go as planned."

It sounded to me like Rhine had been conspiring with Scott, no matter how much the lawyer denied it.

"Scott went down to the marina," I said, "planning to waylay Rick and Harry. He shot at Rick and hit Harry instead. Then the boat blew up, probably because of a propane leak, probably ignited by Harry's cigarette or lighter."

Now Rhine actually smiled, with mordant humor. "Tobacco kills. Scott called me because he wants money from me, even though he screwed things up royally. Rick still has the money, Harry's dead, and my client's boat is a total loss. Now I have a couple of Sonoma County homicide investigators asking me lots of questions."

"And me."

He nodded. "And you."

"All right, Mr. Rhine. I want Rick Newman."

"Is he your missing person?"

"No. But he may very well know where my missing person is."

Rhine thought about it for a moment. "Scott says Rick has been hiding in a cabin on some land west of Graton."

I dismissed this with a wave of my hand. "Old news, counselor. I've been to the cabin. Rick's not there."

"Then there's another possibility. Rick has a friend named Tony Busto."

"Would that be Anthony Busto? The pot grower you defended last year on charges of growing marijuana on state land, namely Annadel State Park?"

"You are thorough," Rhine said. "Yes, that would be the same Tony Busto."

"I understand he's not in the same location. Where can I find him?"

Rhine finished the last of his cappuccino. "He moved to Guerneville."

"A lot of countryside around Guerneville. I need specifics. Just where is Busto's latest pot plantation?"

"I have no personal knowledge of the location." Rhine sounded like the lawyer he was. "My information comes from Scott. He says Tony's pot plantation is near Guerneville, on the north side of Sweetwater Springs Road. Access is up a dirt road, which is about half a mile south of some old mine."

He paused. "If you're going to make a move, I would say time is of the essence. Scott has turned into a loose cannon. He says he's going to go up to Busto's place and make another try for Rick and the money."

THIRTY-TWO

"THE GUY'S A FUCKING LIABILITY." THE VOICE, A LOW growl, belonged to the man who owned this place. He and the other man, Rick Newman, were in the kitchen.

I have to get out of here, he thought. They're not going to let me go. They're going to kill me.

At least he wasn't handcuffed anymore. He was locked in a small space that had once been a storage closet or a pantry. It was furnished with a narrow cot. At the foot of the cot was a bucket to be used as a toilet, and a couple of large bottles of water. Every now and then a man who didn't speak unlocked the closet, fetched the bucket, and brought it back empty. A different man, also silent, brought him food and plastic bottles of water to drink.

As they'd brought him from the vehicle to the building, he realized what this was. A pot plantation. He'd heard about these places, read that they were all over Northern California.

He was in an old house. When they'd brought him inside early that morning, he'd had time for a brief look at his surroundings. The front part of the house was a living room–dining room arrangement. A hallway led to the back and he'd glimpsed a bathroom at the end of the hall. The kitchen was a walk-through, and the closet where he was locked up was in back of this, near a back door at the rear of the house.

It was dark when they'd arrived at the house, escorted by the men with guns. But he'd seen enough on the drive up here that he thought he knew where they were.

If I could just get loose, he told himself, I'm sure I could get out of here.

He tested the door. The two men were still in the kitchen. He heard the sound of something sizzling on the stove, smelled cooking meat. The man with the low growl said, "I say we shoot him, and dump the body down at the old mine."

It was up to him to get away and save himself. He didn't have much time.

THIRTY-THREE

RHINE LEFT THE STARBUCKS BEFORE I DID. I WATCHED him get into his silver BMW and drive away. Then I used the coffee shop's rest room before returning to my car. I pulled out my cell phone and Detective Griffin's business card. He was in his office.

"Carla Vann called me," he said. "We're making arrangements for her to identify her brother's body. Thanks for your help on this."

"I have information that leads me to believe that Harry Vann was shot by a man named Scott Cruz," I told him. "Cruz works as a mechanic at Vann's Motorcycle Shop. I also have information concerning my brother's whereabouts. I can give you more details. I'm in Petaluma right now, heading for Santa Rosa now."

"Good. I want to hear what you have to say. Meet me at my office as soon as you can get up here."

I headed back up Lakeville Highway and got on the freeway headed north. I called Donna back, bringing her up to date with what I'd learned that afternoon, from Willow, Carla, and now Rhine.

"The person I was tailing, Scott Cruz, met up with Rhine, the attorney who represented Busto last year. It looks like Rick Newman was hiding at the cabin on his grandfather's property, planning to get away on the boat. Brian went up there and—"

"I get the picture," Donna said. "So Brian walks in on these people and they grab him. Maybe they were planning to leave him at the marina when they left on the boat."

"Maybe." I didn't express my deeper fear, which was that Rick and Harry had killed Brian back on Friday, when he'd gone to the cabin.

"Scott had figured out Rick was alive and offered to get back the money Rick stole. He went to the marina and shot Harry. Rick ran. He's friends with Busto. Maybe he went up there and took Brian with him."

"You could be right," Donna said. "Listen, I'm on River Road, probably fifteen minutes from Santa Rosa. I'll meet you at the sheriff's office. Given my past encounter with Busto, I figure I'll horn in on this investigation."

Donna was waiting for me outside the front door. We gave our names to the deputy at the lobby window, who called up to the Investigations Division.

"If this guy Busto is growing pot on state land again, I want to nail him," Donna said. "The problems we've had, both state land and federal. These people are planting in the tens of thousands of pot plants. Marijuana needs lots of light and lots of water. To get the light, the growers are cutting down trees. To get the water, they're diverting creeks with dams and sucking out all the water. Each pot plant needs up to fifteen gallons a day. Multiply that by forty thousand plants."

I did the math. "Six hundred thousand gallons. Damn. And we're in a drought."

"And the damage. Hell, Jeri, you wouldn't believe the stuff

I've seen. Huge amounts of trash strewn all over the landscape. And the ground drenched in toxic crap like herbicides, fungicides, and fertilizers. The contaminated soil has to be scraped up and carted off. The growers kill animals to keep them away from the plants. Even if the grow isn't on public land, it's still a Fish and Wildlife issue. Because they're killing the fish and the wildlife."

This time it was Harris who came to meet us. Donna stuck out her hand. "Agent Doyle, California Department of Fish and Wildlife. I have an interest in the case."

Harris took us back to the office where Griffin waited. Donna introduced herself and disclosed our family relationship.

I told the two detectives about Willow and the cabin on her grandfather's land—and the likelihood that Brian had gone up there. I also told them what I'd learned from Rhine, whom I didn't name, at least not at this point.

"My informant says Rick Newman stole a large sum of money, a quarter of a million dollars. Then Rick faked his death back in June, with Harry Vann's help. Since then, he's been hiding out at the cabin. Brian must have gone up there last Friday, and walked in on them. Rick was planning to take the boat from the marina and get out of the country. Maybe Harry was coming with him. But Scott Cruz, the mechanic who works for Carla and Harry Vann, learned that Rick was alive. Scott wanted to get his hands on the money. He went to the marina early Sunday morning. His target was Rick, but he shot Harry instead. Both Rick and Harry are smokers. I assume the propane explosion was set off by a match or a cigarette lighter."

"Cigarette lighter," Harris said. "We found one on the scene. Near the body, like we found your brother's MedicAlert bracelet."

I showed them the link that I'd found at the cabin. "I believe this link goes with the band of Brian's bracelet. I think the band broke when it got caught on something, Harry picked up the bracelet, and put it in his pocket."

Griffin looked as though he were turning all this over in his mind. "Okay, if Newman isn't dead, where is he now?"

"Rick has a friend named Anthony Busto, who's a large-scale pot grower. In fact, Rick's sister told me Rick was hoping to use their grandfather's land for a marijuana plantation, going into partnership with his buddy. Busto already has a pot plantation. It's located outside of Guerneville, on the north side of Sweetwater Springs Road."

"Busto and I have met before," Donna added. "He had a big grow operation in the east part of the county. He was initially on private land and then he expanded his grow onto state land at Annadel State Park. Aerial photography showed us the location and the extent of the operation. Marijuana grows have a distinct green color that distinguishes them from the surrounding forest. I was part of the raid that shut down Busto's operation last year. That was a joint operation with the feds and Sonoma County. Some of your people were involved in that."

Harris was nodding. "I remember that one. Sergeant Lewis was in on that raid."

"Call him," Griffin said. "He might want to be in on this one. So Busto's moved to West County."

"Looks like it," I said. "I was told that there's a dirt road leading up to the place, about half a mile south of an old mine. If Rick Newman and Harry Vann captured Brian when he stumbled on them at the cabin, I think it's likely my brother is with Newman, at Busto's plantation." I told them about the red paint I'd found on the gate where Hargis Ranch Road met Green Valley Road. "Who else would know about that road except Willow, and her brother?"

"That would explain a few things," Griffin said. "That's not far from where your brother's Jeep was found, near Forestville." He unfolded a Sonoma County map and spread it across the surface of his desk, tracing a line with his finger. "Here's Sweetwater Springs Road. I ride my bike up there. The road starts here, at Westside Road southwest of Healdsburg and goes all the way to Armstrong Woods Road outside of Guerneville. Definitely rugged and forested the closer you get to Guerneville." He pointed. "The old mine's been there since the nineteenth century. They used to mine quicksilver, which is what they called mercury in those days."

Donna bent over the map. "The location Jeri's talking about is really close to Armstrong Redwoods State Reserve and Austin Creek State Recreation Area. The two are contiguous. Given Busto's history, I'm concerned that he might be encroaching on state land again."

"You could be right," Griffin said.

Harris was at the computer. "Here's a shot of the mine." He clicked into a picture of the old mercury mine as it looked now, with its derelict buildings and tailings, enclosed by a fence.

Now he clicked into a map that showed the area and zoomed in closer. "You're right about it being close to the state park. Not far at all as the crow flies." He pointed at the screen. "Sweetwater Creek follows the road. Redwood Creek is here, to the west. Fife Creek is north of that. Sweetwater Creek is too close to the road. My bet is Busto's located his plantation close to Redwood Creek or Fife Creek, so he can draw water from one or both creeks."

"Fife Creek flows through both state parks," Donna said. "If he's polluting that stream with all that toxic junk the growers use, my department definitely has a stake in this case."

Griffin clicked from the map view to the satellite view, and zoomed in even closer. "I don't see a road, but I see some buildings up there, in a clearing. Could be a house, some outbuildings. There are people living up there, in various places off Sweetwater Creek Road. This map doesn't get me close enough."

"Let's keep an eye on Cruz," Griffin said. "I don't want him going up there and tipping off Newman or Busto."

Harris scribbled on a nearby pad. "I'll check property records to see if any parcels on Sweetwater Springs Road have sold recently. And start working on a warrant. Got plenty of probable cause. Newman's a material witness in the murder of Harry Vann. And if he's got your brother, that's kidnapping." He looked at his watch. "It's after five. We won't be able to do this till tomorrow morning at the earliest."

"Are we invited to the party?" I asked.

The two detectives exchanged glances. "Agent Doyle, yes. She represents state interests. As for you, Ms. Howard, you're a citizen, not law enforcement. We'll see what we can do."

Before leaving the building, Donna and I conferred in the lobby. "I don't know that they'll let you go along on the raid," she said. "I'm law enforcement, you're not. And these pot growers are armed, though they'd have to be crazy to fire on us. But you never know when you'll get some hothead with a gun. I'm sure you'll be able to come up right after."

"I just hope I'm right, and Brian's up there. Or maybe he's been able to get away."

Donna and I looked at each other, without my voicing the concern that was nagging at me. I was guessing that Rick had gone to his second bolt-hole, Busto's pot plantation, on Sunday, after things went sour at the marina. It was now Thursday afternoon, four days later. Would they keep Brian a prisoner there? What if they decided that Brian was a liability? What if they killed him?

I drove home to Oakland. I still hadn't stowed away my hiking gear from the trip to Lassen. Now I loaded everything into the trunk of my car—hiking boots, hiking poles, binoculars, and a backpack stuffed with the essentials. I carried several water bottles, a couple of bandannas, a small first-aid kit, and an assortment of food, including trail mix, jerky and candy bars. I tossed in a small jar of peanut butter, a pack of crackers, and several of the Gravenstein apples I'd gotten from Pat as well. If I had to hike into the woods to find Brian, I'd be ready.

When I'd finished loading the car, I called Dan on his cell phone and told him what I'd learned since our lunch together in Graton. "Things are starting to happen. It looks like the detectives are going to raid the pot plantation tomorrow. I'm hoping I'll be able to go up with them. If I'm right, Brian's up there."

"I was planning to hike Armstrong Woods Park anyway," Dan said. "So I'll be in Guerneville. I'll be ready to help, any way that I can."

THIRTY-FOUR

A FEW YEARS AGO, HIS SISTER HAD TAUGHT HIM HOW to pick a lock. She knew about such things. He thought it would be a lark to learn how.

He never figured he'd have to use the knowledge.

The cot he'd been sleeping on had a thin mattress covered with a plain sheet, a pillow, and a blanket. He pulled off the mattress and took a look at the frame. It was plain metal, with flat linked springs. He set to work, loosening one of the coiled springs that held the flat springs to the frame. It took him a while, but finally he worked one free.

He'd been saving food from the ration they brought him, and saving water in one of the bottles as well. He'd be ready to go, as soon as he picked the lock.

He maneuvered the spring into the lock, hoping he could escape before someone decided to kill him.

THIRTY-FIVE

I WAITED IMPATIENTLY IN MY TOYOTA, PARKED ON THE shoulder of Sweetwater Springs Road, where a narrow dirt road led up to Tony Busto's marijuana plantation. Earlier this Friday morning, a team of Sonoma County law enforcement personnel and Fish and Wildlife agents had executed the search warrant. The minutes dragged by. Fifteen minutes, half an hour. Finally Donna called my cell phone.

"We've got Rick Newman and Tony Busto in custody," Donna said. "Along with a bunch of workers."

"What about Brian?"

"Not here. At least so far we haven't found him."

I slumped back against the passenger seat. "I'm coming up. I want to talk to Rick."

I ended the call, not waiting for her reply. I started my Toyota and headed up the dirt road into the woods. It was a mile of ruts, furrows, and twisting turns, gaining in elevation. Both sides of the road were bordered by trees—oaks, California buckeyes, and manzanita.

I emerged into a small meadow, where I saw two buildings, one of them an old house that looked as though it was falling down, and behind that, an old barn that appeared to be in the same state of repair. "Appeared" was the operative word. Solar power collectors had been fastened to the roofs of both buildings. I wondered if they were powering an indoor grow.

I recalled what Harris had said that morning. His check of county property records showed that someone named Boland had purchased this land earlier this year, but we were all guessing that Boland, whoever he or she was, had been fronting for Busto.

All around me were vehicles and people in uniforms. I got out of my Toyota and looked around, shaking my head. Donna's earlier comments had prepared me for the destruction, but what I was now seeing with my own eyes was appalling. The pot growers had clear-cut this meadow, removing the smaller trees and planting marijuana. Larger trees had been girdled by removing a wide strip of bark from the entire circumference of each tree. This meant that those trees would die and eventually fall, clearing more land for pot cultivation.

The slope above the house had been graded and terraced. To the west of the house and barn was Redwood Creek. Busto and his growers had built a crude dam. Plastic tubing spread out like spider webs, diverting water to the grow. Below the dam, the creek was a mere trickle. Between the house and the barn I saw tents where the growers had been living. Trash was everywhere I looked. I saw hundreds of containers—insecticides, herbicides, rodenticides.

To my left, I saw the remains of several small animals, squirrels, a raccoon, who had fallen victim to the toxic chemicals. The growers had shot several animals. To my disgust, a bobcat had been used for target practice. A dead wild turkey hung from a hook outside the barn, presumably destined for the same fate as the wild pig whose remains littered the ground near a propane barbecue. The carcass of a black-tailed mule deer lay on the bare ground near the front porch of the old house.

Donna walked to meet me. She got there at the same time as one of the Sonoma County deputies, who approached me, hand on the gun at his hip, wanting to know who I was and why I was there.

"She's with me," Donna said. The deputy nodded and turned away.

Donna waved her hand around, eyes flashing with indignation. "Look at this mess. Anything that runs off into this creek heads downstream and winds up in Sweetwater Creek."

"Which ultimately drains into the Russian River," I said, "which then drains into the Pacific Ocean."

"Yeah. Watch where you step and don't touch anything. The whole damn place is toxic."

Donna led the way toward the house, where several deputies had collected the growers. I counted nine men in handcuffs.

"That's Busto." She indicated a short, tough-looking man with a shaved head and a goatee, gold rings in each earlobe. He wore a white athletic T-shirt, black jeans, and hiking boots. Tattoos ran down his bare, well-muscled arms, now handcuffed behind his back.

Busto must have recognized Donna from his arrest last year. He glared at her, venom radiating from him as he snarled at her. "You bitch. I'm not on state land this time."

Donna glared back and gestured at the deer carcass. "I'll bet whoever shot that deer didn't have a license."

Detective Harris loomed in the doorway of the old house. He beckoned us inside. We entered the building. Its outward ramshackle appearance was deceptive. Inside, it was far from falling down. It had been modified so that someone, probably Busto, could live here, overseeing his pot-growing enterprise. It looked as though the wall separating the living room from the dining room had been knocked out. The living room had an assortment of old, stained furniture and the dining room held a scarred table and several mismatched chairs. Behind the dining area I saw a small walk-through kitchen, with a back door. A hallway led back to a small bathroom and there were a couple of doors that must lead to bedrooms. No wonder Rick Newman thought of this place as a second bolt-hole. It had more comforts than the rough cabin on his grandfather's land.

Just this side of the dining room table, Griffin and another deputy stood over a man seated on a low-backed chair, his wrists cuffed behind him. Rick had grown a beard, but I could see an echo of his father's face in his features. He wore faded blue jeans, a T-shirt, a pair of dirty white sneakers.

"I want to talk with Newman," I said.

"We asked him about your brother," Griffin said. "Busto, too. Neither one of them would say anything."

"Maybe he'll talk with me."

Griffin shrugged. "It's worth a try."

I walked over to Rick. He looked up at me with red-rimmed hazel eyes.

"Your sister will be glad to know you're alive," I said.

He stared at me. Then he snorted derisively. "No, she won't."

"Why do you say that?"

He shook his head. "I just complicate her life."

"Still, she's your sister. She was upset when you supposedly died. She told me so." He didn't say anything. "That's the thing about brothers and sisters. No matter what happens, you're still family. My name's Jeri. My brother Brian is the man you surprised at the cabin at the Hargis ranch. I've been looking for him for days. I'd sure like to find him. Did you bring him here?"

Rick didn't say anything for a moment. Then he sighed. "I was going to let him go. Just leave him there at the marina while Harry and I took the boat. Then things went to hell in a handbasket. I never expected things to go down the way they did. I couldn't go back to the cabin. So yeah, I brought him here. We had him locked up in the pantry back of the kitchen."

"What were you going to do with him?" I asked. "Did you have a backup plan?"

He shook his head. "Get away from here, that was my plan. Tony was working on something, to get me down to Mexico." He hesitated. "Your brother, he must have heard us talking about…"

I leaned in closer. "Heard you talking about what?"

Rick looked out the door, then back at me. "Tony wanted to kill him. Tony was royally pissed off when I brought the guy up here. Said he was a liability, knew too much. I didn't want to do that. I got enough on my plate as it is."

I'd suspected this was a danger, that Brian's life might be in jeopardy. But it was another thing entirely to hear him voice it. Thank God, Brian had gotten away from these guys before getting a bullet in the back of the head.

"I said no," Rick continued. "I figured when I left, we could let your brother loose somewhere. Then yesterday, he got out of the pantry and took off."

"Any idea when? What time did you discover him gone?"

"Shit, I don't know when." Rick shook his head. "It must have been after lunch. One of the guys took him some chow around noon. Went back to give him some dinner. I don't remember what time it was. Maybe six, six-thirty. He was gone. We went looking for him, but we couldn't find him. It was evening. It gets dark later this time of year, but up here in these hills, once the sun gets low… It's pretty dark. We gave up the search. I just didn't think he could get far with that head…" He stopped.

I recalled the blood spots I'd seen at the cabin, on the mattress ticking and the knob on the old iron bedstead. I'd guessed that it was Brian's blood. I didn't see any wounds visible on Rick. "What about his head? Is he hurt?"

Rick seemed reluctant to answer. Then he nodded. "He hit his head."

"How did he hit his head? And how badly was he hurt?"

"When Harry and me tackled him at the cabin. He fell and hit his head on that old iron bedstead. It bled some. When he came to, he had a headache, said he was dizzy. After that, he didn't have much appetite. Couldn't keep much on his stomach. We kept him doped up so he wouldn't give us any hassles. Maybe that was upsetting his stomach."

"Doped up with what?"

"Some sleep stuff, Tylenol PM and then later, some Xanax. So that kept him kinda mellow, he slept a lot. But he must have figured it out. He picked the damn lock and went out the back door. We found a bunch of those tablets jammed inside the mattress. He was putting them in his mouth and spitting them out."

Rick was getting downright loquacious. Maybe he figured to make the case for treating Brian well during his captivity.

Brian must have a concussion. Headache and dizziness were symptoms, and so was nausea. And based on what Rick had told me, he'd ingested some serious sedatives. The Tylenol contained a painkiller and a non-prescription sleep aid, mostly harmless. But the Xanax was heavy-duty stuff, with serious side effects.

But I had a more immediate worry. Brian had escaped his captors yesterday afternoon. So he had spent the night out in these hills, in rugged country. It was hot, and I was guessing he hadn't had much to eat or drink. Unless he'd managed to take some food and water with him, he was in trouble.

Where had he gone? I considered the terrain and the location of the pot plantation. The grow was located here along Redwood Creek. He could walk downstream along the creek. But that would be an obvious route, no doubt one of the first places Tony Busto and his men had looked. But they hadn't found him. If he'd gone east, he would have intersected with Sweetwater Springs Road. Again, a route that Busto would check.

I recalled the brochure I'd found on Brian's desk, the one about Armstrong Redwoods and Austin Creek. He'd been researching the two state parks as places to camp and hike. If he recalled something about the trails and terrain, he might have headed west, toward state land.

If he knew where he was. That was the caveat. Did Brian, with a head injury and some disorientation, know where Rick had taken him?

"We're taking him in now," Griffin said. He and a deputy pulled Rick to his feet. "We've got people searching the immediate area. If they find your brother, we'll let you know."

"What about a helicopter, searching farther out?"

"Getting one in the air would take some time," he said.

As they led Rick away, I looked at Donna. "I don't want to wait for a chopper. I'm betting Brian's gone west."

"That's what I'd do, if I knew where I was."

"You've got topo maps for this area, and the state parks?"

"Sure." We left the old house and walked to her truck. She opened the rear door and took out several rolled topographical maps. "The Guerneville topo shows where we are now. And the Cazadero topo shows the parks."

I studied the maps and the elevations showing the changes in topography, as well as Sweetwater Springs Road and the boundaries of the parks. A narrow finger of the Austin Creek area pointed south. Immediately west of this was the Armstrong Redwoods State Reserve.

I pointed at the map. "Here's where we are, roughly. If he crossed Redwood Creek and then continued west, he could connect with Fife Creek and come down the creek bed into the park."

If, if, if. Brian was injured and out there in rugged terrain. It was August, summer, hot outside. The creeks were running low. That would make following the creek bed easier. But he was without food or water, unless he'd managed to take something with him.

Donna had another map open, this one showing Armstrong Redwoods and Austin Creek. "Fife Creek enters the park here, close to a fire road. And that leads down to Armstrong Woods Road, which goes through the park all the way to the Bullfrog Pond Campground. The creek also intersects with the East Ridge Trail, here."

"So he could go several directions," I said. "The creek bed, the fire road, or the trail."

"Let's go," Donna said.

Donna conferred with some of her Fish and Wildlife colleagues. Then we headed down the dirt road, me in front and
Donna following in her state pickup truck. I got out my cell phone
and called Dan. "Where are you?"

"Guerneville, at the Coffee Bazaar. Where are you?"

"Heading for Armstrong Redwoods. Brian got away from the
bad guys. I think there's a chance he headed into the park."

"I'll meet you at the visitor center," Dan said.

THIRTY-SIX

WHEN DONNA AND I DROVE INTO THE PARKING LOT
at the Armstrong Redwoods Visitor Center. Dan was waiting for us,
leaning against his Subaru. I parked my Toyota in a nearby slot and
Donna pulled her state truck in next to my car. Dan had already collected park brochures from the visitor center. I introduced them.
Then we opened a brochure and spread it out on the hood of the
Subaru, map side up.

I briefed Dan. "Brian picked a lock and got out of the house
where they were keeping him. He took off sometime yesterday
afternoon, no idea when, so he's been in the woods all night. We
think maybe he's headed west into the park. If that's the case, at
some point he'll connect with Fife Creek."

Dan studied the map. "I see what you're thinking. He could
follow the creek down into the park, then take the fire road or the
trail. But if he's on the trail, he could go either way."

"It's likely he'd go south," I said. "That's the way to the visitor
center. In fact, the trailhead's right over there."

As I spoke, two hikers came out of the visitor center and started toward the trailhead. Surely if Brian was on the trail and he
met any hikers, they'd help him. I just hoped I was right, that he
was heading for the park, and that he wasn't lying hurt—or dead—
at the bottom of a hill. Just in case, I jogged over to the hikers

and told them we were looking for a missing man, showing them Brian's photo. Then I returned to the car.

"If he went northeast," Dan said, "he could get close to the road here."

He pointed at the map, a location marked Pond Farm Pottery. According to a note on the other side of the brochure, the pottery had been used by ceramic artist Marguerite Wildenhain, who moved to the area after World War II and lived and worked at the farm until her death in 1985. Now the property was part of the Austin Creek reserve.

"Agreed." I tapped the map. "All right, let's go up to this parking area and I'll start hiking the East Ridge Trail. You go up to the pottery and access the trail there. Donna's going to the fire road."

"According to the map," Donna said, "there's a locked gate across the entrance to that fire road. I'll find a ranger so I can get access."

The visitor center was staffed by a volunteer, but there was a ranger's office across the road. Donna walked over there. While she was gone, I unlocked the trunk of my car. Dan, too, had brought hiking gear. We put on our boots and checked the contents of our packs. I slathered on a layer of sunscreen and put on my hat. I tied a bright red bandanna around my neck, and then put on my binoculars.

Donna returned to the parking lot, accompanied by two state park rangers. They introduced themselves. The woman was Lori Ellis, the man Tom Balsinger.

"I'll start up East Ridge Trail from here," Ranger Ellis said. "One of you can head north on East Ridge where it intersects with the Waterfall Trail. Tom here will help Agent Doyle check the fire road."

"Agreed." We traded cell phone numbers and made sure everyone had plenty of water, replenishing our bottles from a faucet and taking extra water, just in case any of us found Brian. Ranger Ellis set out for the trailhead just beyond the visitor center. The rest of us got into our vehicles. We left the parking lot and drove past the entry kiosk, heading up Armstrong Woods Road.

The valley floor was cool and dark. Fife Creek meandered alongside the road. Here and there I saw people walking on one of the hiking trails. Tall first-growth redwoods were interspersed with other trees—tanbark oaks, California bay laurels, and big-leaf maples—all of them filtering the sunlight and the August heat. Under the forest canopy, the ground was covered with moss, red-wood orchid, lichen and mushrooms. A side road led to the Colonel Armstrong Tree, a massive old first-growth redwood named for the man who had preserved these redwoods from logging. We drove another half mile up the road, to an area with picnic tables and a rest room.

Here the road forked. Dan, Donna and the ranger continued up the road, bearing left and heading uphill. Donna and the ranger were headed for the gate leading to the fire road. Dan's destination, the Pond Farm Pottery, was beyond that.

I took the right fork of the road, which led to a parking area, another rest room, the park volunteer office and a maintenance facility. I got out, locked my bag in my trunk, and tucked my cell phone in my pocket. Then I shouldered the pack and set out.

The Waterfall Trail was a short and easy hike. I crossed a bridge over Fife Creek and headed up the trail. When I reached the T-junction where East Ridge Trail went north and south, I stopped and took my water bottle from my pack. I took a drink. Then I cupped my hands around my mouth and called my brother's name, hoping, just hoping, that Brian would hear me.

No response.

I put the bottle into the pack and started walking north toward my eventual destination, the junction where the trail intersected with the fire road and Fife Creek. The trail undulated through forested hills. I climbed and then descended, and climbed again. I was glad of the shade provided by the canopy of trees, because the afternoon was hot. I felt sweat trickling between my shoulder blades.

At the top of another hill, I stopped and drank some water. In the distance I glimpsed a mountain. I consulted the map and identified this as McCray Mountain. It was on private property,

just west of the park boundary and north of the Fife Creek headwaters. Then I raised my binoculars to my eyes and scanned the
trees, searching the dappled shade of the forest for movement. I
saw a scrub jay flitting from branch to branch in a tree, and behind
me I heard the *rat-tat-tat* of a woodpecker.

I took another drink, then I stowed my water bottle in my
pack and did some stretches. Despite the fact that I'd hiked with
Dan only last week, the muscles in my legs were aching.

And I was tired. I hadn't been getting enough sleep, what with
my week-long search for Brian. Tension, worry, late nights, early
mornings—all of these were taking their toll.

I'd felt an adrenaline burst earlier today, when I was sure
Brian was being held prisoner at Tony Busto's pot plantation. I
was right, but now the euphoria had departed. Once again, I'd
gotten close to the truth—and my brother—only to find that the
prize was still elusive.

Now doubt crept in. Brian had gotten away from his captors,
but my theory that he was hiking west into the park was just that,
a theory. I had nothing to base it on. I was going with my gut. If it
were me, that's what I'd do. Would Brian do it?

Even if Brian was headed for the park, what if he was confused, unsure of his location? What if he'd headed in a different
direction? What if he was more badly injured than I thought, having difficulty managing this terrain?

What if? What if? Stop it, Jeri, just keep walking.

I called out to Brian again. No response. I started down the
hill. Then my cell phone rang, reminding me that, hills and forests
notwithstanding, I was still close enough to civilization to get a
signal. I stopped and hit the button to answer the call.

It was Dan. "I parked at Pond Farm Pottery. Now I'm headed
south on the East Ridge Trail to where it meets up with the fire
road. I've been calling out, hoping Brian might hear me. But I
haven't seen any hikers up here on this section."

"Thanks. I've been calling out, too, but I haven't heard anything. No hikers, either. I'll check in with you later." I disconnected and called Donna.

"I'm at the fire road, where it crosses the creek," she said.
"No sign of Brian, or any other hikers. Ranger Ellis checked in.
She's moving north and she hasn't seen him on her section. She
encountered some hikers heading south, and they hadn't seen him
either."

"Thanks for the update," I said. "Dan's on the trail from Pond
Farm, heading your way. I'm about halfway up my section of the
trail."

"Okay," Donna said. "There's an intermittent stream here, a
little creek that feeds into Fife Creek, but it's dry right now. I'm
going to hike upstream here, at least for a ways, and see what I see.
Then I'll start down the trail to meet you."

I tucked my cell phone in my pocket and continued down the
hill, then up another. I called out to Brian over and over again, but
the only sounds I heard were my own footsteps, and birds sing-
ing in the trees. A breeze came up, rustling the branches of the
trees, a welcome respite to the heat. I lost all sense of time as I
walked.

Finally I emerged from the forest. I was at the edge of a meadow that sloped downhill. From this vista point, I looked down into
the densely forested canyon where I'd started this journey, thick
with tall, majestic old-growth redwoods. A turkey vulture coasted
overhead, riding the thermals.

I raised my binoculars and scanned the scene. My pulse
quickened when I saw movement in the trees at the edge of the
meadow. But it wasn't human. A mule deer, a common sight here
in these oak woodlands, stepped out of the trees, its black tail
twitching, This one was a doe, and she was followed by a good-
sized fawn whose spots were fading. The deer paused, then moved
slowly across the meadow and disappeared into another stand of
trees.

I turned, keeping my binoculars in front of my eyes, sweep-
ing my gaze along the edge of the meadow. Down below I spotted Fife Creek and the fire road. I didn't see Donna, though. I
scanned uphill, looking for movement.

Nothing. But wait. I saw movement in the trees. It was another mule deer, this time a buck. He was young, his antlers small. He trotted out of the trees and stopped, poised for movement. It was as though something had startled him, something that was still in the forest.

I lowered the binoculars and set off walking down the slope, shouting Brian's name. My voice galvanized the buck into flight. He took off, running toward the creek. I called out to Brian again. I waited. Called again. Then...

What was that? I thought I heard something. Again I shouted, "Brian!"

A human voice called in response, hoarse, unarticulated, but definitely human. At the spot where I'd seen the buck, a lone figure stumbled out of the trees into the meadow. I raised the binoculars and focused on the figure, impatient to see who it was.

Brian.

He had a week-old beard and his face was dirty, streaked with sweat, dust, the leaves and duff of the forest floor. His T shirt and khaki hiking pants were filthy. Even at this distance I could see the effects of weariness, dehydration, lack of food, and the head injury. He moved toward me in a slow, shambling walk, stumbling but determined, putting one foot in front of the other.

I quickly untied the red bandanna, pulled it from my neck and tied it to one of my hiking poles. Then I lifted it high, waving it back and forth.

Had Brian seen me? Yes, he had. He raised his arms and waved back.

I started down the slope again, moving as fast as I could. When I reached Brian, I dropped the poles and threw my arms around him. I felt his arms encircle me, hugging me tightly, as though I was a life preserver.

Thank God, I thought. Thank God.

Then I laughed. "Hey, baby bro, you're smelling a bit ripe."

He chuckled. Then he said in a raspy, tired voice, "Hey, sis. I knew I could count on you to find me. And make some wise-ass remark."

THIRTY-SEVEN

I SAT BRIAN DOWN ON THE GRASS. I KNELT BESIDE HIM and opened my pack. I took out the extra bottle of water and twisted off the top, handing it to him. "Don't drink that too fast, or it'll come back up."

He took the water and tilted it back to his mouth. He sighed with relief, waited, then took another drink. "Food?" he asked between sips. "You got anything to eat? I had some, but it's long gone. Good thing I was studying up on edible mushrooms. That's what I ate this morning."

"Granola bars, apples, some jerky." I pulled them from the pack, opened the jerky, and tore off a small strip. "For starters, just suck on that for a while."

He put the jerky in his mouth. I opened one of the granola bars and broke it into small pieces, setting it on the grass next to him.

I pulled my cell phone from my pocket and called Donna. "I found him. I'm in a meadow, must be near the fire road."

"Yes, you are," Donna said. "Dan's with me and we're heading your way."

I saw movement at the lower end of the meadow. Two people, Donna and Dan. I grabbed the hiking stick with the bandanna tied to the top and waved it.

Donna's voice crackled from my cell phone. "I see you."

"He's hurt, dehydrated," I said. "We need to get him some medical attention."

"I'll head back to my vehicle and call the rangers. Dan's coming up to help you."

The two figures at the bottom of the meadow separated. Donna headed back to the fire road. Dan kept climbing, moving quickly to cover the distance between us.

"I want to hear all about it," I told Brian. "But first we need to get you to a doctor."

I MADE SURE to tell the medical staff at the emergency room in Santa Rosa about Brian's penicillin allergy. Then I went outside with my cell phone in hand and called Sheila. When I told her the news, she screamed, and then shouted, "I'm on my way." I called Dad next, getting much the same response.

Then I called the Sonoma County Sheriff's Department. "Good work," Griffin said. "I'm glad your brother's okay."

"My guess is, they'll keep him here at the hospital overnight," I said. "He's got a concussion and he's dehydrated."

"We'll be over later to talk with him. Things are popping here, so it will probably be tomorrow morning. He's no longer a suspect, but he's a material witness to Harry Vann's murder. I'm hoping he can identify Scott Cruz as the shooter."

My parents and Aunt Caro arrived first, since they were here in Santa Rosa. But Sheila wasn't far behind. She had the children with her, the two youngsters talking excitedly about seeing their daddy. Caro took them in charge, assuring them that they could visit with Brian as soon as the doctors had finished working on him.

One of the ER doctors came out to talk with us, giving an update on Brian's condition. He'd had an X ray for the head injury and now he was getting fluids. The doctors were admitting him to the hospital, an overnight stay, just to keep an eye on him. "If he does well over the next twenty-four hours," the doctor said, "he can go home tomorrow."

Once the ER had him stabilized, Brian was moved to a room. The other bed was empty and the family gathered around. Brian looked exhausted, ready to sleep. He held Sheila's hand and after a while told her to take the children and go home. She did, promising to be back first thing in the morning. Caro left as well, taking Mother and Dad with her. I lingered, out in the hospital corridor with Donna and Dan. Finally they, too, departed. I sat in the hospital room next to Brian's bed, watching him sleep. He woke up around seven-thirty, looking at me with a wobbly smile.

"How are you feeling?" I asked.

"My head still hurts. And I'm really tired."

"You've had quite an ordeal. Two detectives from the Sonoma County Sheriff's Department will be here sometime tomorrow, to interview you." I paused. "I need to hear what happened. Before you tell the detectives."

He fumbled for the control on the side of the hospital bed and found the right button. He pressed it and raised the head of the bed. "How much do you know? About me and Sheila?"

"A lot. When I get into investigation mode, I dig out everything I can. It doesn't matter if you're related to me or not. I know you two have been having some problems and I know why. I also know why you left Sonoma. I've talked with Sheila, at length. I've also talked with Lance and Becca. Nancy Parsons over in Sonoma told me about your problems at your last school, and the student. And I talked with Willow."

He sighed and closed his eyes, his face pale against the pillow. Then he opened his eyes again. "I was upset that Sheila has been spending so much time away from home. And I feel guilty for feeling that way. Does that make any sense?"

"Yes, it does."

"I know she's had a rough time with her father being sick. But with all the stuff going on at my last school in Sonoma, I felt like she wasn't there for me. I'd try to talk with her, and she tuned me out. She didn't understand, or she didn't want to understand, that I had to get out of the job in Sonoma. I told her I was going to look for another job and I didn't care where. She didn't say anything. She didn't take me seriously." He paused. "But I was serious. When the position came up in the Petaluma schools, I jumped at it. I didn't think Sheila would react the way she did. She was so angry about moving. It took me by surprise."

Communication, I thought, or lack of it. It was so damned important in any relationship, and in this case, both Brian and Sheila had dropped the ball.

"Tell me about Willow."

"It wasn't a romance, really. I had a feeling Willow would have

liked it to be. But not on my side. You've got to believe that. I love
Sheila, even if we have been going through a rough patch these
past few months."

"I know that. But Willow was someone sympathetic to talk
with."

"Yes. That's exactly it." He stopped and reached for the water
container, taking a sip. "I met Willow last spring, at a craft fair in
Sonoma. She had some nice-looking pottery. A lot of it was too expensive for my blood. But I bought a coffee mug. She kept looking
at me and finally she told me I looked a lot like her brother. I stood
there talking with her for a while. That was that. I never thought
I'd see her again."

"But you did."

"Yes. It was just a few weeks later, after that student I was so
concerned about tried to kill himself. I ran into Willow in downtown Sonoma. She said I looked terrible and asked me what was
wrong. So we found a place to have coffee and we sat there and
talked. I told her about my student, how I was sure the kid had
attempted suicide because he was being bullied, and I couldn't
get my principal to listen to me. I said the job in Sonoma had gone
sour and I was looking to get out. I thought, I'm talking to this
woman I hardly know. What's wrong with this picture? But Willow
was listening to me, and Sheila wasn't."

"You had coffee with her several times after that," I said. Willow had already told me this, but I wanted to hear it from Brian.

"Yes. We started texting each other. I always deleted those
texts." He shook his head, and winced at the movement. "Looking
back on it, I see that...well, it's water under the bridge. So yes, we
met again when I came over to Petaluma to interview for the new
job. After the interview, I wanted to talk about it. I couldn't talk
with Sheila. I knew she was opposed to moving. She didn't even
know I'd applied for the job. I could have talked with Lance. But
he was out of the office. So I texted Willow. She drove down from
Occidental and we met downtown. Becca saw us. So that's how she
knew. From the look on her face, I was sure she thought Willow
and I were having an affair."

"Sheila thought you were," I said.

"How did she even find out?" Brian asked. "Did Becca tell her?"

"No. Willow wrote you a note, when you moved to Petaluma."

He looked chagrined. "The note? I thought I'd gotten rid of it. I remember reading it, then tossing it in the recycling bin."

"Amy found it. She thought the picture of the bird on the front of the card was pretty. So she fished it out of the bin and took it to her room. Sheila found it there and read the note."

"Hell," Brian said. "It was just a friendship."

Just friendship, but Brian hadn't felt he could tell Sheila about it. From my conversations with Willow, I thought perhaps she had hoped for more, despite her protestations to the contrary. It was possible Brian's feelings for Willow weren't as innocent as he claimed. I wasn't going to put my two cents in about his relationship with the potter, though. He'd been through enough already. Brian and Sheila would have to sort out the trouble in the marriage on their own.

"A couple of weeks after we moved to Petaluma," he said, "Willow texted me and invited me over to the gallery in Occidental, to see her pottery. So I went. I looked at the gallery, then we went down the street and had coffee. She'd moved into the house at the ranch her grandfather left her. She'd built a kiln and was turning the barn into her workshop. She invited me to the ranch to show me what she'd done, but I said no. I thought it was a bad idea. I didn't see her again until a few days after Sheila left for Firebaugh."

"How did you wind up going to the cabin on the ranch?"

Brian took another sip from the water container. "I was really pissed when Sheila extended her trip. I had to cancel our camping trip to Plumas County, after I'd booked the campsite and made all the plans. So I decided to go camping on my own. But…it's summer, close to the weekend. Every place I checked, all the campsites were taken. So I thought I'd just do some day hikes locally. That Thursday, I drove up to Sebastopol and hiked the West County Trail, from Occidental Road to Forestville and back.

On the way home, I stopped at Andy's Market to get a few things. While I was shopping, I ran into Willow."

THIRTY-EIGHT

BRIAN PARKED IN THE LOT AT ANDY'S MARKET ON Highway 116 north of Sebastopol. He took a couple of canvas shopping bags from the stash in the back of his Jeep Wrangler, grabbed a shopping cart, and wheeled it past a display of new-crop Gravenstein apples.

I should have stopped at Cousin Pat's place, he thought. She grows Gravensteins. She would have given me a bag of apples.

But truth be told, he didn't feel like talking with anyone in the family. There would be the inevitable questions about Sheila and the kids. He was pretty sure he'd mentioned the plans for the August camping trip up to Plumas County when he was at Aunt Caro's Fourth of July barbecue. Now that the trip had been canceled, he didn't want to talk about it. Or the fact that Sheila had gone away yet again, extending her trip even longer. He was tired of the whole damn ball of wax.

He picked out several apples, bagged them, and circled through the open air section of the store, with its abundant displays of fruits, vegetables and nuts. He piloted the cart into the store, speculating about what to have for dinner. Here was a display of pies from Kozlowski Farms, which was located up the road between Graton and Forestville. He'd hiked right past it on the West County Trail. He could have stopped there and bought something, but he hadn't thought of it. Besides, how would a pie fit into his pack?

Now he was thinking about it. The pies looked great and he was hungry.

Why not? He thought. I'm batching it for the foreseeable future. I can eat any damn thing I want.

He chose a crumb-topped apple pie—made with Graven-steins, of course—and put it in the cart. He headed for the cheese section. He picked out some cheddar and jack, and took some salami from another refrigerated case. Then he circled around the fresh produce, picking up lettuce, tomatoes, bell peppers, an avocado, and other things for salad. He grabbed a couple of baskets of strawberries as well.

He moved into another section of the store and picked out crackers to go with the cheese, and debated about tortilla chips and salsa. Sure, why not? He could use the avocado to make guacamole.

Of course he had to have ice cream for his pie. He moved the cart to frozen foods and took out a half gallon of French vanilla. Then he walked down to the meat section and grabbed a couple of steaks.

He assessed the contents of the shopping cart. Did he need anything else? No. This should do it. He headed for the checkout stands.

"Brian?"

He turned and saw Willow. She was dressed in a pair of faded jeans and a purple T-shirt, her long, curly hair caught back and tied, as it frequently was, with a purple scarf. She must have just come into the market. Her shopping cart was empty except for an assortment of cloth bags.

He felt suddenly tongue-tied. He was glad to see her and angry with himself for feeling that way. "Hi. How are you? Didn't know you shopped here."

"Oh, Andy's is the best," Willow said. "Now that I've moved into my grandfather's house, it's not far. What brings you here?"

"I just hiked the West County Trail."

She nodded. "That's the one that follows the old Petaluma and Santa Rosa Railroad line. It's nice that they've turned the railroad right-of-way into a path."

"It's an easy hike," Brian said. "Mostly flat and paved. Tomorrow I want more of a challenge. I thought I'd head up to Armstrong Woods and check out some of the trails there."

"It's pretty up there, with the redwoods." Willow moved out

of the path of a mother with a toddler, angling her shopping cart closer to a display of crackers. She reached for a box and examined it, then put the box back on the display. She cocked her head to one side. "Wait a minute. Weren't you and your family going camping up in Plumas County? That was this week, right? Before you start the new job?"

He hesitated, frowning. "I had to cancel the trip."

"Why?"

Suddenly it all came pouring out, all the anger and frustration that had built up over the past few months. He shouldn't be telling her this. He shouldn't be glad to see her, and the sympathetic look on her face.

"I'm sorry things didn't work out." Willow's face brightened. "Hey, I have an idea. If you really want to get out of town for a few days, you can use the cabin at the ranch. From Graton it's not far to Guerneville, and Armstrong Redwoods is just north of there. You could even go over to the coast."

"Well, I don't know," Brian said, looking doubtful. It wouldn't do for him to spend too much time in proximity to Willow.

She looked at him, as though she knew what he was thinking. "It's okay, Brian. I won't be there. I'm heading up the coast myself. I'm going to spend a few days with a friend in Mendocino. I plan to leave tomorrow. I haven't really decided how long I'm staying, but I should be back sometime next week."

That put a different light on it. It was tempting, Brian thought. If he stayed at Willow's property, he'd be twenty-five miles closer to several of the state parks he'd been planning to explore.

"I didn't know you had a cabin on the property," he said. "I thought it was just the farmhouse and the barn."

"My great-grandfather built the cabin," Willow said. "At least that's what my grandfather told me. The family came to Graton way back before World War One. They bought land and then added to it. They did some logging up there in the woods. And they hunted, deer, wild pig, wild turkeys. So that's what Grandpa used it for. Rick, too, when he was alive. Anyway, there are trails up there, from the hunting days."

"So where is this cabin located?"

"About a mile from the farmhouse. The road continues up through the timber to the cabin. It goes further than that, just a narrow track really, and comes out on Green Valley Road, west of Forestville. I've never driven all the way up there. I think the road's fairly rough, might even be impassable. For a car, I mean. You could certainly hike it."

"Sounds nice," Brian said.

"I think it would be great. It's in good condition. One room, and there's an outhouse that Grandpa put in. No running water, of course, unless you count the creek, and you don't want to drink that. So you'll need to bring in drinking water. There are a couple of old beds with mattresses. You can throw your sleeping bag on one of those. I don't know about a table or chair. It hasn't been that long since Rick used it. He was up there earlier in the spring, around Easter."

Still Brian hesitated. Willow pressed her case. "You'd be doing me a favor to go up and look around. I haven't been up there to look at the place since I moved onto the ranch, after Rick died. I'm wondering what I'm going to do with the land that isn't planted in apple orchards. That area where the cabin is, it's hilly and forested, very pretty. I thought about donating that section. Maybe the county could use it as a park, although I grant you it's a bit remote for that kind of use. But every bit of open space is important. I'd rather donate it than sell it to some winery. You could take a look at the trails, let me know what you think."

"It sounds great," Brian said with a smile. "Okay, I'll do it."

"Wonderful. Now, I have a gate on the road, just below the house. And I have an extra key." Willow rummaged through the large quilted bag she carried. She took out her key ring, removed one of the keys, and handed it to Brian. "I'm leaving first thing in the morning. So come on up whenever you're ready."

"Sure. I'll pack up my gear and head up there tomorrow morning, probably. I'll just stay a couple of nights, Friday and Saturday. Sheila and the kids are due back on Sunday." If she doesn't extend her trip again, he thought.

Brian put the key on his own key ring. Then he said good-bye to Willow and paid for his groceries. When he arrived at home in

Petaluma, he went to the garage and pulled the camp stove and the big cooler off the shelf, along with the plastic tub that held his sleeping bag.

Before leaving the house on Friday, he left a note for Sheila. Then he loaded the car with his camping gear, extra water, and a cooler full of ice and food. He drove to Graton and headed west through the little town. Midway to Occidental, he turned off on Hargis Ranch Road and headed up past the apple orchard to the locked gate. He unlocked it and drove through, then locked it again.

Past the farmhouse, the road narrowed and wound through more apple trees, then gave way to oak and pine. Creek, bridge. Finally he saw the cabin, in a small clearing. He parked close to the cabin and got out, looking around. The road continued to the north. Willow had said it wound around and eventually came out at Green Valley Road. She didn't know whether the road was usable. It looked all right to Brian. It was narrow, yes, but he thought his Jeep could manage it. He'd have to explore, take a hike down that way, and see what was there.

The cabin door was unlocked. He opened the door and walked inside. Then he stopped, frowning as he surveyed the interior. Someone was living in the cabin.

THIRTY-NINE

THE CABIN WAS ONE BIG ROOM, ABOUT TWELVE FEET square, with a single door, the one Brian had just entered. He took a few steps in and looked around, taking stock of what he saw.

A two-burner camp stove had been set up on a rectangular table on the far wall. At one end of the table were two metal folding chairs. An empty tuna can had been used as an ashtray, and it was full of cigarette butts.

A red plastic crate underneath the table held a frying pan, a saucepan, a coffeepot, and an assortment of utensils. A big cool-

er was on the floor to one side. Next to this, three wooden fruit
crates had been stacked one atop the other to make shelves that
contained canned goods. Whoever was living here, Brian thought,
must like tuna, tortilla chips and salsa. There were plenty of all
three, as well as boxes of crackers and cereal. A can of ground coffee sat on the top shelf, next to metal salt and pepper shakers, and
a small plastic dishpan containing a couple of plates, bowls and a
mixture of flatware.

To his left, Brian saw two single beds. The old iron bedsteads
had knobs on each of the four corners. The bedsteads had been
painted white, but now the paint was flaking and peeling to show
the black metal underneath. Each bed contained a mattress, thin,
covered with blue-and-white ticking. The bed in the far corner
held two pillows and a sleeping bag. Between the two beds was
a wooden stool holding a large battery-operated lantern on top.
Another fruit crate, standing on end between the far bed and the
wall, held a small battery-operated radio.

Somebody's been living here long enough to settle in and be
comfortable, Brian thought. Surely Willow didn't know about the
cabin's resident. Otherwise she wouldn't have suggested that he
use the cabin for the weekend.

Just as well he hadn't unloaded the Jeep. He might as well go
home. He turned to go. As he reached the door, he heard a vehicle
getting closer. He stepped outside and looked in the direction he'd
come from, the road that went down past the farmhouse and out
to Graton Road. But the vehicle was a silver SUV, and it was ap-
proaching from the narrow road that led the other way, to Green
Valley Road.

The SUV stopped and two men got out. They walked toward
him. The one who had been on the passenger side moved closer,
scowling at Brian. "Who are you? What the hell are you doing
here?"

Brian felt as though he'd stepped through the looking glass.
The man in front of him, dressed in jeans and a T-shirt, was his
height, his build, and his coloring. Despite the long hair and beard,
he knew who this was. "You're Rick Newman. You're supposed to
be dead."

"Son of a bitch," the driver said, pitching a cigarette butt to the ground. "This fucks up everything."

"This is a mistake," Brian said. Why did these guys look so hostile? "Willow told me I could use the cabin for the weekend. I'm sure she doesn't know you're here."

"You're damn right she doesn't know I'm here," Rick said. "And she's not gonna know."

Brian raised both hands, fighting down the panic that enveloped him. "It's cool. I'll just leave now. I'll go on home, and I won't say a word to her."

"You're not going anywhere." The driver reached behind him and pulled out a gun that must have been tucked in the waistband of his pants.

"Harry, wait a minute," Rick said.

The driver—Harry—looked at Rick. "What do you mean, wait? We gotta do something."

Brian spun around and ran toward the Jeep. But Rick and Harry were quicker. Rick grabbed Brian's left arm, twisting it behind him. Harry shoved the gun back in his pants, then he seized Brian's right arm. Together they manhandled Brian toward the cabin. As the men shoved the struggling Brian through the doorway, his MedicAlert bracelet caught on a nail just inside. The nail scraped him on the wrist and the bracelet's band separated. He heard the bracelet and some of the links fall to the floor. Harry picked up the bracelet and shoved it into his pocket.

Once they were inside, Harry set the gun on the table. Then the two men searched Brian's pockets, taking out his cell phone, wallet, and the keys to his Jeep. Brian twisted and grabbed for the keys. Harry shoved him hard.

As he fell, Brian saw the knobbed end of the iron bedstead looming at him like an enormous ball. He felt, and heard, the crack as his head slammed against the knob. Pain shot through his head like daggers of lightning. He went limp, seeing stars. Then everything turned black.

When Brian woke up again, he was on one of the beds, the one with the bare mattress. His head throbbed, and it felt wet and cold. He realized there was a damp towel on his forehead, with a cold lump that must be a piece of ice. He opened his eyes. The light was too bright and little pinpoints swam in his field of vision. He closed his eyes, heard the metallic clink of a lighter, and smelled cigarette smoke. He listened as the two men talked.

"I don't like it." Harry was speaking, his voice deeper than Rick's. "Somebody's gonna be missing this guy. You saw the wedding ring. He's got a wife somewhere."

"Willow told him he could use the cabin for the weekend," Rick said. "The weekend, right? So nobody's gonna miss him till Sunday night. Don't sweat it. By then we'll be long gone."

"So, what, you're gonna keep him here?" Harry sounded skeptical.

"Thirty-six hours, tops," Rick said. "We do it just like we planned, only we take him with us and leave him at the marina. Somebody finds him eventually. By the time anybody figures out what happened, we're on our way to Mexico, just us and that case full of money."

Harry grumbled. "If Rhine ever finds out we've got his money…"

"He's not gonna find out. As far as he knows, I'm dead."

Harry laughed. "Come on. Show it to me again. I want to see what a quarter of a million dollars looks like."

Brian opened his eyes. He'd never seen a quarter of a million dollars either. Where did someone like Rick get that kind of money? Stole it, probably. Maybe someone was after him, because of the money. That must be why he'd staged his death and why he and Harry were heading for Mexico.

Rick left the cabin and returned a few minutes later, carrying a shiny briefcase that looked like it was made of lightweight aluminum. Rick set the case on the table and unlocked it with a key that he wore on a chain around his neck.

Harry whistled. "Look at all that green. Sure is pretty."

"We can go a long way on this once we get to Baja," Rick said. "Like I said, thirty-six hours. We head for the marina and sail that baby down the river to the bay. We're home free."

"Almost," Harry said. He shot a look at Brian, who shut his

eyes, feigning sleep. "We got to get rid of that Jeep. We're only a mile or so from the house and your sister's living there now."

"Take it up to Tony's place?"

"No, it's red. Too damn visible. Tony wouldn't like that. I say we just ditch it. But let's get his stuff out of it first. Then we can take it. Got any ideas?"

"I know a place," Rick said. "That quarry outside of Forestville. There's a back way in. Nobody uses that road much. We can ditch the Jeep there."

The two men got up and left the cabin. Brian opened his eyes again. Still the light hurt. He moved his left hand and discovered that he was wearing handcuffs, one end around his left wrist and the other fastened to the bedstead. The cuff was irritating the place on his wrist where he'd scraped it against the nail. With his right hand he lifted the damp towel from his head and saw streaks of blood on the light blue terrycloth. He explored the tender spot with his fingers. It felt spongy. Damn, he'd hit his head hard. Did he have a concussion?

The two men returned to the cabin. Through half-closed eyes Brian watched as they carried his camping gear and supplies inside and set them on the floor. Then they left. He heard two engines turn over outside and figured they were taking his Jeep and the SUV.

The two men were gone several hours. During that time, Brian tried to free himself from the handcuff, but he couldn't manage it. If he could just get out of the cuff, he could hike down the way he'd come, back to Willow's house.

Each time he moved, though, his head hammered with pain. He fell into an uneasy sleep. When he woke again, the men were back. He needed to use the outhouse. They unlocked him and escorted him to the primitive structure. Then, back in the cabin, they opened a can of tuna and let him eat. Rick thrust a bottle of Tylenol PM at him, along with a bottle of water. "Here, take some of these. I'm sorry about your head."

Brian was familiar with the over-the-counter painkiller. He'd taken it before, a mixture of acetaminophen and a mild sedative.

"Just let me go. I won't tell anyone you're here."

Rick scratched his beard. "I'll let you go tomorrow night. We'll leave you at the marina. Now take the pills. I want to see you swallow them. You'll be better off if you just sleep. Time will go faster."

Rick shook four of the tablets from the bottle. The recommended dose was two, Brian knew. Two would make him drowsy. Four would knock him out completely. He was sure that's what Rick had in mind.

Brian took the tablets from Rick's hand. He put them in his mouth. As he took the bottle of water from Rick, Brian tucked two of the tablets into the corner of the mouth. He swallowed the other two. As soon as Rick turned away, Brian spat out the remaining tablets, catching them in his free hand. He stuck them into the pocket of his khakis.

Then he lay back on the mattress. Over the next half hour or so, he fought the oncoming drowsiness, listening as the men talked. He overheard enough to piece together what had happened. Rick Newman had taken some money that didn't belong to him. Evidently it belonged to a man named Rhine. At least, Rick and Harry were worried about Rhine, that he might locate them.

The theft was the reason Rick and Harry had staged the motorcycle accident last June, when Rick supposedly died. Since then, Rick had been living here at the cabin, plotting his escape to Mexico. On a boat that was berthed at a marina. Brian knew from talking with Willow that her father owned Newman's Marina and Roadhouse down in Lakeville.

Then Harry left and Rick stretched out on the other bed. Soon he was snoring loudly. Brian renewed his efforts to get free of the handcuffs. But the two tablets he'd swallowed took effect and he fell asleep.

On Saturday morning, Rick scrambled eggs on the camp stove and scraped half of them onto a plate for Brian. Rick ate the other half, spreading his liberally with salsa and using tortilla chips to push the food onto his fork. When the meal was over, Rick repeated the process with the tablets, insisting that Brian take four tablets. Again, Brian managed to take two and hide the others. He slept again, his head feeling worse.

Harry showed up again late Saturday afternoon. The two men loaded gear and equipment into the SUV. They cleared out the cabin, leaving little evidence that they'd been there. It was after dark when they unlocked the handcuffs holding Brian to the bedstead. Again, Rick insisted he take the Tylenol PM. This time Brian put the tablets in his mouth but he didn't swallow them. They cuffed his hands behind his back. As they walked him out of the cabin toward the SUV, Brian spat out the tablets, hoping they wouldn't see.

They put him in the backseat of the SUV, making him lie down. Harry drove, with Rick slumped down in the passenger seat. Brian managed to shift his position, so that he was propped up enough to see where they were going. Harry drove the SUV out of the clearing, on the narrow road that led to Green Valley Road. He turned right onto Highway 116, heading through Forestville. Then he cut over to River Road, just below the Russian River, and drove east toward Santa Rosa. Once on U.S. 101, he headed south, to Petaluma. Harry took the Lakeville exit. City lights gave way to countryside darkness on the Lakeville Highway.

Ahead, Brian saw more lights, the marina, he guessed. Harry slowed and turned off the highway. The SUV bumped down a gravel road, then made a three-point turn and backed up. Harry cut the engine. He and Rick got out of the SUV, walked to the rear, and opened the door. They didn't speak as they unloaded gear and supplies. Brian turned his head, wincing because it still hurt. In the distance he could hear music, as though someone on one of the boats was having a party. Then he heard the roar of a motorcycle, loud, then diminishing as someone left the roadhouse.

This end of the marina was dark, although there were overhead lights near the dock, illuminating the boats. There were cottages here, some with interior lights on.

He heard Rick and Harry talking, but they were too far away for him to make out the words. They were still transporting supplies onto the boat. From what Brian could see, it looked like a good-sized cabin cruiser. They were going to take it to Mexico, that's what Rick had said. They would leave him here at the marina. Surely someone would find him. Or he could head for one of those cottages and pound on the door. Soon this nightmare would be over.

Brian must have dozed off. He came awake suddenly, when he heard the sound of an engine nearby. Another car, he guessed, maybe someone headed for the roadhouse. He turned in the back seat of the SUV, twisting around to see the boat. He could make out two figures on the deck. He shifted position again, looking past the front of the SUV.

He saw a vehicle, though he couldn't tell what make or model. It hadn't been there before. Someone got out and walked toward the SUV. It was a young man with dark hair, wearing dark clothes. As he passed the SUV, the man glanced inside and saw Brian. Then he turned away and headed for the dock. Brian twisted around in the seat, looking back toward the boat. Now he saw three figures. The two on the boat's deck he figured were Rick and Harry. The man who was on the dock was the new arrival.

He heard voices again, fragments of conversation as all three men talked.

"Scott? What the hell are you doin' here?"

"I didn't tell him. He must have—"

"What the fuck?"

Then they were all talking at once, arguing, their voices getting louder, more agitated. He couldn't tell who was saying what, but he could make out some of the words.

"I don't care—"

"You got it all wrong—"

"Look, we'll cut you in—"

"What the hell? Are you crazy?"

The man who'd just arrived was visible in a pool of light. He raised his hand and light glinted off metal. My God, he's got a gun, Brian thought.

The shot sounded incredibly loud. Brian was surprised people in the nearby cottages didn't react. Then there was a louder bang. Flames leapt from the boat, shooting into the sky, illuminating the scene. The man with the gun ran past the SUV.

The explosion and fire got the attention that the gunshot hadn't. A man came out of the nearest cottage and ran toward the dock. People were streaming this way from the other cottages, and the roadhouse.

Then another figure opened the driver's-side door of the SUV and threw in the briefcase containing the money. Rick Newman climbed into the driver's seat and keyed the ignition. He drove away from the dock.

"You were going to let me go," Brian said as the SUV slewed onto the pavement. "Just let me go."

"Shut the fuck up," Rick shouted. "I gotta think, I gotta think."

He sped north on Lakeville Highway. Sirens and flashing red lights up ahead signaled the coming of the fire department, heading for the marina. Rick didn't say anything as he piloted the SUV onto U.S. 101, heading north again. As near as Brian could tell, Rick was driving aimlessly, as though he was unsure of where to go.

Brian fell asleep again. When he woke up, the SUV was still moving. The sun was moving up the eastern horizon. Where were they? Brian thought he recognized a few landmarks. This looked like River Road, outside of Guerneville.

Rick guided the SUV off the road, onto the shoulder. He turned and pointed the gun at Brian. "Get down. And don't make a sound."

Brian obeyed. He scrunched down on the seat, keeping his head as high as he dared, trying to see as much as possible in the faint light of dawn.

Rick drove back onto the road. The SUV entered the outskirts of a town, looking sleepy and deserted in the early morning hours.

I was right, Brian thought. We're in Guerneville.

Rick took a right turn. They passed a building. COFFEE BA-ZAAR, read the sign. This is Armstrong Woods Road, Brian realized. Heading north, toward the park. Where is he going? He must know someone who lives up here.

Rick turned right again, but Brian couldn't see a street sign. Then they were outside of Guerneville. Okay, Brian thought.

We're heading east, maybe northeast, on a twisty road with no lights and no oncoming traffic. Now Rick slowed the SUV. Brian scooted up as far as he dared, and looked outside. Now Rick took a left turn off the pavement and onto a dirt road. They jolted along, maybe a mile, or a mile and a half, Brian thought. Suddenly Rick stopped. Several armed men surrounded the SUV.

"Tell Tony it's Rick."

FORTY

"THE GUY'S A FUCKING LIABILITY." BRIAN RECOGNIZED the voice coming from the kitchen—Tony, the guy in charge.

Brian had seen Tony when he and Rick had arrived earlier today, as the sun was coming up. The man was short, muscular, with a shaved head, a black goatee, and a scowl that appeared to be permanent. He had a gold ring in each earlobe, and he carried a gun tucked in the back waistband of his black pants.

Tony wasn't happy about Rick being here. And he was angry about Brian's presence.

At least Brian wasn't handcuffed anymore. He was locked in a pantry in back of the kitchen. There was a cot with a thin mattress, covered with a plain sheet, a pillow, and a blanket.

At the foot of the cot was a bucket to be used as a toilet, and a couple of large bottles of water. A couple of hours ago, a man who didn't speak had unlocked the closet, fetched the bucket, and brought it back empty. An hour or so later, a different man, also silent, brought him food and more water bottles. When the second man had opened the door, Brian saw that it was getting dark outside. Sunday evening. He'd left a note for Sheila saying he would be home Sunday. She'd be worried when he didn't show up.

Tony and Rick were the only ones he'd heard speaking English. The other men, six or eight of them, he thought, spoke Spanish. When he and Rick had driven up to the buildings, he'd heard the men talking among themselves. In his years of teaching, he'd picked up enough Spanish to understand that they were talking about him, wondering what he was doing here.

They'd brought him into the house, past the tents where the Spanish-speaking men were living. There was trash strewn all over the place, and cans of what looked liked pesticides.

It was then that he realized what this place was. A pot plantation. He'd heard about these places, read that they were all over Northern California.

He was in an old house. When they'd brought him inside, he'd had time to glance around, assessing his surroundings. The front part of the house was a living room–dining room arrangement. A hallway led to the back and he'd glimpsed a bathroom at the end of the hall. The kitchen was a walk-through, and the pantry was near the back door.

He'd seen enough on the drive up here that he thought he knew where they were. He didn't know the name of the road, but he guessed that they were northeast of Guerneville, which meant east of Armstrong Redwoods State Park.

I have to get out of here, he thought. I could disappear into the trees, hike into the park.

He moved to the door, leaning his head against it. He heard something sizzling on the stove, smelled meat cooking in a skillet. Tony and Rick were still in the kitchen.

Tony spoke, his words dispassionate. "We shoot him, and dump the body at the mine."

"Can't do that, man," Rick said. "I don't want a murder rap on top of everything else."

"Hell, you're already in crap up to your belly button," Tony said. "First you rip off that briefcase full of cash. Then you get Harry killed and blow up the boat on top of it."

"It's like I told you, man. Scott killed Harry. Just walked up bold as brass and shot him. And I didn't blow up the boat. I don't know why the damn thing blew up. Propane leak, maybe. Harry was firing up a cigarette when Scott shot him. He fell back into the cabin. If there was propane leaking in there, that would do it."

Brian heard scraping sounds as something was lifted from the skillet. "I don't care how it happened," Tony said. "The shit has hit the fan but good. You're a liability and that guy you brought with you is a liability. I don't need anything that's going to bring the cops down on me. The sooner you're both out of here, the better."

The voices moved out of range as the two men left the kitchen. Brian leaned against the door. He had to get out of here before that guy Tony decided to kill him.

But he was tired, so very tired. His head hurt. And once again, Rick was forcing him to take pills. But it wasn't Tylenol PM this time. Rick had gotten his hands on a more potent drug, Xanax, and the stuff was knocking Brian out and making him dizzy. Brian had slept most of the afternoon, waking only when someone unlocked his prison.

He was hungry, too. A short time later, Brian heard sounds coming from the kitchen, smells, too. Then Rick unlocked the door and handed Brian a plate piled with scrambled eggs and hamburger. Brian wolfed it down. Then they went through the drill with the pills again. He slept hard during the night, awakening when Rick delivered a breakfast of scrambled eggs and some toast.

As the days stretched out into two, three, he slept, dosed with the pills. Several times he managed to fake swallowing the pills, spitting them out and concealing them. He'd torn a hole in the mattress and stuffed the pills inside.

He pleaded for some apples, figuring he needed food he could take with him when he escaped. "I can't just live on scrambled eggs," he said.

"I can," Rick said.

The next time Rick brought food there were two apples, a hunk of cheddar cheese, a handful of chocolate chip cookies. Brian ate one of the apples, a small bite of cheese, two of the cookies. He saved the rest, including one of the bottles of water, hiding his provisions in the mattress.

I don't have much time, he thought. Tony and Rick had argued again, about what to do with Brian.

A few years ago, his sister, Jeri, had taught him how to pick a lock. She knew about such things. He thought it would be a lark to learn how. So she'd showed him how to do it, with a variety of implements. He'd done all right in the trials she had set for him. He never figured he'd have to use the knowledge to save his life.

He pulled the mattress from the cot and looked at the frame. It was plain metal, with flat linked springs. He set to work, loosening one of the coiled springs that held the flat springs to the frame. It took him hours, over a couple of days, but finally he worked one of the coils free.

He straightened one end, then maneuvered the spring into the lock, moving it gently, delicately, hoping he could escape before someone decided to kill him.

FORTY-ONE

"I WASN'T SURE HOW MANY DAYS HAD PASSED," BRIAN told me that evening in the hospital. "Time just seemed to blur. That damned Xanax was knocking me out, so I slept most of the time, unless I could manage to fake swallowing the pills. The day I left...that was yesterday, although it seems like a long time ago. I knew it was afternoon, because they'd brought me breakfast and lunch."

"So when you were ready, you picked the lock." I leaned back in the chair, feeling tired but wanting to hear the rest of my brother's story.

He nodded. "I listened. The house was usually quiet after lunch. I'd at least figured that out. I don't know why. Maybe they were all out doing whatever they did with their pot crop. Or maybe they were taking siestas. Hell, I didn't know. But I was ready to go. I stuffed the food I'd saved and the water bottle in my pocket and I stuck the spring into the lock, moving it around the way you taught me. Once I got the door open, I found out the back door leading out of the house wasn't locked. It wasn't even closed all the way."

"They got careless."

Brian nodded. "Maybe they figured I wouldn't try to get away. I listened and I didn't hear anyone. So I eased out that back door and headed for the trees. Every step I took, I expected to hear a gun and feel a bullet in my back."

"You were lucky to get away. I don't know how much longer Rick could have kept Tony from killing you."

Brian reached for the water and took a sip, then lay back against the pillow. "I had a good idea where I was. By coincidence, I'd been thinking about going hiking at Armstrong Redwoods, so I'd studied the map. I knew if I could get to Fife Creek I could follow it into the park."

"I knew you wouldn't go down Redwood Creek. That's the first place they would look. So you went cross-country, looking for Fife Creek."

"Yeah. I figured if I found the creek and hiked downstream, eventually I'd find a trail. I'm not sure how far I was from the park when I started, though. The terrain was rough. And it got cold up there once the sun went down. I spent the night in a little cave I found, then started hiking again in the morning." He smiled. "I didn't have very much to eat. I was rationing out the stuff I'd saved. And looking for mushrooms. It's a good thing I had been studying edible mushrooms, because I found some. I hadn't found the creek, though. I knew if I kept heading west, I would run into it. I was still looking for the creek when I saw you."

He looked exhausted, as though telling the tale had taken more out of him. I leaned over and took his hand. "You're found now. I'd better let you sleep. I'll be back in the morning."

━━━

I WAS THERE the next day when Griffin and Harris interviewed Brian. As Griffin hoped, Brian was able to identify Scott Cruz as the man who had fired the shot that killed Harry Vann. I didn't know what happened to the aluminum briefcase full of money that

Rick Newman stole, the money that had precipitated the whole sorry episode. The cash presumably belonged to Lowell Rhine's client, but getting it back was Rhine's problem, not mine.

The doctors let Brian go home late Saturday afternoon. He'd made a quick recovery once he was properly fed and hydrated, and the Xanax was out of his system. The concussion he'd sustained was minor. The doctors did recommend some counseling, and I told my brother he should consider it. He might have some leftover stress due to being held prisoner for a week.

Brian didn't commit to the counseling, talking instead about how he was looking forward to starting his new job, getting on with his life as soon as possible. He seemed resilient, ready to leave the whole horrible incident behind and get on with his life, as though nothing had happened.

But it *had* happened. It might come back to haunt him later on. I concurred with the need for counseling for several reasons. As much as Brian wanted to get back to normal, I wasn't sure Sheila had made her peace with the changes in their lives, the changes that had led to the problems they were experiencing.

It was up to the two of them to figure out how to patch the holes in their marriage.

Brian went home, and so did my parents, leaving Aunt Caro's home on Sunday afternoon. Mom went back to Monterey, Dad went back to Castro Valley—and I went home to Oakland, but just for one night.

On Monday, I drove up to Bodega Bay, to spend a few days with Dan at his friends' house overlooking the bay. Our trip to Lassen had been cut short, but we enjoyed those few days walking along the beach looking at the ocean.

Before I went to the coast, however, I went to Occidental.

It was midafternoon when I detoured off Highway 12 onto Bohemian Highway, and drove along the winding two-lane road that led through the redwoods to Occidental. When I reached the town, I parked in front of Hestia Gallery and went inside. Dad's birthday was coming up and I'd decided to get him the watercolor of the hummingbird that I'd seen there earlier.

The painting was still there. I took it off the wall. Then I heard someone say my name. I turned. It was Willow. She was dressed in purple as usual, with a lavender scarf holding back her dark hair.

"You found Brian," she said.

"I did. And your brother. I'm sorry you won't have clear title to the land."

She made a face. Then she shrugged. "Who knows how that's going to turn out? It looks like Rick's going to be in jail for a while. I've hired a lawyer to deal with it. I've got more important things to do, like my pottery." She paused. "I'm really glad Brian is all right, and home with his family. I like him a lot. Probably more than I should. I won't be seeing him again."

"I think that's a good idea."

Willow nodded, then looked critically at the watercolor I was holding. "That's really lovely. The artist does good work."

"It's a birthday present for my father," I said. "He's a birder. I'm sure he'll enjoy it."

"I'm sure he will, too. But you should get something for yourself."

"Maybe I will."

I watched as Willow went outside and got into her car. As she drove off, I turned and walked back to the cash register, setting the watercolor on the glass surface near the cash register.

Then I stepped over to the shelves displaying Willow's pottery. I picked up the asymmetrical green platter I liked so much and carried it to the counter.

AUTHOR'S AFTERWORD
⊷⇒◎⇐⊷

THE CULTIVATION OF MARIJUANA ON PUBLIC LAND is a major problem in California, where pot plantations have been found on state and federal property. Courtesy of Neal Benson, who is a retired forester from the California Division of Forestry, I learned of this US Forest Service video on YouTube, which shows vivid and disturbing scenes of the horrific environmental destruction caused by these farms: https://www.youtube.com/watch?v=IFNe_KZhPZw

These are public lands. That means they belong to all of us, and these lands are being trashed for financial gain.

ABOUT THE AUTHOR

JANET DAWSON IS THE AUTHOR OF THE JERI HOWARD private eye series, which includes *Kindred Crimes*, winner of the St. Martin's Press/Private Eye Writers of America contest for Best First Private Eye Novel, and most recently, *Bit Player*, which was nominated for a Golden Nugget award for Best California Mystery. In addition to a suspense novel, *What You Wish For*, Janet has written *Death Rides the Zephyr*, a historical novel set aboard a train, the historic streamliner known as the *California Zephyr*—with a sequel soon to follow.

A past president of NorCal MWA, Dawson lives in the East Bay region. She welcomes visitors at www.janetdawson.com and at her blogs.

More Traditional Mysteries from Perseverance Press
For the New Golden Age

Diana Killian
POETIC DEATH SERIES
Docketful of Poesy
ISBN 978-1-880284-97-1

Janet LaPierre
PORT SILVA SERIES
Baby Mine
ISBN 978-1-880284-32-2
Keepers
Shamus Award nominee, Best Paperback Original
ISBN 978-1-880284-44-5
Death Duties
ISBN 978-1-880284-74-2
Family Business
ISBN 978-1-880284-85-8
Run a Crooked Mile
ISBN 978-1-880284-88-9

Hailey Lind
ART LOVER'S SERIES
Arsenic and Old Paint
ISBN 978-1-56474-490-6

Lev Raphael
NICK HOFFMAN SERIES
Tropic of Murder
ISBN 978-1-880284-68-1
Hot Rocks
ISBN 978-1-880284-83-4

Lora Roberts
BRIDGET MONTROSE SERIES
Another Fine Mess
ISBN 978-1-880284-54-4

SHERLOCK HOLMES SERIES
The Affair of the Incognito Tenant
ISBN 978-1-880284-67-4

Rebecca Rothenberg
BOTANICAL SERIES
The Tumbleweed Murders
(completed by Taffy Cannon)
ISBN 978-1-880284-43-8

Sheila Simonson
LATOUCHE COUNTY SERIES
Buffalo Bill's Defunct
WILLA Award, Best Softcover Fiction
ISBN 978-1-880284-96-4
An Old Chaos
ISBN 978-1-880284-99-5
Beyond Confusion
ISBN 978-1-56474-519-4

Shelley Singer
JAKE SAMSON & ROSIE VICENTE SERIES
Royal Flush
ISBN 978-1-880284-33-9

Lea Wait
SHADOWS ANTIQUES SERIES
Shadows of a Down East Summer
ISBN 978-1-56474-497-5
Shadows on a Cape Cod Wedding
ISBN 1-978-56474-531-6
Shadows on a Maine Christmas
ISBN 978-1-56474-531-6

Eric Wright
JOE BARLEY SERIES
The Kidnapping of Rosie Dawn
Barry Award, Best Paperback Original. Edgar,
Ellis, and Anthony awards nominee
ISBN 978-1-880284-40-7

Nancy Means Wright
MARY WOLLSTONECRAFT SERIES
Midnight Fires
ISBN 978-1-56474-488-3
The Nightmare
ISBN 978-1-56474-509-5

REFERENCE/MYSTERY WRITING
Kathy Lynn Emerson
How To Write Killer Historical Mysteries:
The Art and Adventure of Sleuthing
Through the Past
Agatha Award, Best Nonfiction. Anthony and
Macavity awards nominee
ISBN 978-1-880284-92-6

Carolyn Wheat
How To Write Killer Fiction:
The Funhouse of Mystery & the Roller
Coaster of Suspense
ISBN 978-1-880284-62-9

Available from your local books
or from Perseverance Press/John Daniel & Comp
(800) 662–8351 or www.danielpublishing.com/persevera